Seeing

Calvin

Coolidge

in a

Dream

Seeing Calvin Coolidge in a Dream

John Derbyshire

To enter in these bonds, is to be free . . .
—John Donne, "To His Mistris Going to Bed"

St. Martin's Press
🐾 New York

Design by Ellen R. Sasahara

Library of Congress Cataloging-in-Publication Data

Derbyshire, John.
    Seeing Calvin Coolidge in a dream / by John Derbyshire. —1st ed.
      p.   cm.
     ISBN 0–312–14044–4
     I. Title.
    PS3554.E47S44 1996
    813'.54—dc20   95–25613

First edition: April 1996

10 9 8 7 6 5 4 3 2 1

Author's Note

For best results (as the makers of my bedtime malted drink powders say—referring, I hope, to the quality of the dreams induced) the conscientious reader should attempt the following sounds, none of which occurs in the American language.

Mandarin *q:*   Halfway between American *ch* and *ts.*

Mandarin *x:*   Halfway between American *s* and *sh.*

Mandarin *zh:*   An American *j,* but with the tip of the tongue pulled as far back along the roof of the mouth as you can manage.

Cantonese *eu:*   As in French *veuve* or German *schön.*

Cantonese *ue:*   As in French *lune* or German *Glück.*

Both these Cantonese sounds are pure vowels, not diphthongs. The first, but not the second, can be joined with *i* (always pronounced like American *ee*) to make a diphthong: *eui.*

Ng is always pronounced, in all Chinese dialects, as in American *singer,* never *linger.*

For Rosie

Seeing

Calvin

Coolidge

in a

Dream

1. Moon Cake

Come look at the moon!

After putting Hetty to bed we had played a game of Scrabble, according to our custom. This took us through the ten o'clock news to the rerun of *Cheers* on Channel 11. It's a show Ding likes a lot. Myself, somewhat less. And this was one we had seen before, not one of the better ones. After the second break I had picked up my book, quite forgetting about August Moon, though we had eaten moon cake as a dessert earlier in the evening. Perhaps we had both forgotten. Perhaps it was only when Ding went to lock the patio door that she recalled.

Come look at the moon on the deck! So beautiful!

I got up, crossed the living room and dining room, and went out on to the deck. The moon was high, shining down on us, on the back of our house, on the deck. The light of the moon, bright and silver, gave the deck an odd metallic look.

Actually the deck was wood, of course. It had been made for us the previous year, after we bought the house. Ding had decided right away that she wanted a deck, with a sliding glass patio door, an Andersen door, leading out onto the deck. So we hired a fellow who'd advertised himself in the local Pennysaver. He came in with a colleague, two rough-looking but amiable young men with long hair and pumped-up muscles, and they made us a deck in two days. It took them half a day to make the footings, after which they disappeared for a week, to let the concrete set in the footings. Then one day, while I was out at work, they came back and built the whole deck. Ding said it looked as though they had it down to an art—like soldiers doing drill, she said. This impressed her very much, because she is an army brat. So we hired them to do a couple more small jobs, but they made a mess of them. Apparently decks were what they knew how to do, nothing else. Well, they made us a good deck. We won't complain about the other things, which were not very important.

We stood on the deck, appreciating the moon. So bright! Our moon shadows were sharp and clear, the sky almost purple. Jip came out behind us. He sniffed around on the lawn for a while, following the scent of a squirrel perhaps, then came back to lie down on the deck under the moon.

I fetched some wine and moon cake and we sat there drinking and appreciating the moon. The air was warm. August Moon falls on the fifteenth day of the eighth lunar month. This lunar year had started early, before the end of January, and there was no intercalary month, so we were sitting on our well-built deck appreciating the moon, eating moon cake and drinking generic Chablis in warm early September, with our dog curled up at our feet. I felt like Mr. Boswell: This is as much as can be made of life.

As a matter of fact this is my favorite time of year. Ding comes from Chongqing, a famously hot and humid city, one of the so-called Three Ovens of China. I, however, was raised in the Northeast, near the Korean border, and the New York summers are too much for me. Springtime is very pleasant of course, and I have no argument with the various poets who have praised that season, nor with the sages of ancient times, in all cultures, who determined that a new year truly begins when the worst of winter is past. Yet for me, fall is the season.

Not only beautiful in itself, but bringing with it relief from the summer.

After sipping twice at her wine and swallowing some moon cake, Ding recited Su Dongpo's well-known poem, written for another August Moon nine hundred years ago.

> Mortals have sorrow and joy, parting and uniting.
> The moon has clouded and clear, crescent and full.
> So it has been since ancient times . . .

Ding knows all the old poems. In a literary way she is well educated. In other matters—history, geography, all the sciences—her ignorance is really disgraceful. However, this is not her fault. She was born in 1962, so her education took place entirely during the Great Cultural Revolution when teachers and scholars were horribly persecuted and examinations all abolished. Later, after the Chairman died and the examinations were reestablished, she went to college and made up some lost ground. But of course nothing can replace sound training in the formative years. However, I should not speak slightingly of Ding. She married me, though I was so much older than she, without any compulsion, when she could have married anybody. Because I knew you were a good man, she said when later I asked her, and tears leapt to my eyes for the simple clarity of her soul. I hope I may always keep that faith with her. And I believe I shall, thanks to President Coolidge.

I felt I should recite a poem in response to hers, but nothing came to mind. It has been some years since I read the old poems. There was a time when I read little else—when I wallowed in the long heartbreaking rhythms of Bo Juyi, the lush melancholy imagery of Li Shangyin. But that was long ago, in another place. I think that the only ones I can now recite without preparation are the ones everyone knows: Li

Bai's "Night Thoughts," Zhang Ji's "Mooring at Maple Bridge," and so on. Ding would think me very gauche if I recited one of those. Yet I could think of nothing else. Moon, moonlight—how many poems have been written to the moon? A hundred thousand, at least; but all I could come up with at last was a disconnected fragment.

> A rafter glows in the setting moon.
> It seems, for a moment, to be your face.

What is that? I asked Ding. I really can't place it.

Why, it's Du Fu, of course. "Seeing Li Bai in a Dream." The first one, where he hears the rumor that Li Bai has drowned, but refuses to believe it. Then it goes

> The water is deep, the waves are broad.
> Oh, don't let the sea dragons take you!

I suppose I must have known these following lines at some point, but kind forgetfulness had dissolved them for me. Now, from that moon-silvered deck behind a small suburban house on the North Shore of Long Island, I was flung again into the black still ocean, soundless but for my own weary splashing, twenty years and ten thousand miles away.

Ding read my thought. I guess you are thinking about your swim to Hong Kong, she said.

I spoke lightly, to show that it wasn't important. I didn't want Ding to know too much about Hong Kong. Well, I said, the sea dragons couldn't catch *me*.

If you'd waited a few years you could have come out in a normal way, said Ding.

4

I let the matter drop, and reached for some moon cake. The crickets were very loud. The sound they make comes from rubbing their legs against their wing cases. English has a special word for this: *stridulating*. What a marvelous language! To have a special word for such a thing! Chinese can approach this phenomenon only by onomatopoeia: *ji-ji*. So crass! I said something about it to Ding, and taught her this word *stridulate*.

I don't think they're crickets, said Ding. I think they're . . . *zhi-liao*.

Cicadas.

Yes, yes. Cicadas.

Really? I said. Now you mention it, I'm not sure.

She laughed in the way she has, mocking me affectionately. How like you to know the word but not the thing!

Words are the daughters of Earth, but things are the sons of Heaven. This was to argue against myself, but the quotation was too apt to leave unsaid.

She snorted at my pedantry. Then: What were you reading?

I told her I was reading Mr. Paul Johnson's *Modern Times*, the chapter about America in the 1920s. This chapter is called "The Last Arcadia." It deals with Presidents Harding and Coolidge.

Arcadia? What is Arcadia?

I said that Arcadia was the Peach Blossom Country, and at once felt pleased with myself for drawing such an exact analogy with so little thought. Here is the story of the Peach Blossom Country.

> A fisherman was in his boat on the river when he saw peach blossoms floating on the water. He thought he would like some peaches, so he paddled in the direction the blossoms came from. This led him into a cave with a glimmer of light at the other end. When he had passed through the cave he came out into a beautiful country. Here the people worked the fields in peace and contentment. Children played happily in the woods and streams. There was no illness and no war, no officials or tax gatherers. The people had fled there some centuries before, to escape the disorders which followed the Qin dynasty. The fisherman lived among them for a while. Then he decided to fetch his family. So he went back through the cave, back to his home village. He packed all his family and their belongings in the boat, and they set off for the source of the peach blossoms. But there were no peach blossoms now, and he could not find that cave. He searched all his life, but he never found it again.

This story was told by Tao Yuanming, a poet who lived in the terrible fourth century. Myself, I have always thought it had the flavor of a folktale, and perhaps the poet took it from the oral tradition, but I don't know whether there is any evidence for this.

Harding, said Ding. And . . . who?

Coolidge.

Coolidge. Well, what about these guys? Were they good presidents?

About Harding, I'm not clear. I think he was a good man in

himself, but he did not take care in choosing his friends and colleagues, and so his government fell into scandal. Mr. Coolidge was a Puritan from New England, very honest and upright. Under him the country was very prosperous. More than ever before. Also peaceful, both inside and outside. That's why Mr. Johnson calls it "The Last Arcadia."

In that case, I'm surprised he is not more famous. I have never heard of him.

Sweetheart, you hadn't heard of either of the Roosevelts until we went to their houses. And I'm sure you still don't know which one is which.

Ding sniffed, waving her wineglass back and forth in a rather tipsy way, to dismiss the Roosevelts and all their works. She uttered a Chinese idiom, which being translated means *fretting about emperors dead and dynasties past.* It is hopeless to try to interest her in American history. In her heart, she thinks Americans are barbarians.

2. *Westward Journey*

We had debated, the three of us, whether it would be wiser to make our attempt by moonlight or in complete darkness. We did not know whether Hong Kong would be visible across the sea. If it was not visible we would need moonlight to show us the land. On the other hand, we had heard that the coast guard patrolled the sea at night, and shot with machine guns at any swimmers they found. On a moonless night it would be easier to evade the coast guard.

Sitting around in the park in Canton, in the muggy heat of late summer, we tried to weigh the relative dangers. But we just didn't have enough information; and not knowing anyone in that place, we were afraid to ask. At last Huang Jen took the initiative. Come on! Let's just go and take our chances! Better to die in the sea than live in this godforsaken country! That was his nature, that was how he spoke—very forthright, not giving a damn for anyone. A real northeasterner. We had been Red Guards together, but he was always much bolder and fiercer than I. So we slipped into the sea—it was warm as soup, I recall—under a waxing moon three-quarters full, to swim the four miles to Hong Kong.

I never knew what happened to Huang Jen. Little Tan drowned, I know. We heard him drowning, far out from the shore where we could have done nothing to help him. I heard his cries behind me—I hear them still. Only a kid, seventeen years old.

After the cries stopped, I could still hear Huang Jen's regular splashing, at eight o'clock behind me. I heard it for a long time, until I entered a sort of dream state of exhaustion and despair, in which I thought I could still hear it . . . but when consciousness returned, I was alone on the infinite sea, somehow still swimming, my arms and legs like concrete posts, yet still moving.

The sea was smooth but with a long, slow swell. The swell was too long to perceive directly. Only that at times I was at the bottom of a great bowl of black glass, and at other times gazing out across the world at a far-glimmering strip of moonlit land which never changed in appearance or proximity.

It seemed to me, in my dream state, that the great slow swell was a kind of breathing, the sea itself a living thing. By no means a malevolent one, either. In my desperation I thought it not altogether a bad idea to stop my hopeless swimming and give myself to the warm black sea. Why I did not do so, I cannot say. At such times your own most inward and essential nature governs your fate. Mine is difficult and stubborn, toward friend and enemy alike. So long as I could move my limbs I would not yield to the sea.

I have always wondered what became of Huang Jen. Perhaps the sea dragons took him, as Du Fu warned. Perhaps he took a cramp and drowned. Perhaps his most inward nature was, after all, less stubborn than mine, and he yielded to the warm sea. Or possibly we just swam apart, out of hearing from each other, and he made it to Hong Kong after all. I think this most probable. He was much stronger than I, and four miles is not a very great distance to swim, in a calm sea on a warm night.

When I was settled in Hong Kong I tried to find him, going back to Deep Water Bay to talk with the fishermen, but nothing came of it. The fishermen just shrugged. There were so many swimmers, so many. I went through the telephone books, looking for his name. It is a rather common name, and there were three or four Huang Jens, but none was him. However, it is possible he changed his name, as I did for a time.

Those fishing folk take Guan Yin as their patron deity, calling her Queen of Heaven and Bodhisattva of the Southern Ocean, begging her for protection against storms and typhoons. Every little fishing village, every rocky island, has a temple to her. When I went to those places, for whatever purpose—to talk to the fishermen, or for a picnic party with friends, or with Selina, or later, alone, to escape the noise and stink of the city—I would always make an offering to Guan Yin. I would place an orange on her altar, burn some joss, and shake out the lucky sticks, always hoping for some sign to help me find Huang Jen. I hoped he was not dead. If he had really drowned in Deep Water Bay his ghost might feel some resentment against me for not helping him. Little Tan definitely did drown, and I supposed his ghost would be resentful, too. But somehow I felt that Little Tan, so shy and mild, would not produce a very terrifying ghost. The ghost of Huang Jen would be another matter altogether.

There is a shrine to Guan Yin in New York City, in Chinatown. There she is not called Queen of Heaven, only Goddess of Mercy, Who Hears the Cries of the World. I hope she heard Little Tan's cries, when he was drowning, and Huang Jen's, if he truly suffered that fate. I hope she heard their cries and gave them her mercy.

My memory of ending my swim is very vague. I came up, in the furthest extremity of exhaustion, on a steep stony beach, in the early light of morning. I crawled a few yards, the stones cutting my hands and legs, then fell unconscious. Fortunately the tide was going out, and the sea left me alone. Not so the sun, which burnt me badly, though it was some hours before I really suffered the effects.

When I came to, I opened the bag that I had been towing behind me, to find my clothes all soaked. There was some dried cuttlefish and jujubes, likewise soaked, but I ate them anyway, and set off along a path leading inland.

How naive I was! I had never seen a map of Hong Kong—there were none available in the Mainland at that time—and I knew nothing about the place. I thought it was just a seaside city, like Dalian. I didn't know about the New Territories, stretching back twenty miles to the border and Deep Water Bay. I should have had a long walk indeed; but it was a Sunday, and I met some students from Kowloon on a picnic, and from simple kindness they took me back with them. When I saw them paying the minibus driver I felt ashamed and stupid. I had not even known that Hong Kong has its own currency. So naive! And I had towed ninety yuan of Chinese money with me across Deep Water Bay! I begged twenty dollars in Hong Kong money from the students, and made them write down their names and addresses for me so that I could repay them. I did repay them, too, every one, and in only a month.

I shall never forget my first hours in the city. Mr. Charles Dickens, stepping out at the age of twelve into the clamorous, stinking streets of old London, was not more bewitched or befuddled than I. The minibus left me in Kowloon, at the southeast corner of Nathan Road and Waterloo Road. I think I stood there for quite a long time, dazzled and astounded. Ten thousand cars! Ten thousand stores, all lit up! And looking down Nathan Road to the south, ten thousand signs hanging out over the street, glowing in every color of the spectrum, some flashing or fizzling—merging together, down to the south, in a glorious pandemonium of form and color! And all this, at nine o'clock in the evening, when our northern cities were silent and dark, except perhaps for the occasional rattle of a bicycle. The vitality of the place, the noise and color and bustle, overwhelmed all my senses, thrilled and terrified me all at once.

It was easy to find work. There were factories everywhere—at that time, all the way down Kowloon to the Star Ferry. All of them would take anyone who asked for a job, at piecework rates. The pay was not much, of course, but to a *daailukjai*—a Mainland boy—who had lived most of his life on the edge of starvation, it seemed just fine. I took a room in a single men's hostel in Samseuipo, worked the night shifts, which paid a little more, and fell in love with that raucous, ruthless, beautiful city.

Hong Kong in the early seventies was still a Cantonese city, hardly touched by the presence of foreigners. Under the arcades in Yaumadei and Mong-gok—my main stamping grounds—were crammed tiny stores called Unity Restored or Remembrance of Harmony; noodle shops and herbal pharmacies; tearooms with an awesomely bare lobby—any empty space more than a meter square was striking to the eye in Hong Kong—all dark lacquered wood, with the single character TEA on the wall by the receptionist's desk and a flight of stairs leading up. There were tobacconists, and fortune-tellers, and pawnshops with the big PAWN character in gold on red, and tiny bookshops selling knight-errant adventure stories and weepy romances with titles like *Brief Dream* or *Fragrant Dust,* and out on the sidewalks old grannies who'd remove the hairs from your face with a piece of string. At night, if you walked the back streets, you might come across a Cantonese opera troupe performing in a square, or open-air food stalls selling all those bizarre delicacies the Cantonese love—owl's brain, raccoon tail, heron's gizzard.

Hong Kong was at that time probably the freest place in the world. There was no government to speak of. There was, to be sure, a governor, sent over from Britain to supervise the affairs of the Colony, but I do not know how he filled the hours of his day. There were no restrictions, no regulations, no taxes. If you wanted to start a factory, you cleared some space on your living-room floor. If you wanted to hire people, you put out an ad. If you wanted to fire them, you fired them—and we considered ourselves lucky if we got outstanding wages paid. The schools were private. If you wanted to send your child to school, you paid. If you didn't want to, that was your business. The police were just a nuisance. Nobody—at any rate, nobody in the working-class areas where I lived—ever called the police for anything. If you called them they would just ask you for money. Then they would probably arrest you anyway, in the hope of getting more money from your family.

It was not Arcadia—any more, I suppose, than President Coolidge's America was. There were gangs everywhere who felt they had the right to take money off you by asking, and to kill you if you refused. There was poverty unrelieved and disease untreated, and money could get you anything you wanted: five dollars for a whore (not the slack-eyed needle-tracked disease carrier of a Western city, but a pretty young girl fresh from the Mainland), twenty dollars for a driver's license, fifty dollars to have your enemy arrested, one hundred dollars to have him killed.

What Victorians called the Battle of Life was waged here with full vigor, and the casualties were plentiful, though for the most part kept decently out of sight. The hostels I stayed at were mostly just made-over apartments in residential blocks. Going home to one of these places one morning I missed its door and went along the corridor too far, to another door. This door was open. Inside, in a room about twelve feet square, were thirty or forty old men. They were stacked up on broad shelves going up the walls all around, the shelves a couple of feet apart, four or five old men on each shelf. One of them was coughing—the terrible, liquid cough of the consumptive. Some of them looked at me without any expression. Most just lay there, though a couple of more spirited ones were playing Chinese chess on a sheet of paper. I found out later that these were just old men nobody wanted, who got a bit of shelf space for two dollars a week. Hong Kong dollars, that is—about thirty cents U.S. at that time. There were other rooms behind the one I saw. Every month a couple of the old men died.

But I was young, single, and healthy, and I put these things out of my mind. I suppose if you were sick, or old, or lazy, then Hong Kong was pretty awful. But for a fellow like me it really was a kind of Arcadia. Quite apart from Selina—indeed, in spite of her—I have maintained a deep love for that city.

There were no real restrictions on immigration from the Mainland. The authorities practiced a policy called Touch the Crease. This comes from cricket, the national game of the British. The crease is a line in front of the wicket, which is to say the base. When you are running to the wicket you can be thrown out by the other side getting the ball there first. However, if you can reach out and touch the crease, you are home, and can't be given out.

Well, the authorities considered that if they caught a swimmer in Deep Water Bay, they had a right to send him back to China. Even if you were caught in the New Territories near the bay, you could be arrested and sent back. But once you reached the city, unless you got into trouble, they would not send you back. My fellow workers told me I could get a Hong Kong ID card if I asked. For a long time I refused to believe them. I had—I still have—the Mainlander's aversion to entering any government office for any purpose. But when I went at last, they gave me a card for the asking.

Doing factory work I used false names, from that chronic fear and suspicion that everyone from the Mainland carries. When I registered for my Hong Kong ID card, however, I used my real name. I thought they might check the details I wrote on the form. Actually they had no way to check. They relied on fingerprints to prevent fraud.

They transliterated my name as Chai, though it should more properly be Zhai. This turned out for the best. Everything followed from my Hong Kong ID card—passport, U.S. visa, green card—and Chai is much more user-friendly for foreigners than Zhai. They don't know what to do with that *zh*. Low-class people just ignore the *h* and say Zai, which is not too far from the Chinese, at any rate in a southern pronunciation like Ding's. Educated foreigners make a French *j*, a sound which does not occur in any Chinese dialect. Thus—as we say in Chinese—do the smarties outsmart themselves.

Actually, as a Chinese surname, Chai is quite classy. It's rare, which is worth several points, and ancient—one of the original Hundred Names. It means Pheasant, and its character shows two feathered wings over one of the bird symbols. With a different pronunciation—*Di*—it was the name of a country in very ancient times, before China was unified, and also the forename of the philosopher Mo Tzu, who preached economy of expenditures and the abolition of music. So much in a name! But China is a very old country, and everything—every name, every place, every thought—is encrusted with connotations and accretions like this. That is why it is so difficult for us to make any progress. In everything we do we are cumbered by this dark calciferous mass of associations from the past.

Everyone has some feeling about his name, hasn't he? Ding, whose surname is Li, likes to boast that she is descended from the emperors of the Glorious Tang, whose dynasty carried that surname. Since the Tang were on the throne three hundred years, practicing polygamy the whole time, and since a further thousand years have elapsed since the last of the Tang princes were all hanged in a batch by the unspeakable Zhu Quan-zhong, I am sure she is right. But Li is such a common name there is nothing impressive about her claim. Selina bore the surname Guo, also rather commonplace; but the guy she married had the remarkable name Rui, pronounced Yoy in Cantonese. I had never heard of this name before she told me.

Yoy?

Yoy.

What kind of name is that, Yoy? We were speaking Cantonese at the time.

It's a name. The Grass radical over Interior. (Describing the form of the written character by its components.)

What part of China does that come from?

She shrugged. His people are from the Four Towns, same as mine.

The Four Towns is a district in Guangdong Province, next to Hong Kong.

I laughed, I remember. Yoy! Yoy! It looks to me like a barbarian name. Barbarian, from the grasslands of the far interior, you see? Your fiancé is a Lolo.

The Lolo are a very primitive tribe in the mountains of south-west China. They wear no clothes and practice cannibalism.

Well, after I got my ID card I was a real Hong Konger. I forgot about the Mainland altogether. I have never bothered much about it since. When I am reading a newspaper, I skip over the stuff about China. I can't feel any interest in it. And to tell the truth, I feel somewhat ashamed of it. What, after all, does China news amount to? A palace intrigue, a warlord brought to heel, an episode of prosperity, an episode of famine. Nothing important or interesting has ever happened in China, and nothing ever will, *ex Sinica numquam aliquid novi.*

Ding says I am an anti-Chinese Chinese. Well, so far as human beings are concerned, this is nonsense. People are the same everywhere. But human societies are not. Chinese society took a wrong turn somewhere, thousands of years ago, and is now too far lost in the wilderness of despotism to ever become worthy of the best in human nature. That society can only promote the worst, and this will always be so.

There is a saying in Chinese: Old men don't read *Three Kingdoms,* young men don't read *Westward Journey. Three Kingdoms* is an ancient novel, what in English would be called a swashbuckler—fearless warriors, the ebb and flow of military encounters, the skill of strategists, the play of fortune. *Westward Journey* is another novel, of the same period but very different. It is the adventures of a little group of men— men and animals, actually—who journeyed to the far West to seek Buddhist scriptures. The adventures are mostly very preposterous, but the whole book is redeemed by a quality of Buddhist otherworldliness, of spiritual resignation. Such an attitude is, of course, beyond the understanding of young men. Contrariwise, an older man who has survived a few decades in Chinese society does not want to read about courage, which he knows is useless, or dignity, which he knows will only get you killed.

The force of gravity operates differently in China, acquiring more influence the longer you live there. When you first go to China—or in early childhood, if you are a native Chinese—

you can walk upright. After a time, however, you are forced to your knees. Then Chinese gravity becomes stronger, until you must crawl on all fours. At last you are brought down onto your belly, with your face in the dirt, in the barren lifeless yellow dust of China.

3. *Weaned on a Pickle*

Boris called me into his office. Boris is my boss. He is very big—more than three hundred pounds—with a voice of equivalent size.

What he actually said was: Get your yellow ass in here, Chai. This is his normal mode of address. Boris has worked on Wall Street all his life. He is nearly sixty now, and has been put out to pasture in back-office work, but in his youth he was a trader, and he has carried the rough language and manners of the trading floor with him into these later years. Many people are intimidated by him, but those of us who work with him know that he is kindly and generous. Like the great Dr. Samuel Johnson, he has nothing of the bear but his skin. He is, in fact, a sensitive soul, with a very well developed aesthetic sensibility, and an apartment on Central Park East full of beautiful things acquired by endless diligent browsing in the catalogs of Messrs. Sotheby, Christie, and so on.

Boris told me a disgusting joke about a homosexualist buying underwear in a department store. Then he told me I was having a direct line put into my office.

For Info Serve. It's one of these (he waggled his big fat hands in front of him, to indicate something awesome and incomprehensible) networks. You get access to . . . to what? They told me, but I can't remember all this goddamn jargon.

Databases.

Right. That's what you get. Humongous great databases.
Market information, Dun & Bradstreet, Moody's, all that crap.

We have that already on the Quotron and Bloomberg.

Yeah, yeah. But this has some other stuff, too. Don't ask me.
It's just policy, that's all. Everyone with rank of AVP and up
gets the stupid thing.

I said I was sure it would prove very useful to me in my work.

Don't brownnose me, Chai, you slitty-eyed creep. How's your
beautiful wife? And the little princess?

I said that Ding and Hetty were both fine. I told him about
August Moon. He asked what we had done, other than eat
moon cake.

Well, we recited poems about the moon.

Oh, yeah? You want moon? I'll give you moon.

Swaying his huge bulk from side to side, the chair cracking
and groaning under him, he sang "By the Light of the Silvery
Moon." Boris is not a man of deep literary interests.

A word of advice, Boris?

What.

Keep the day job.

Kiss mine, pal.

Say, Boris. What do you know about Calvin Coolidge?

What, Silent Cal? The business of America is business.

I'm sorry?

The business of America is business. That's what he said. He was famous for saying that.

Anything else?

Nothing. He said nothing else. That's why they called him Silent Cal.

Okay. How about his presidency? I mean, what is he mainly remembered for?

How should I know? What am I, the goddamn *Columbia Desk Encyclopedia?*

I just thought that perhaps, as an American, you might have studied him when you were at school.

Whatever they taught us at school is so far behind me I don't care to think about it.

Americans care so little about history. Even their own—so far as the history of other countries is concerned, they are a perfect blank. But this is because they are an optimistic, forward-looking people, who fled from an old world to build a new one. This is a form of ignorance one can excuse, insofar as ignorance is ever excusable.

At lunchtime I went to the public library on Murray Street. The downtown area is hardly residential, and I suppose the library is designed to cater mostly to office workers looking for something to enliven their commute. They have not much in the way of serious books. Still, I thought I would find something in the biography section. President Coolidge was, after all, a president, and not so very long ago. Within living memory? Certainly. But the biographies here were mostly of show business people and murderers.

The only mention of the thirtieth president in that whole place was in the tiny reference section. There I found a book called *Facts about the Presidents.* This proved somewhat unsatisfactory. It was written in a flippant and disrespectful manner. The author's intention seemed to be to embarrass the presidents, or their memories. Washington's wooden teeth, Jefferson's black mistress, Lincoln's dirty jokes. I did not think this very interesting. Of President Coolidge there was only some raw biographical information, then this.

> An undersized, repressed man, called Great Stone Face by his contemporaries. Coolidge handed the country over to business interests, pulled down the shades in the White House, and dozed for five years. The United States was run—in so far as it *was* run—by Andrew W. Mellon the banker, Coolidge's treasury secretary, "under whom three presidents served." The only exercise Coolidge took was riding a mechanical horse he had had installed in his White House bedroom. His greatest pleasure was to have breakfast in bed while a valet rubbed Vaseline into his hair. He could not whistle. His wife had a pet raccoon called Rebecca which she liked to walk in the White House grounds, calling out greetings to passersby. Seeing a depression on the horizon, Coolidge declined to run for a third term in 1928. Rated thirty-first.

The last sentence referred to some poll of Eminent Historians the author had conducted, asking them to rank the first forty presidents. Coolidge was placed thirty-first by these very learned persons. Yet Mr. Paul Johnson had described him as the most single-minded and consistent of all modern presidents, superintendent of the Last Arcadia. Such a puzzle! And he could not whistle—say what? What was that sentence doing in there? How was that important, even for derogatory purposes?

Along with these rather offhand comments was a photograph, I think the first I ever saw of Mr. Coolidge. It was the standard presidential thing, the kind of picture they put on the wall in foreign consulates, so that folk like me who grew up prostrating themselves before God-Kings, Great Helmsmen, Defenders of the Faith, Descendants of the Prophet, Little Fathers of the People, and so on may see what the chief functionary in a republic of free men looks like. Head and shoulders against a plain dark background, the gaze off-camera to the viewer's right.

I studied the face for some time. There was a great deal in it. At a first glance you could see what the Eminent Historians were thinking of. It was a bank manager sort of face—prim, careful, a little out of its depth, desiccating silently above a high starched collar. Not the kind of face that intellectuals would go for. Not glamorous. Weaned on a pickle, Mr. Johnson had quoted someone-or-other as having said. Weaned on a pickle—just so.

Closer study revealed some interesting harmonics. Humor, certainly. Something in the turn of the mouth . . . something impish, irreverent, boyish. Yet a steadiness in the eyes—a certitude weightier than mere smugness. Beneath the clerkishness, great strength and wisdom. I trusted this man at once, and wanted to know him better.

Foregoing lunch altogether, I walked up to the Chatham Square branch in Chinatown, which I knew had an extensive section of biographies. Constantine, Conway, Cook, Coolidge. *Meet Calvin Coolidge,* a collection of newspaper and magazine pieces, mainly memorial or obituary. *A Puritan in Babylon,* by William Allen White, which seemed to be a genuine biography. I took both books.

That evening, after we had put Hetty to bed, Ding and I played a game of Scrabble. It is a favorite game with both of us. We do not play it in that very artificial way that is seen in international tournaments, all *eb* and *ut* and *ai.* There is an understanding between us that only reasonably commonplace words are allowed. Furthermore, because my vocabulary is much bigger than hers, I spot her fifty points. As a matter of fact, I try to use the game to improve her English. I pick some word from the newspapers or magazines that I think it would be useful for her to know, and introduce it into the game, sometimes sacrificing several goes to do so. When she challenges it as *too strange,* I show her the newspaper or magazine and try to persuade her that it is really not too strange. Then it becomes part of our stock of allowed words.

Actually, fifty points is rather generous. Although her vocabulary is much inferior to mine, she makes up for her deficiency by cunning. I am really not a good player of games. I have no guile. I suspect Ding of having guile. On this occasion, for example, she set down the word USUAL in such a way as to render both U's useless for further play. Now, it happened that I was holding a Q, and had been waiting several turns, hoping for a U. Here she was with two U's, and she had killed them both stone dead. I could not but suspect her of teasing me, though I don't see how she could have known I had the Q. There were plenty of letters still in the bag. And, yes!—glancing up from my letters as she added her score, I thought I saw a mischievous smile pass across her face. Well, it is only a game.

How old is Walter? I asked her, stifling my suspicions. Walter is our neighbor across the street. He and his wife, Abby, though both advanced in age, are very kind to us, helping out with baby- and dog-sitting, bringing over pies and cookies for us, and so on.

He is eighty-one, said Ding, who can be depended on to know things of this sort.

Eighty-one. Then he was born in nineteen twelve. Seventeen when Coolidge stepped down.

What? What are you talking about?

President Coolidge. "The Last Arcadia." Remember last night, when you asked me what I was reading?

Oh. Ding went back to contemplating her letters.

This President Coolidge seems to have vanished without trace.

Well, perhaps people just don't find him very interesting. We allow EL, don't we?

Certainly. Mr. Tom Wolfe and Mr. James Baldwin both use EL. *Sister Carrie*—the word EL is in there, I am sure.

Ding was frowning, rearranging her letters.

I wonder if Walter remembers him, I wondered aloud.

Remembers Mr. Carrie?

SISTER Carrie. No, no. Mr. Coolidge.

Oh. I don't know. Seventeen? Who was in charge of China when I was seventeen?

Hua Guofeng. Do you remember him?

Sure. I remember him. He looked like a horse.

Well, then, I should think Walter remembers President Coolidge. As I was saying this, Ding put down the word TUNE, making TO and UP with the end of COP. Another murdered U! But how does she *know* when I have a Q?

I thought you wanted to make EL.

No, I wanted to stop you making it.

Well, this is perfectly all right, of course—all part of the game. I just can't think like that. I said nothing, just concentrating on my letters. QRRLIIE.

Are you going to ask him?

Ask whom what?

Walter. About this president.

Oh, certainly. But not tonight. Too late. RILE? LIER? MILE? Nothing much to be made. That damn Q.

I hope this President Coolidge won't become another obsession. Like Mr. Johnson.

Dr. Johnson. *Mr. Paul* Johnson wrote *Modern Times. Dr. Samuel* Johnson wrote the *Dictionary* and *Lives of the Poets* and *Rasselas.*

Now I must explain that from time to time I am taken up with a great enthusiasm for some historical or literary figure. I want to know everything about that person, to get inside his mind, to *understand* him.

It happened first when I was in high school. That first infatuation was for Lu Xun, a Chinese writer of the twenties and thirties. He was practically the only modern Chinese writer of any quality whom the Party approved of, though I think they would certainly have shot him if he had had the misfortune to survive into the People's Republic. He hated all orthodoxies and bowed his head to no one. How could they have let him live? But he died in 1936, on good terms with the Party as it then was, needing all the friends it could get, and they canonized him, and his writings—suitably bowdlerized, of course—were easily available in China in the early sixties. I had better say no more about Lu Xun, or I will fill this memoir with him.

The next was Kang Youwei, a nineteenth-century reformer and writer probably of little interest to foreigners. Kang was very elusive, to the degree that I suspect him of having deliberately covered his tracks. I wasted a great deal of time in my college years pursuing him in the college library. He took part in the so-called Hundred Days, a failed attempt to reform the old imperial government at the end of the last century. In his later years he traveled the world in the company of a teenage concubine, stopping at places of historical interest to write rather good poems in the classical style. He resembled somewhat the more eccentric style of British aristocrat. But he was Chinese, perfectly Chinese. He was the last important person who believed in the emperor system. His last manuscript—he died in 1927, during Mr. Coolidge's presidency—was a memorial to the ex-emperor, composed in full court style, all the characters which referred to himself written with a small brush, all those denoting the emperor separated out from the main columns of text.

And—oh, there were others. The British philosopher Mr. Bertrand Russell; the Jewish-Hungarian writer Mr. Arthur Koestler. But the only infatuation of this sort since I married (and therefore the only one witnessed by Ding) has been my two-year affair with Dr. Samuel Johnson, the eighteenth-century British gentleman, who made the first full dictionary of this remarkable language and served as the subject of Mr. James Boswell's famous biography. At one time I contemplated purchasing the entire Yale University Press edition of Johnson's works, priced at twenty-four hundred dollars, but Ding disapproved rather strongly when I discussed the matter with her, and I yielded to her disapproval. She was right, of course. She was three months pregnant with Hetty at the time, and we had to begin thinking about college funds and life insurance, topics which had not much exercised us up to that time. But my enthusiasm for Dr. Johnson was very great, even to the degree that I worked my way through a Latin primer in the hope—vain, as it turned out—that I might attain sufficient knowledge of that noble tongue to allow me to read Dr. Johnson's Latin poems without effort.

Ding has diagnosed these odd obsessions with dead thinkers as the result of my having been raised, for the most part, without a father. My father died in the Korean War, when I was very small. He was a fleck of spume on one of those Human Waves your own father told you about. I am inclined to trust Ding's intuition on these matters of personality and motivation, having little interest in such things myself.

Now I see my father. He is fixing the bogie of my train. I had a little wooden train—it was painted some bright color, but oddly enough I cannot remember the color. Perhaps it was yellow. The wheels went round; and at the front was a swiveling bogie, with four tiny wheels of its own, which also went round. But the bogie fell off—whether frequently, or only once, I cannot remember—and my father fixed it. While he fixed it, he sang a song, a song about a runaway train. In the song he had to imitate the train whistle, which he did very well. Woo-woo! It made me laugh. When I laughed, it made him laugh, too. We laughed together, my father and I, while he fixed the bogie of my train. Woo-woo! Woo-woo!

Now I see my mother: weeping, weeping, weeping.

4. *Hua Tuo Reborn*

It was Mr. Chan who prompted me to get a Hong Kong ID card. That was after I joined the bank, of course. The way I joined the bank was like this.

I was working night shift at a toy factory in Mong-gok, living in a hostel near the Jordan Road ferry. Coming home one morning I saw a minibus shoot out of Soy Street onto Nathan Road, hitting a young man who had stepped off the sidewalk to avoid a crowd around a peddler. Above all the din of Nathan Road I could clearly hear the sound of the minibus hitting the young man—a very unpleasant sound, something more than just an inanimate thud, a sound containing immediate pain and injury.

I hurried over to the young man, who was lying still. He was not dead, but blood was dribbling from his nose and ears, so I guessed he had a skull fracture. The minibus driver had stopped—a fairly gracious act, by Hong Kong standards—and we took the young man in the minibus to Queen Elizabeth Hospital.

He had been carrying a green zippered plastic pouch, and I put this in the minibus with him. On the way to the hospital he became conscious again, and started feeling around anxiously with a hand. I put the pouch in his hand, and saw that he was very relieved. He was a messenger for one of the big international banks, he told me. The pouch was to be delivered to their office on the other side of the harbor. I promised to deliver it for him. I don't think he was altogether happy about this, but I did it anyway, riding over the harbor on the Star Ferry to Hong Kong Island.

Who that has ever made that ride can forget it! You take the ferry from the tip of Kowloon. Facing you is Hong Kong Island, which is really just a mountain sticking up out of the sea. Scattered up the face of the mountain are white towers— apartment blocks—vanishing, on a cloudy day, into the mists that veil the peak in humid weather. Those mists! They close in the space about the Colony, so that you are living in a great room. A Hong Kong poet—yes, there are poets too in Hong Kong—has celebrated those mists, in a poem about drinking with a friend at New Year:

> . . . And Immortals above will smile to see us
> And slap their thighs, and laugh, and toast us
> Raising a glass to old friends in the sky,
> Far above these New Year mists.

All along the waterfront is the great bustle of trade, ships of every kind, buildings of every shape and size, all at the foot of that wonderful mountain. There is no sight like it on earth. There are, of course, better natural prospects, and better human ones, too; but nowhere have Nature and Man built together in such wild harmony. Oh, I used to love to ride the ferry! There is a word in English—not much used now, I think—to indicate everything clean and well ordered: *shipshape*. I learned this word from an English colleague in Hong Kong, and at once, and forever, fixed it to the image of the Star Ferry. The Star Ferry was always shipshape, even down to the second-class deck where you stood open to the weather: the woodwork all lacquered, the brasses all shining, neat white notices with old-style characters, and phrased with such delicacy!—Please Do Not Spit expressed not with the insolent Mainland party secretary bark *bu zhun!* but a courteous *qing wu* . . .

When I reached the bank the doorman directed me to a small office at the back. There were three or four young fellows lounging about on benches, and a small desk with a telephone. At the desk was Mr. Chan, who was in charge of the messenger office. He looked the same then as he did when last we met, twenty years later—at least, so my memory tells me. Small and wiry, with a lean, mischievous face—as soon as I saw him I thought of Sun Wusong, the Monkey spirit in our ancient story *Westward Journey*. Mr. Chan watched my approach with wry calculation, no doubt cooking up some scathing or insulting remark; but when I told him what had happened, he was at once concerned. He telephoned Queen Elizabeth, then logged in the green pouch and had one of the boys take it upstairs.

You a Mainland boy, right? From the North, I guess.

I told him he was correct on both points.

How long you been in Hong Kong?

Less than a month.

Swimmer?

Yes. I came across Deep Water Bay.

He nodded, with some respect on his face. What was in the pouch?

How should I know? *Ngo dim ji?* I was starting to pick up these snappy, aggressive Cantonese phrases.

You didn't look?

No, I didn't look.

How did you know it wasn't money?

I don't know. I didn't think about it.

All this seemed very satisfactory to Mr. Chan. He asked me if I wanted a job. I asked him about the conditions.

Twenty bucks a day, Monday to Saturday. No work Sunday.

Twenty Hong Kong dollars was at that time around four dollars American. This was wonderful, much better than I had been doing at factory work. Of course I did not show how pleased I was. I pretended to consider. Mr. Chan pretended to believe that I was considering.

I said it sounded all right, but I wanted to sleep because I'd been working all night.

No problem. Come here tomorrow, eight o'clock.

I went away, shaking hands with myself (as we say in Chinese). And that was how I got into banking. From that came the slow climb into office work, the transfer to New York, the green card, the house on Long Island, Ding and little Hetty, Jip the puppy—everything that has meaning for me. Everything I might have lost, but for President Coolidge. But of course I didn't know anything about that at the time. All I knew was that I would have more money the next week than I had had the previous week.

Mr. Chan educated me about Hong Kong. He had lived there all his life, except for the period of the Japanese occupation, when he had fled north into Guangdong Province to hide. He knew everything about Hong Kong: every street, every store, every temple, every cinema, every restaurant. The messengers all called him Uncle Chan, and came to him for everything. He could tell you where to go if you were in any kind of trouble, he would help out with ten or twenty bucks when you needed a loan, and locked in his desk he kept a sensational stash of porn magazines—illegal in the Colony at that time.

He taught me to speak good Cantonese, too. Like most northerners, I had heard it occasionally, but never thought of it as anything but a peasant dialect, not worth serious attention. Now, in Hong Kong, I saw millionaires in air-conditioned limousines doing business in Cantonese. I saw movie stars on TV—far more glamorous than anything we were allowed to see on the Mainland—being interviewed in Cantonese. I heard officials of the bank carrying on international phone calls in Cantonese. So I developed some respect for it. It is a tongue full of color and vigor, capable of brilliant flights of eloquence. It is also a very filthy language. It is difficult to swear in Mandarin. Aside from a few rather colorless expletives, our national language has little to offer in this line. Cantonese, by contrast, has at least a dozen different ways to violate your mother, and some imaginative and colorful expressions of salacity—*pig on a slab,* for example, to indicate a loose woman. Male masturbation is *anti-aircraft,* female is *polishing the peony* or *teasing the rabbit.* And so on.

Mr. Chan is a master of the language, never at a loss for words. His Mandarin is not very good, though he can understand and make himself understood. He can sing Cantonese opera, too, and do tai chi exercises, both with swords and without. After work each Saturday we used to climb up the steep alleys behind Queens Road to a somewhat expensive Western-style bar called the Saddle, and sit drinking Heineken and eating bar snacks. Sometimes we would sit talking until late, talking about everything under the sun. We talked about the people at the bank. We talked about China. We talked about public affairs—*Tian xia da shi*, as we say in Chinese: great matters under heaven.

The work, though well paid by my previous standards, was rather easy. You sat around in the messenger room gossiping or looking through Mr. Chan's porn magazines until some delivery was required. If it was outgoing, you checked it out with Mr. Chan. Then you took a cab or a ferry as necessary to get to the other party. The only job requirements were that you be reasonably large and healthy-looking—to deter any opportunist thief who might like the look of your package— and honest. You could goof off to a certain extent. Mr. Chan had a shrewd idea what travel time should be to the small number of locations we served, but you could always take time out for some shopping or a bowl of noodles, and plead bad traffic or trouble getting a sign-off.

That was how I met Selina. I had taken a mild stomach infection, probably from one of the noodle stands, and went looking for a doctor. I had made a delivery to the bank's Mong-gok branch, so I went into the back streets behind Tongmei Road until I saw a doctor's sign. The doctor was up two flights of unlit concrete steps. He had a small, windowless waiting room with some suitably clinical-looking chairs, made of steel tubing and vinyl, and various character scrolls hung around. One of them was a testimonial, calling the doctor Hua Tuo Reborn—Hua Tuo being a legendary physician of the Three Kingdoms period.

Selina was the receptionist. She had a little desk over in one corner of the waiting room, under the Hua Tuo Reborn scroll. She seemed very shy, not looking at me at all while I gave her my details. She wanted me to make an appointment, but I explained that because of my job my whereabouts were unpredictable. She went in to see the doctor, then came out and told me to wait. I took one of the chairs, the nearest one. There were no other patients waiting. I took my chance.

Guleung, what time do you finish work? I used a Cantonese honorific, to show her I was an educated man.

She still did not look up. I'm not supposed to talk to the patients, she said. Except to register them.

But there, you see, I said, you have already broken the rule to tell me that. Rules are like hearts: once broken, they can't be mended.

Teacher Ouyang used to say: If you're not strong at twenty, handsome at thirty, rich at forty, and wise at fifty, then you will never be strong, or handsome, or rich, or wise. Well, I have never been rich, and I suppose never shall be. The others worked out all right, though, so I will not complain. Now, coming toward fifty, I have even got some wisdom at last, thanks to President Coolidge. Just a little—not enough to be a teacher myself. But enough to live my life the right way—and what else is wisdom for?

But at that time I was not wise, not wise at all. I was strong, though—strong enough to survive childhood as an orphan. Strong enough to stay alive in the Three Bad Years 1959–61 when thirty million of my countrymen starved to death. (The greatest human calamity of our century, after World War II—but who has heard of it? They were only Asiatics, after all. My uncle and all his children died with their mouths full of white clay, a kind of soil supposed to have nutritive properties.) Strong enough to work the hemp pits in a northeastern winter, up to my waist in icy water all day—work you could not do, actually physically could not do, unless you had first numbed yourself to insensibility with white liquor. Strong enough to come through the Great Cultural Revolution with my mind and body intact. Strong enough to swim across Deep Water Bay for my freedom. As for handsome—well, at that time, midway from twenty to thirty, I was handsome enough. Not a movie star—my teeth not straight, my skin not smooth—but tall (which counts for a great deal with Chinese people), well built, confident. I had survived everything, I feared nothing, and I believed myself indestructible. I was pretty cocky, I guess.

5. Sea of Words

The weekend was warm. Walter and Abby across the street were sitting out on their porch. I went over and sat with them. Walter asked me if I wanted a martini. This is a drink popular with middle-class white Americans some decades ago. Walter has offered it to me before, and I always think it very droll to sit with them, this kindly old couple, drinking their antique drink and listening to the small sounds of suburban afternoon.

I asked Walter if he recalled President Coolidge.

Oh, sure. Great man. Also a good man.

So! A great man! So much for the panel of Eminent Historians! However, I restrained myself. To keep Walter on a topic you have to proceed slowly and gently.

I have heard it said that he slept through all five years in office.

Well, if he did, it was the right thing to do. Country got along just fine.

Why did you say a good man?

'Cause he was straight. Never lied, never cheated. Didn't put himself up as a superman, didn't make big promises. Didn't make any promises at all, as I recall. Just said vote for me, and things will go along all right. Well, we did, and they did. Not me, of course. Too young. But pretty much everybody else. Why, he even carried New York City—last Republican to do that, I think.

But in that case, why is he so little remembered?

Oh, well, you know. The Wall Street crash happened right after Coolidge left office. Then the depression. Folks felt Coolidge might have done something to stop it. And even the folks that didn't feel that way, well, the depression changed everything so much the twenties just seemed like a different age. Seemed like something far in the past. Y'know, when there's some terrific upheaval like that, it makes people forget everything that went before.

It's hard to keep Walter's mind on track, but well worth the effort. If you can hold him to a topic for five or ten minutes, he talks wonderful good sense. Now I was thinking of the speech before Agincourt in *Henry V*, and Dr. Johnson's commentary on it:

> *Crispin Crispian shall ne'er go by,*
> *From this day to the ending of the world,*
> *But we in it shall be remembered.*

> It may be observed that we are apt to promise to ourselves a more lasting memory than the changing state of human things admits. This prediction is not verified; the feast of *Crispin* passes by without any mention of *Agincourt*. Late events obliterate the former: the civil wars have left in this nation scarcely any tradition of more ancient history.

But while I was indulging myself in this pleasant and altogether appropriate remembrance, Walter had slipped into a rambling anecdote about a job he had held in the thirties, and I knew we had lost President Coolidge.

That evening Meng and his wife came for dinner. Meng comes from my own hometown in northeast China. Our families knew each other distantly. When he came to America in 1987 it was my responsibility to look after him, to show him how things were done. Now he has a good job with the Public Health Department in New York City. He married a girl also from the Northeast who works for one of the credit card companies. They have two small children, but Meng brought his mother over to live with them, so they don't have to worry about baby-sitters.

Ding cooked one of her specialties: alternate slices of lotus root and fat beef, arranged in a circle round the plate, all in a delicious brown sauce on a bed of crisp green beans. Several other dishes, too, of course. She is a terrific cook. Meng's wife can't cook at all. I think that's another reason he brought his mother over. When we go to visit them, it seems that Meng and his mother do all the cooking.

To tell the truth, we have not much in common with the Mengs, other than us all being Chinese. Even that doesn't really count for much, as none of us is much interested in Chinese public affairs. Still, it's an opportunity to get out of the house (for them, on this particular occasion).

Also to speak Chinese. Ding and I generally speak English to each other. If this seems odd, it really isn't. We first met at work, where of course everything is done in English. And then, she wanted very much to improve her English (which at that point was Dinglish), and looked up to me because of my fluency, and always wanted me to teach her better English. Sometimes, if one of us (usually she) is stuck for a mode of expression in English, or if we want to quote something, or use one of our language's colorful four-character idioms, we will fall back on Chinese. But for everyday matters we speak English.

Other matters aside, English is just smarter, more sophisticated, and more powerful. Once you have mastered English, Chinese seems very second-rate and . . . I don't know. Puerile. Volcano is *fire-mountain*. Saliva is *mouth-water*. Giraffe is *long-neck-deer*. Asbestos is *stone-cotton*. Do you know what the ring finger is called in Chinese? *Wu-ming-zhi*—the no-name finger. Five thousand years of civilization, and nobody could stir himself to think of a name for the fourth finger on every blessed human hand! Chinese is all like that. Monday, Tuesday, Wednesday are *One-day, Two-day, Three-day*. January, February, March? *One-month, Two-month, Three-month*. It's embarrassing. I think foreigners who learn Chinese must spend a lot of time laughing. And those characters! Ay ay ay, what a stupid way to write a language! You have to memorize thousands of the damn things, and for each one not only the meaning, but also the pronunciation. So primitive! To be sure, it makes the language difficult to learn, and that impresses some people. Not the unfoxable Dr. Samuel Johnson, of course.

> It is only more difficult from its rudeness; as there is more labour in hewing down a tree with a stone than with an axe.

Meng and his wife have quite different attitudes to ours. To my way of thinking, they have never adjusted properly to living in America. Meng is always putting down this country and its manners and institutions. I sometimes feel like saying to him: Why did you leave China, if you only intended to find fault with your new nation? The answer, of course, is that in America there is a good standard of living, very little chance of a dictator taking over and dragging the whole country through thirty years of lunacy, and no need to go begging on your knees to arrogant, corrupt officials for every form and permit. But you can like all that about a country without liking its people or its culture. This is the situation of the Mengs.

On this particular evening Meng is complaining, over dinner, about his neighborhood school. The Mengs live in Queens. Their eldest child has just started school. The other kids are giving him a hard time.

They call him Chink and flat face, said Meng. Especially the *heigui*. They're the worst.

There's a *heigui* district right next to ours, explained Meng's wife.

Their mothers', said Meng. I don't know why the Americans put up with them.

I said I thought it was the black person who had more to put up with, using *ren*—"person"—instead of *gui*—"demon." I don't like this *gui* stuff. Not that it really amounts to much. In Cantonese it carries no weight at all. They call all foreigners *gui*: a guy is a *guilou*, a woman a *guipo*, and even little boys and girls are *guijai* and *guileui*. I have heard an old Cantonese lady refer to cheese (very exotic to us Chinese until recently) as *gui daufu*—devil tofu. Northerners used to *gui* everything foreign, too, earlier in this century; but they were shamed out of it, except in reference to the Japanese, who were still *gui* in the propaganda texts of my childhood. Now the Party bosses want Japanese money, so *gui* is no longer used at all in Mainland Mandarin, except when someone is speaking facetiously. I don't know how it slipped back into the talk of New York Chinese. I don't use it myself, and neither does Ding. We are educated people, for heaven's sake.

Yes, said Ding—partly in support of me, partly to lighten the talk—for example, they have to put up with white Americans. I chuckled, though I did not altogether approve of the remark. Meng grinned despite himself; and his wife actually laughed, putting up a hand, palm inward, to hide her rotten teeth. I believe this was the first time I ever saw Mrs. Meng laugh.

Meng shut up about the *heigui*, anyway. I was glad. I really don't get into this race thing he has. But that is typical of Meng. He has, as I said, made no adjustment at all. He carries China around with him like body odor. He has all that appalling racial arrogance that caused Mr. Rudyard Kipling to suggest that his countrymen might be wise to exterminate the Chinese nation while they had the power to do so.

Meng's wife is an even worse case. Although she has been seven years in America, she still looks like a Mainlander. She wears slacks that are too short and too tight, ill-fitting blouses in meaningless colors, ugly unfashionable shoes, and ankle-highs. Ankle-highs! Ding used to wear knee-highs, which I even found quite attractive, or at any rate erotic, for a while. But I talked her out of them by showing her a newspaper article that said they caused phlebitis. But ankle-highs! And those heavy old-style spectacle frames—where does she get them? She must go out of her way to get them. Or have them sent from China. *She must like them!* And that awful perm. The women in China itself are better presented than this nowadays. (They are indeed, I sometimes think, when I encounter one of the newer arrivals, better presented than American women.) She looks as though she hasn't been to a dentist since she got off the plane. She is a fossil, a perfect specimen of middle-class thirtyish provincial Chinese womanhood circa 1985.

Her English stinks, too. Ding and I, between ourselves, call her Gu Nai. This is not her name. Her name is Zhao Lijun. But she has never mastered the art of pronouncing a consonant at the end of a syllable, so when she says good night (which was about all she did say when we first knew her) it comes out as gu nai. She learned just as much English as she needed to survive, made just as much concession to the weird, terrifying realm of not-China as she had to make, then shrank back into her cocoon.

I suppose this sounds cruel. Well, it is cruel, and I am ashamed. Meng's wife is actually in poor health. She was brought up in Fushun, a big industrial center in the Northeast. The air there is so polluted, it destroys everyone's lungs. Everyone in that town has respiratory disease. Most of them die in middle age. Mrs. Meng herself suffers from asthma. Over dinner she told us about some treatment she is getting in Chinatown.

That's another Chinese thing about the Mengs: they are suckers for any kind of medical quackery. Ding herself has tendencies in this direction, I am sorry to say. I have corrected her to a great extent, but still she occasionally expresses approval of acupuncture, moxibustion, or one of those other varieties of low-grade magic that have such a regrettable hold on the imaginations of my fellow countrymen. Then I have to remind her of what any sensible person who has looked into these matters knows: that Chinese medicine is to medicine as Chinese politics is to politics. And that Lu Xun, one of the wisest Chinese of modern times, was so horrified by the death of his father at the hands of traditional Chinese doctors that he left his country at the first opportunity to study Western medicine.

This time with Mrs. Meng it was some kind of autosuggestive therapy. Something like hypnosis, she said. But the guy gave her a drug first. To make her more suggestible.

What, you mean like a truth drug? asked Ding.

Not really. It's just something to open your mind. Make you more willing to go along with the therapist.

I'm surprised that's permitted, I said. Is this guy a qualified medical practitioner? Stupid question.

I'm not sure, said Mrs. Meng. He has some kind of qualifications. From Singapore, I think.

I'm surprised he's allowed to administer a drug like that, I said. I was thinking: It's probably a placebo.

Oh, said Meng laughing, you can get anything in Chinatown, you know.

Does he inject it? asked Ding.

No, you drink it. It's a kind of clear liquid. Astringent taste—something like a persimmon.

Very handy for seduction, I should think, I said.

Everybody laughed. Meng laughed a bit too loud, looking at Ding. He lusts after Ding, I know. All my friends do. It is a very crass thing to boast of one's wife, but there is no doubt Ding is very pretty. On this particular occasion she was wearing a stylish jogging suit that hid her figure, such as it is. But she cannot hide the smallness and delicacy of her features, her tiny hands and feet, her large mobile eyes, the clean grace of her every movement. Aware of Meng's lust, I felt lust rising myself, and decided I would embrace Ding when we went to bed. Seeing me looking at her with this thought in my mind, she read the thought at once and dropped her eyes from natural modesty, thus tripling the force of the thought instantly, to the degree that I began to experience some physical discomfort. For remedy I glanced at Meng's poor frumpy wife, whom no one would bother to seduce, and felt sorry for her, and ashamed of my many uncharitable thoughts about her.

Ding went upstairs to check on Hetty, who tends to kick off her little quilt when settling down for the night. I took the Mengs into the living room and poured more wine for him. We had already established that she was driving them home. Mrs. Meng never drinks much anyway. Along with her other afflictions, she has that unfortunate condition—quite common among the Chinese—which reacts to even small quantities of alcohol with fierce blushing. We say that alcohol affects a person in one of five ways, depending on the person's constitution. It goes to the heart to produce maudlin emotions; or to the liver to incite pugnacity; or to the stomach to cause drowsiness and blushing; or to the lungs to induce hilarity; or to the kidneys to excite lust. In myself it goes to the kidneys, so long as I do not overindulge. Ding is similarly affected, which accounts for our rather disgraceful rate of consumption of wine. But poor Mrs. Meng, poor Gu Nai, just droops and blushes.

My Coolidge books were on the coffee table in front of our sofa. Meng picked up each one, examined the title and riffled the interior pages, then set them down. Coolidge, he said. Thirtieth president.

This stunned me. I would have been sufficiently astonished to hear that he knew of Washington and Lincoln—but Coolidge?

I memorized all the presidents, explained Meng at my query. It's the kind of thing they might ask you for citizenship. And it impresses Americans very much. They know nothing about their own history, you know, and of course never memorize anything. I memorized the tenth, twentieth, thirtieth, and fortieth, then the ones in between. Easiest way. "To study the bamboo, start with the joints." Also the capitals of the states. If you know the presidents, and the capitals of the states, Americans will think you're smart. You already know more about their country than most of *them* know.

I thought this a cheap trick, based on a misunderstanding of the American educational system, which aims at breadth rather than depth. But Meng was full of himself now, and there was no stopping him. Ask me a state, he said, and I'll tell you the capital.

Suppose I ask you to tell me something about Mr. Coolidge, other than his presidential number.

Meng laughed. Sorry. The number is all I know. But ask me a state.

Ding came back down the stairs. She is fast asleep, she said, meaning Hetty. What's this about states?

My old man is showing off, said Mrs. Meng. He knows the capitals of all the states.

I don't see the use of that. Ding walked through to the dining room for her wineglass. I don't even know the capitals of the Chinese provinces.

I bet Meng doesn't, either. It was a bit spiteful, to spoil his dumb party trick. But I could see at once that I was right.

Mrs. Meng rode to her husband's rescue. Why are you reading about this guy? What's his name? What is it in Chinese, I mean?

Well, he seems to have been an excellent president. And now, quite unaccountably, he is forgotten. (I could not very well say *I like his face.*) As for his Chinese name, I really don't know. Perhaps your husband knows. He memorized them all.

No, said Meng, I did it from an American book.

All right. I'll look him up in *Sea of Words,* I said, getting up and walking to the study. Our house is old, as these things go in America—built in 1925. A Coolidge house!—it occurred to me suddenly, walking to the study. The first people who bought it lived there more than fifty years. The old boy at last became crippled with arthritis and could not climb the stairs. He had a little annex built off from the main living room, with its own bathroom attached, and lived there his last few years. I had made this annex into a study, all lined with bookshelves. Among my books were two *Sea of Words,* the generic title for any Chinese encyclopedia. I took down the later one, a Mainland edition from 1979, and carried it back to the living room. There was a special index of Western names and their Chinese transcriptions.

> *Kelizhi.* U.S. President 1923–1929. Republican. Senator and governor of Massachusetts. Elected vice-president 1920. Succeeded to the presidency 1923 following death of President Harding. While in office carried out the *Daoweisi* plan, propping up Germany, allowing U.S. power to advance into Europe.

I read this out to the company, who wanted to know what the *Daoweisi* plan was. I pursued the cross-reference, which was to a politician called Dawes, Mr. Coolidge's vice-president, who had worked out some scheme to reschedule German reparations from World War I.

Not very exciting, said Mrs. Meng.

I could see that Ding agreed with her. But Ding will always support my enthusiasms in company, however sarcastic she may be in private. Try the other one, she said, meaning the other *Sea of Words*. Perhaps it's more informative. I went back to the study and pulled down the older *Sea of Words*. This one is from the Nationalist period, the forties. I found it in a secondhand bookstore in Hong Kong many years ago. It is out-of-date, of course, but has a certain charm which pleases me. All the entries are in classical Chinese, a very abbreviated language, originally intended not for the communication of new ideas but as a mnemonic device for calling to mind old ones. It is, for example, considered very stylish in classical Chinese to omit the subject of a sentence altogether—and the main verb too, if possible.

> *Guliqi.* 30th pres. U.S. Graduated Anmaisite College. Entered law, served as congressman & governor of Mass. Serious & principled in conduct of duties. 1920 Republican Party chose him vice-president. 1923 Harding died suddenly and unexpectedly, became president. Retired 1929.

For "died suddenly and unexpectedly" this *Sea of Words* used the single archaic character *zu,* which thrilled me very much. But I translated it to modern Chinese when I read it out, sure that no one but me would know *zu,* and not wanting to embarrass the others. They had all had their educations destroyed by the Great Cultural Revolution. It wasn't their fault.

Well, said Meng, it's kinder than the other one.

The other one is from the seventies, I said. Of course they must find some fault with any American president.

Amherst College, said Mrs. Meng in English. I know that. In Massachusetts.

Mrs. Meng is very ambitious for her kids. The oldest one's only just in grade school, and already she's been reading up colleges.

If you want to read about a president, why not choose Abraham Lincoln or George Washington? said Meng. They are much more important. This guy seems like a real nonentity.

It was a good period in American history, said Ding, helping out. The Peach Blossom Country.

The Peach Blossom Country is in the next world, not in this one, said Meng.

When they had gone I was overcome with lust and embraced Ding on the sofa. A little the worse for drink, Ding was enthusiastic and rather noisy. Afterward I told her our house was a Coolidge house.

She laughed, stroking my hair. I have to share you with these old dead men. One after another.

But with no one else, I said.

No, said Ding. I don't mind the old dead men. But I couldn't bear anyone else.

6.   *Compassion Boat Temple*

The first place I embraced Selina was on top of a mountain.
The mountain is called Big Hat Mountain. It is in the New
Territories behind Hong Kong, north and west of Kowloon,
overlooking the town of Chuen Wan.

I still had no place of my own where I could take her. I was
living in a single men's hostel. Of course, I could not take her
there. And she herself was reluctant to be alone with me. She
did not trust me—quite correctly, of course. Our first date, the
only thing she would consent to was, we went to the Aberdeen
cemetery with her uncle and his family. It was the Chongyang
festival, the ninth of the ninth lunar month, when Chinese
people pay respects to their dead. Selina's uncle and his wife,
and their numerous children, and Selina, and myself, took a
bus out to the cemetery. We climbed up through the graves to
where Selina's uncle's parents were buried.

As a general rule I am not fond of cemeteries. Most
northerners feel the same way. When I was sent down to the
countryside following the suppression of the Red Guards, I
lived in a production brigade too poor and out-of-the-way to
have any movie shows. To see a movie we had to trek several
miles. Part of the way was through a hillside cemetery. There
was a cliff above and a bog below, so there was no way to avoid
going through the cemetery. We didn't mind so much in the
daylight, but coming back after the movie it was pitch dark.
Can you imagine walking through a cemetery in darkness? I

certainly would not do it nowadays. When you are young you don't mind things so much. Even so, we used to run as fast as we could, leaping over the gravestones, screaming at the tops of our voices to keep the ghosts at bay.

Southerners, or at any rate Hong Kongers, are not so scared of ghosts. Selina used to read ghost stories for pleasure. Myself, I could not even get far into *Strange Stories from Liao's Studio,* though it is a classic, written in the classical idiom, and Teacher Ouyang had recommended it to me. In the comic-strip sections of Hong Kong newspapers there were often jokes about graves and ghosts—a thing you would never see in North China, even today I think.

Well, I was speaking of the Chongyang festival, of going to the cemetery with Selina's uncle. The uncle was a decent sort. He was Selina's nearest relative now in the Colony and had agreed to provide a bunk bed for her until her U.S. visa came through. He was not particularly protective of her and displayed little interest in her comings and goings. On that first meeting she introduced me to him simply as *pangyau:* a friend. He accepted this with a smile and a handshake, and off we went to the cemetery.

While the uncle and his family were laying out food on the grave and burning hell money, I walked off a little way with Selina and tried to get some conversation going. Her mother was in China, I learned. Her father had disappeared in one of the movements—the Hundred Flowers, I think. He had been a schoolteacher. The Hundred Flowers was a movement in which people were encouraged to criticize the Party. Selina's father had written a letter to the local newspaper commenting on the corruption and dishonesty of the Party bosses in their town. Soon afterward he disappeared. He was either dead, or breaking rocks in Tibet.

Selina was angry toward her father. He shouldn't have done that, she said. He should have known better. He wasn't smart. The result was, his wife and child were left with no support.

I could see her point of view. But also his, of course. Selina saw her father as a provider: a father, a husband, a man about the house. The poor schnook saw himself as a responsible member of society, with larger duties, beyond the merely domestic. I could all too easily imagine myself doing what he did.

That happened when she was an infant. Then, in the dreadful famine of 1959–61, her grandmother and aunt had fled to Hong Kong with Selina. Her mother had stayed behind in China, for reasons I never knew. The aunt had fixed up a marriage with a guy who had relatives in the States. The year before I met Selina the aunt and grandmother had gone over to San Francisco. Selina's case was taking longer to settle, because the relationship was so indirect. She omitted to mention fiancé Yoy at this point.

None of this was very unusual—a typical Hong Kong story, in fact. But I showed sincere interest, murmured words of sympathy, and got a smile out of her before we went back to the grave to join her uncle's party. They had finished paying respects and were eating the food they had laid out for the ancestors. Why let it go to waste? We Chinese are a practical people.

I told Chan about all this the following Monday at work. Better get your own place, said Chan. No point having a girl if you can't make hotcakes with her.

I said I couldn't afford it.

Let me see what I can find out, said Chan.

Our next date was a movie, a Chinese weepy. I can still remember the damn thing.

> Jifung liked the good life. His people were well-off and spoiled him. What he liked most of all was driving expensive cars too fast. There was an accident and he was blinded. Waisuen came from a poor background, but she loved Jifung and meant to marry him, in spite of her parents' disapproval. After the accident she told him his blindness made no difference to her. But because he loved her he wouldn't let her sacrifice herself for him, and he sent her away. She kept coming to see him. Eventually he threw a screaming fit and told her he never wanted to hear her voice again. Poor Waisuen! She went off and married a decent, boring guy her parents introduced. They had children and humdrum domesticity. After many years Jifung was sent to an eye surgeon in the States, who restored his sight with some new technique. Jifung and Waisuen met by chance. He told her he'd always loved her. He asked her to come back. She ran home. There was hubby with kids. She agonized. She went to places she knew Jifung might be, and watched him from a distance. He found out where she lived and came to the house when she was alone. They talked. He left. She cried. She left the house and walked for miles, to a beach. Turner sunset. She walked into the sea.

I think she should have left her husband, I said as we were walking back up Nathan Road to her uncle's. The way it worked out, her husband lost her anyway, so it would all be the same so far as he was concerned.

Oh, no, said Selina. She did the right thing. There was no other way. And I thought: This is a very serious girl.

The third time we walked out was Big Hat Mountain. It was Double Tenth—tenth of October, that is, on the Western calendar. It's a big holiday for the Nationalists, commemorating the 1911 uprising, when the old imperial system was overthrown by Dr. Sun Yat-sen and his revolutionaries. The Communists regard their own revolution as definitive. They play down 1911 and celebrate a different National Day, October first. Well, on Double Tenth—it was a Sunday—I had arranged to go walking in the New Territories with Selina. Mr. Chan had suggested this. There was a pretty temple, he told me, called Compassion Boat Temple, in the hills above Chuen Wan.

We took a minibus out of the city and walked up through the villages scattered over the lower slopes of the mountain. Because it was Double Tenth there were Nationalist flags everywhere—white sun on blue sky—and pictures of Dr. Sun. He always looks so sad, said Selina, referring to Dr. Sun.

Because nobody would listen to him. That's what made him sad, I replied. The truth, as always in public affairs, is much more complicated than that. Selina had done well in school, and her people were of Nationalist sympathies, so I'm sure she knew I was oversimplifying. But she did not correct me.

Compassion Boat Temple is actually shaped like a boat, though it is halfway up a mountain. The idea is that Guan Yin, the Goddess of Compassion and Bodhisattva of the Southern Ocean, ferries dead souls into the other world on a boat. There is a statue of Guan Yin, and a very find one of Duke Guan— no relation—the Taoist God of War, Money, and Literature. Also some other statues of Buddhist and Taoist deities, and a little shrine to Confucius. What a mess Chinese religion is!

When we had exhausted the pleasures of the temple we ventured farther up the mountain. The villages petered out at last, and we climbed up a steep track to a ridge overlooking the bay. Chuen Wan was far below us, only some stray distorted mechanical sounds finding their way up the mountainside, remote hummings and clankings. We had seen no one since leaving the villages behind five hundred feet below. We sat on the grass, looking out across the bay to Ching-yi Island. After half an hour Selina permitted me to kiss her; and an hour later, after many refusals and some tears, she yielded to me altogether, on the grass high up there on the ridge, on Big Hat Mountain, our only witness a solitary grasshopper who materialized, without any movement at all, in my field of vision just before the moment of release and left— same freeze-frame instantaneity—as I was returning to earth.

It was one of our few adventures in alfresco copulation. Hong Kong is a very crowded place: spot density in Mong-gok hits one person per square meter. You need to climb a fairly large mountain to be sure of solitude. Such efforts, while worthwhile in their own way, were soon no longer necessary. The week after Double Tenth Mr. Chan took me to check out an apartment in Temple Street, back of Nathan Road. It was tiny and unfurnished, up four flights of unlit stairs, its only window looking out across two feet of space to a blank wall. (Building codes were not taken very seriously in Hong Kong.) However, Mr. Chan knew the brother of the owner's wife, and he got a deal I could just afford, with sufficient left over to buy a bed, a quilt, and a hot plate. I moved in that Friday.

Oh, my little apartment! It was the first place I had ever had of my own—this, at the age of twenty-six. Now, in my mind's eye, twenty years later, I can see it still. And smell it, and hear it. The smell was the Hong Kong smell: food, joss, garbage, and the sea.

The sound effects were at first only the hum of air conditioners and the clatter of mah-jongg tiles from some neighboring apartment. There was always a mah-jongg game going on somewhere within earshot, at any time of the day or night.

Then I bought a cassette player and we could listen to Chinese pop music. There was a singer Selina particularly liked, called Yip Leiyi. This woman modeled her singing style on an American lady called Connie Francis. In fact I believe she later tried to conquer the American market, using the name Francis Yip. But at this date she sang only in Mandarin.

Sweet, sentimental songs, the tunes mostly stolen from the West—the International Copyright Convention was held in even less esteem than the building codes. There was one song I particularly recall: "Can't Forget Our First Love"—in Chinese, "Wo Nan Wang Wo Liang-de Chu-Lian." Many years later I discovered that the tune was "Bésame Mucho," but Miss Yip took it to places Los Paraguayos never knew.

> Wo-o nan wang
> Wo-o nan wa-a-a-a-aaang.
> La la la laaa la la la la
> La la la laaa-aaa-aaa
> Wo liang-de chu-u-u-u- lia-a-a-a-a-a-a-an . . .

The strange potency of cheap music!—as one of Mr. Noel Coward's characters remarks. I can hear that clear, sweet voice now, and see Compassion Boat Temple under an October sky, Guan Yin all in white, the Duke's face and hands glossy dark blood red, one hand grasping his mighty halberd, his long black beard and mustaches and sideburns rippling down over the gold bosses of his breastplate like five black reptilian fingers, Selina shaking out the lucky sticks in one of the side temples, Big Hat Mountain lowering above, waiting for us— patient, silent.

The manager of our Hong Kong operation was in New York last year. He told me Compassion Boat Temple is still there, but the track up through the villages, and the very villages themselves, have been obliterated to make way for the Complete Harmony housing estate. So things pass, so all things pass.

7.   The Scholars

The more I learned of Mr. Coolidge, the more I loved the man.

I grasped very quickly that he was not really a politician at all. He spoke of politicians as a species separate from his own, and with little affection.   ,

> The political mind is the product of men in public life who have been twice spoiled. They have been spoiled with praise and they have been spoiled with abuse. With them nothing is natural, everything is artificial.

This pleased me very much. I do not like politics. Like most Chinese who lived through the movements of the fifties, sixties, and seventies, I think of politics as a fundamentally harmful activity, a destroyer of people's lives. Mr. Coolidge did not see things in that light, of course. It was only that he was by nature not a politician, but a moralist. This I learned from his speeches, a volume of which I found at the Strand bookstore on lower Broadway. None of the speeches referred to any issues. They were lectures on ethics.

> The people cannot look to legislation for success. Industry, thrift, character, are not conferred by act or resolve. Government cannot relieve from toil. It can provide no substitute for the rewards of service. It can, of course, care for the defective and recognize distinguished

merit. The normal must care for themselves. Self-government means self-support.

Work is not a curse, it is the prerogative of intelligence, the only means to manhood, and the measure of civilization. Savages do not work. The growth of a sentiment that despises work is an appeal from civilization to barbarism.

It is conceived that there can be a horizontal elevation of the standards of the nation, immediate and perceptible, by the simple device of new laws. This has never been the case in human experience. Progress is slow and the result of a long and arduous process of self-discipline. Real reform does not begin with a law, it ends with a law. The attempt to dragoon the body when the need is to convince the soul will end only in revolt.

The man was a Confucian, I said to Ding one evening over dinner. Human beings naturally good. Social harmony through the moral perfection of self. Serve the people. Not much need for laws if the leaders give a good example.

What actual policies did he promote? she asked, my practical wife.

I have hardly been able to find any. He didn't think the government should interfere in things unless there was a pressing need.

He must have had *some* policies. He was president for several years, wasn't he?

Five and a half. Well, there was Constructive Economy.

What did that mean?

I think it meant not spending any money. Then there was Allowing Administration to Catch Up with Legislation. That meant not passing any laws. He said it was much more important to kill bad bills than to pass good ones.

I don't know about a Confucian. Sounds to me more like a Taoist. You know: *wuwei wu suo bu wei ye.*

I was surprised, and pleased, to find my wife so familiar with ancient literature. This tag was from the *Morality Classic.* The meaning is: By means of *wuwei* there is nothing that cannot be accomplished. *Wuwei* is a principle, supposedly one of the underlying principles of nature. In a human context it means something like Watchful Inaction.

Hetty was sitting with us at the table, in her high chair, and at this point she ejected a mouthful of milk, and some fast mopping-up was necessary. By the time we settled again I had lost the thread of our talk.

Perhaps, said Ding, there is a Coolidge museum. Like the ones we saw for the Roosevelt presidents.

Presidents Roosevelt, I corrected her. Usage is always her weak point. I think we can easily find out. Mr. Coolidge was born in Vermont. If we call information for Vermont they will be able to tell us.

I did this from the kitchen table, which is within reach of the phone, and learned that there is indeed a Coolidge Foundation in Plymouth Notch, Vermont—Mr. Coolidge's natal place.

I don't think anybody will be there this late in the evening, said Ding.

Well, I shall call them tomorrow.

Perhaps we could go there for the colors. One stone two birds.
New England has beautiful colors. Earlier than New York.

Our custom, since we got married, has been to take a drive up
into New York State to view the fall foliage. We try to catch
the colors at their peak, which in New York is generally late
October. It began as just a Sunday drive; but last year, when
Ding was big with Hetty, we stayed overnight at a lodge on
Lake George to avoid too much continuous driving.

I shall call first thing tomorrow.

Yes, said Ding. Let's find out. I should like to see the colors in
Vermont.

I did call the next morning. A kind lady called Rebecca gave
me the addresses of some motels near the Coolidge homestead
and sold me some Coolidge books. But that was the day of
Boris's party, so now I have to explain about Uncle Sergei and
his catalog.

Boris has an uncle, Uncle Sergei, who is very old and very
eccentric.

The particular form his eccentricity takes is bibliophilia. To be
precise, Uncle Sergei collects Slavic literature. Collected, I
should say. Six years ago he suffered a stroke which, while it
left his faculties unimpaired, demoralized him in some
fashion, so that he gave up collecting. By this time he had
accumulated many thousands of pieces, some of them very
valuable. First editions of Pushkin, the photograph albums of
the czars, ukases and proclamations, and a mass of religious
stuff—fourteenth-century illuminated manuscripts, psalters,
triodions, mineias and meaneons, heirmologions and

tetraevangelions, sticherarions, octoechos in neumes. (Let me show off a little here; I worked hard on this stuff.) The whole of Boris's family is involved with the Russian Orthodox church, in ways I have never bothered to sort out. I think Boris's grandfather was a metropolitan, or a beatitude, or one of those things.

Uncle Sergei never married. He made a small fortune on Wall Street in his younger days and thereafter lived quietly in an apartment on the Upper West Side with all these books and manuscripts. Well, following Uncle Sergei's stroke, after he had sat motionless among this vast priceless collection for a year or two, Boris and his brother Cyril decided to produce a catalog of it, partly with a view to advertising and ultimately—nobody supposed Uncle Sergei would live forever—selling the collection, either in whole or piecemeal, and partly (as Boris said) as their family's contribution to Slavic scholarship.

Uncle Sergei had enough money to do the thing properly, so Boris and Cyril recruited some scholars from the big auction houses and universities and let them loose in Uncle Sergei's collection.

The thing they couldn't get anyone to do was the index. Indexing is dull work, beneath the dignity of real scholars. On the other hand, whoever indexed the catalog needed to be able to read Russian as well as English, to put items in the right categories and the correct order. Well, Boris pulled me in to do it. We agreed a fixed rate and I did it all on one of the office PCs, using a simple set of escape sequences for the Russian and Bulgarian alphabets. Boris and Cyril themselves are both perfectly computer-illiterate. So are all these eminent scholars and antiquarians. It's a point of pride with them, in fact. I can't afford to be so proud. I have to use the damn things, and keep up with all the changes.

Well, the catalog was now complete, and Harvard University Press had completed the first print run. It was really very well done. The paper was archival quality, made by a specialist mill in Massachusetts, the binding a fine red vellum cloth stamped with gold. There were two volumes in a slipcase covered with the same cloth. Boris himself took the photographs, including some fine color plates.

As well as the index, I ghosted the acknowledgments, both Boris and Cyril having high regard for my ability in composition. At the time—this was about a year ago—I was deep into Johnson, reading the *Rambler*s I think, so the thing came out somewhat in the ponderous, Latinate style of the great lexicographer. I even brought him in by name:

> If, as Dr. Johnson tells us, the chief glory of every nation arises from its authors, then the collector of books must be content to shine in reflected glory, whilst those who compile his catalogs should consider themselves fortunate to catch a glimmer twice reflected. . . .

To celebrate the completion of the enterprise, and to show appreciation to all of us who had worked on the catalog, there was to be a party at Boris's apartment, the family paying to fly the Harvard people in from Boston.

Ding engaged a baby-sitter and we drove in to Manhattan. Boris's apartment is in the East Eighties, near the Metropolitan Museum. You can park right outside after 7:00.

Boris's wife took our coats and led us into the living room. Boris trundled over to give Ding a kiss and a sweaty hug. My little lotus blossom, he panted, beaming down at her. Boris, too, lusts after my wife. She quite discommodes him, in fact. When he is speaking with her he glows and trembles, his pudgy hands wabbling in front of him as if he were struggling to restrain himself. This is only amusing. There is no harm in Boris. His own marriage is solid, based on the principle— which seems to be a source of great strength to some couples—that husband and wife should maintain entirely separate social lives, meeting only at home. There is no fathoming other people's marriages.

Cyril was there—an old bachelor, like Uncle Sergei, some kind of corporate lawyer—talking in Russian to a short, stocky fellow with a thick black beard. Seeing us, he waved to bring us over.

Our ghostwriter, said Cyril, beaming at us. Who would have thought a scholarly catalog needed a ghostwriter?

I introduced Ding. Cyril kissed her hand in an exaggerated, but apparently quite sincere, manner. He introduced us to the beard, a theologian from the Ukraine without a single word of English. He was studying at a seminary in upstate New York, and the brothers had hired him to help classify the religious materials. Cyril, who I have always found to be a close man, made some inconsequential small talk, all of which had to be translated into Russian for the beard.

Boris came back and took Ding and me to see some new acquisition he had made from one of the auction houses. It was a beautiful religious painting on boards, the boards hinged in an ingenious way so that the whole thing folded down to carryable size. Apparently there was some kind of reformation in the Orthodox church in the seventeenth century, and the Old Believers were proscribed. To preserve their faith they relied on wandering priests, who had to carry their religious impedimenta with them. Boris explained the difference between Old Believers and New Believers to Ding, at quite unnecessary length. The main thing seemed to be that one group used only two fingers when crossing themselves, the other three. Ding strove to look interested.

When we got back to the main reception room more guests had arrived. I knew these people, at least to the degree of having spoken on the telephone with them. Two of them, who had apparently come together with their wives on the shuttle, were academics from the Department of Slavic Studies at Harvard: Professor Kroll and Dr. Kazinsky. Just arrived were an Irishman who worked the computerized typesetting machines for Harvard University Press, and his large florid wife. Standing off at one side was a beaky Englishwoman called Doris, who worked for one of the auction houses, and who had brought with her a small, shy-looking young woman I had not seen before.

Muff divers, said Boris.

I beg your pardon?

Doris is a dyke. That's her, whaddya call it? Catamite?

Boris, I refuse to participate in the denigration of an inoffensive minority.

Boris guffawed. Ding was squinting in that overattentive way she has when something has passed over her head. She was going to ask about *muff divers*, I knew, so I preempted the query. Boris implies that the two females on the other side are same-sexers, I explained in Chinese.

Ding is marvelous. She didn't move her head to look, not even a millimeter. Only: You really have a beautiful apartment, Boris.

It's yours, honey, slobbered Boris, glowing like a lighthouse. For just one night of bliss.

Ding blushed and looked down, but I could see she was not displeased.

Your man Coolidge, said Boris to me, was a cuckold.

I said I found that hard to believe. My understanding of the president was not yet deep enough for me to issue the strong denial that would really have been more appropriate.

Certainly, Boris continued. His wife had a cicisbeo. Secret Service man. Coolidge found out and fired the guy.

Now I knew the incident Boris referred to, and which he had misrepresented very wildly. There was, in fact, no hanky-panky at all: only a single incident in which Mrs. Coolidge had gone for a walk in the country and got lost. The Coolidge marriage was cloudless. He adored his wife, and she him. One of Mr. Coolidge's few recreations was window-shopping, to buy dresses and gifts for her. However, my attention was snagged on *cicisbeo*.

A married woman's gallant, giggled Boris. From the Italian.

In our relationship Boris is the one long on aesthetics, I am the word man. But he likes to trump me now and again with words. Probably spends hours looking them up. It's a power thing. He's my boss, after all. My satisfaction—which I enjoy in silence, of course—is that he rarely serves one of these aces without a foot fault; in this case, wrongly stressing the first syllable of *gallant*.

At this point Uncle Sergei arrived. The doorbell rang and Boris's wife went up to attend to it. There were voices in the hallway: Boris's wife and another Englishwoman. There were some rattling and clanking sounds, a wheelchair being folded away, I later discerned, then footsteps—very slow footsteps—toward the dining room door. At last Uncle Sergei appeared.

I had never seen Uncle Sergei before, in spite of having spent some hundreds of hours working on his indexes. I knew that he was very old—a year older than the century, Boris always said. He looked to be entirely self-possessed. Holding a stick, but not really leaning on it. Impeccably dressed in the old Wall Street style—sober suit, detachable collar and cuffs, vest and pocket watch. He was very short—one of those people whom the aging process *squashes,* so that his physiognomy was now almost that of a dwarf. But erect and clear-eyed, and with sufficient presence that we all stopped talking to look when he entered the room. Boris's wife came in behind him, turning to beckon in the new Englishwoman, who was apparently Uncle Sergei's nurse.

Boris rolled over to where the old man was standing, surveying us.

Uncle Sergei, surely you didn't walk, did you?

Uncle Sergei stood silent and immobile. The nurse answered for him. We came over in the wheelchair, she said. It's all right, we wrapped up warm. The identificational plural slipped past me at first, and I had a happy little vision of the two of them crammed into one wheelchair.

We can go in to dinner, suggested Boris's wife. Rather than sitting down and then getting up again.

With Boris at one elbow and the nurse at the other, Uncle Sergei was trundled into the dining room, the rest of us shuffling behind. After a great deal of fussing he was seated at the head of the table, Boris and his wife on one side, Cyril and ourselves on the other. The academics occupied the center of the table, with Uncle Sergei's nurse down at the end with the lesbians.

The food was very Russian: freshwater fish, pickled mushrooms, cabbage, beetroot, cucumbers and tomatoes, more fish in a pie. Butter and vinegar; no sauces, not much spice. A harsh red wine.

I am open-minded about food, but I know Ding doesn't really like anything not Chinese. However, she cleaned her plate, and complimented Boris's wife very nicely. There was a lot of talk about mailing lists to promote the catalog. Boris and Cyril had found a firm that specializes in that sort of thing. Dr. Kazinsky made conversation in Russian with the bearded Ukrainian. The beaky Englishwoman and the Irish couple talked over the Irish Problem in that terrifically careful way people have when they do not want to give offense to others whose views they are not quite sure of. Uncle Sergei did not seem inclined to speak. He engaged in only one brief exchange, with Cyril, in Russian. Otherwise he sat eating stolidly, and incredibly slowly.

Professor Kroll's wife was very pretty. Thirty years younger than he, I thought. Kroll was a rather distinguished-looking man, early sixties probably, stooped and gray-haired, but great intelligence in the face. And a sort of canny look—acquired, I suppose, in countless funding battles and interdepartmental squabbles. American academic life, Boris had explained to me once, is intensely political.

Chai here was a Red Guard, said Boris to Kroll. Storm trooper in the Cultural Revolution.

Is that so? Kroll looked amused. Can you recite some of the *Little Red Book* for us?

I really don't care to, I said. It's a part of my life I'd prefer to put firmly behind me.

Are there any Communists left in China now? asked Mrs. Kroll.

Oh, certainly. My wife's father is a dedicated Communist. Lifelong Party member, was a colonel in the People's Liberation Army. Now retired.

And your own father? asked Kroll.

An engineer. Died in the Korean War.

Why, you don't look old enough to have been born before the Korean War, said Mrs. Kroll. I caught something in the eyes— not really any kind of invitation, just a quick erotic flash. Probably just unconscious habit on her part.

How long before we are at war with China again? asked Kroll out of the blue.

Taken aback, I could think of no response. But the remark had stirred a patriotic response in Ding's breast. We don't want to have war with anybody, she said. Never been a conquering power.

No. Not when the outside world was populated by barbarians. Hardly worth the trouble. But what about now, when it's full of *rivals?* There can only be one sun in the sky—isn't that a Chinese saying? Kroll was smiling genially at us to dull the edge of his bold remarks.

I could see that Ding did not care for this talk. She turned to Uncle Sergei and, with that combination of tact and directness she can employ when it pleases her to, said: You must have seen a great many things in your life, sir.

This roused him. He turned his eyes to her. You could tell that he must once have been a formidable man.

I have seen the czar blessing the Neva, said Uncle Sergei. Then, as if in sadness at the thought, he dropped his head to look at his plate, and picked up a fork. His sadness rolled down the table like cold air billowing in from an open door.

What an immense thing it can seem, this human life! Here was Uncle Sergei, born in the last century, eleven years old—already sentient!—when Tolstoy died, witnessed the Russian Revolution, fled the country with Bolsheviks at his heels, his mother's diamonds sewn into her petticoat. (These things I had learned from Boris.) Made a fortune in the twenties boom, got out of the market before the crash, dropped everything—and sold off his first book collection—to serve in the U.S. Navy in World War II. Retired around the time I was born. *I have seen the czar blessing the Neva*. What a span of time! What a mass of experience—of *history*—to be carried about inside one small, fragile ring of bone! Uncle Sergei's eyes might have seen men who saw Napoleon in Moscow. Continue the chain another, what? five or six links, and you are speaking of Black Tooth, the Mongol chieftain to whom Boris's family owe their name.

I noted with approval, as a connoisseur of such things, that Uncle Sergei's English had practically no trace of Russian accent. Only a slight darkening of the laterals and a residual desire to terminate nasals on the palate: *bwessink the Nyeva*. But barely noticeable—which was all the more remarkable, really, since he had presumably suffered some minor brain damage from the stroke, as well as being very old, so that one might expect some regression to infantile forms.

I wonder, did you ever see Calvin Coolidge? The question escaped from me without any thought at all.

Uncle Sergei lifted up to me his saurian gaze. He had taken some cucumber into his mouth and was chewing very slowly—but was obviously going to give me a reply, in the fullness of time.

Our oriental friend here is a Coolidge buff, said Boris to Uncle Sergei, to give him a chance to cope with the cucumber. His manner to Uncle Sergei was deeply deferential—a side of him I had never seen before.

Uncle Sergei continued masticating, a column of vinegar trickling from the far corner of his mouth. Cyril leaned forward with a napkin to stem the flow: and the old fellow still had me locked in his scaly stare.

Ah, Silent Cal, said Dr. Kazinsky. Could be silent in seven languages, so I've heard.

The business of America is business, said Boris's wife.

I shook hands with him, uttered Uncle Sergei.

What? Boris laughed. I never knew that.

Some of us young fellows went on a jaunt. To Washington, D.C. It was the time of the 1924 campaign. We were all for Coolidge, of course. Coolidge or Chaos, that was the slogan. Myself, I had seen enough of chaos.

He stopped, and took his eyes from me. He seemed to consider he had finished.

And so . . . how did you come to shake hands with Mr. Coolidge? I prompted.

Went over to the White House. Coolidge used to come out at twelve-thirty every day to shake hands. With anybody. Anybody wanted his hand shaken, Coolidge would shake it.

Uncle Sergei seemed amused by his own last remark. He cracked a smile and his shoulders trembled.

Did he say anything to you?

No. Not a word.

What was his manner? Happy, bored, or what?

Seemed cheerful enough. That was before his son died, of course. Such a dreadful thing. Broke his heart, I believe. Middle of the twenty-four campaign. Didn't campaign after that. Won anyway, of course. Didn't campaign, but won anyway. Landslide. Fine man, fine president.

Of course, this was very fascinating to me, notwithstanding the very slight content of the story. I was also relishing the word *jaunt*, which I did not think I had heard spoken before. I could see them, these young Wall Street men, swaggering around the streets of Washington in sunlight—hands in their pockets, hats on their heads—smoking cigars, perhaps. A *jaunt*. Well, it was a jaunty age. The Last Arcadia. I was also reflecting that, having shaken hands with Uncle Sergei, I had shaken hands at only one remove with Mr. Coolidge, thus improving my one-remove tally, whose previous star was Generalissimo Chiang Kai-shek. I wanted to ask if Uncle Sergei had witnessed any evidences of Mr. Coolidge's whistling, but could think of no way to frame a polite question.

Here's a Coolidge story, said Cyril. Coolidge was at a function once. The woman seated next to him said: Oh Mr. President, you must make conversation with me. I have made a bet that I can get more than two words out of you. Coolidge: You lose.

This made everybody laugh. Then we all had to wait while Cyril translated it for the Ukrainian. The Ukrainian frowned and asked some questions. Gooleezh? *Kyoo*leezh? Cyril did some explaining. Then Boris did some explaining. It did the Ukrainian no good—he just shook his head at last and bent to his food.

It was inherited, you know, not acquired, I said. The taciturnity. I had learned this from Mr. Gamaliel Bradford's essay on Coolidge, "The Genius of the Average."

Oh, I'm sure that's right, said Kroll. The man was a New Englander, a true Yankee. When there still were such things.

You don't think there are Yankees anymore? asked Boris.

Kroll shook his head. Not the real article. Even in the twenties, that New England was dead. That's why people made such fun of Coolidge. He was a relic. The old New England—the New England of Longfellow and Hawthorne, the New England of Robert Frost—was already gone, as dead as Buffalo Bill's Wild West. Coolidge was a curiosity.

I volunteered another Coolidge story—I had a stock of them from my reading. In this one a group of Amherst men in Spain decided to have a dinner. They thought it would be very grand to have Mr. Coolidge, an Amherst man himself, send them an address to be read at the dinner, so they got in touch with his secretary. Knowing the president's parsimony they made it plain they would pay the entire cable transmission costs for any address he cared to send. A cable duly arrived. At the high point of the dinner, the chairman stood up and announced that it was now his privilege to read to the company an address by the president of the United States. He opened the envelope and read out the message: GENTLEMEN GREETINGS CALVIN COOLIDGE.

I paced the story well and delivered it with some skill, if I may say so. Everybody laughed, including even Uncle Sergei. Doris embarked on a Churchill story we had all heard before. While Cyril was translating for the monk, Boris's wife served dessert—a light cream-colored mousse.

As I was starting on dessert the Ukrainian said something to me. I could not catch it. I can still read Russian, very slowly, but my ear training for the language is all gone.

He wants to know how you find Russian food, said Cyril helpfully.

I praised the food. Catching the spirit of it, Ding joined in.

The Ukrainian rumbled his way through a long monologue.

He never had Chinese food till he came to the States, said Cyril, condensing drastically. He likes it very much.

I thanked Rasputin in my poor Russian, at which he laughed, frankly and good-naturedly.

There is a very excellent Chinese restaurant in Cambridge, said Mrs. Kazinsky. We go there often.

Ah yes, said Kroll, apparently addressing Kazinsky. Our palindromic friend.

Kazinsky frowned incomprehension for a moment, then brightened, and chuckled. Palindromic, yes. This had the character of some private joke.

What is this word? asked Ding. Pali-what?

This is the result of my good training. When I first knew Ding she would never ask for vocabulary assistance from foreigners. If there was something said that she didn't understand, she would let it go, hoping it was not too important. All too many Chinese people are diffident in this way. Our national vice is, if we know something, we have to show it off; and if we don't know something, we would rather die than reveal our ignorance. But you cannot master a language like that, and I taught Ding—forced her, on many occasions—to stop conversation and ask for explanations. In that way, she not only conquers her native reticence, but also gains the advantage that the word or expression in question is set forever in association with some social context—a far more potent aid to memory than mere words in a textbook.

Madam, I'm Adam, said Boris.

A man, a plan, a canal—Panama, said Kroll.

Able was I ere I saw Elba, said beaky Doris.

Norma is as selfless as I am, Ron, offered the Irishman.

Straw? No, too stupid a fad. I put soot on warts, said his rubicund wife. This brought the palindromicity up to some sort of critical mass, and everyone collapsed laughing. Cyril even applauded. Then there was a break for Cyril to explain palindromes to the Ukrainian. He nodded sagely, but made no contribution.

It's something that reads the same backward as forward, I told Ding, while Cyril was at work on the Ukrainian. Madam, I'm Adam—you see? If you start from the back, letter by letter . . .

Yes, yes, I see. Ding had got it. She is really very intelligent. Then she took the opportunity to say, in Chinese, The professor of Slavic studies has been looking at me a lot.

He's a dirty old man, I said, also in Chinese. Look at his young wife. Kroll's wife was really very pretty, as pretty as Ding, though in a different way: pale, blond, Baltic. A Second Wife, for sure. I am glad I married so late. My first wife is my Second Wife. This is very satisfactory. I have all the advantage of a Second Wife, without alimony or visitation problems.

How did we get into palindromes? asked Boris. I think everyone was slightly tipsy at this point. Little conversationettes had started up around the table—like my own dialogue with Ding—while the Ukrainian was being set straight on palindromes. Now the Irishwoman was laughing much too loud at something with Doris, old Dr. Kazinsky was chuckling at something with his wife, and the Irish computer man was making some kind of vigorous point to Doris's fricatrice. Even the Ukrainian looked a little flushed, I thought.

My wife was speaking of a Chinese restaurant in Cambridge, said Dr. Kazinsky in response to Boris's question. Very popular with the faculty. And with our Chinese postgraduates, too, I should say. That's supposed to be the sign of a good Chinese restaurant, isn't it? That the Chinese themselves patronize it. Especially the Cantonese, I think.

Yes, said Ding, and recycled an old Chinese joke: The Cantonese will eat anything with four legs, except a table, and anything that flies, except a plane. It is not very funny in English, but people laughed politely.

I felt a shiver of apprehension. I didn't like to hear any talk about Cantonese people, or their customs or tastes, or Hong

Kong. Those things were in the past. I didn't want Ding to know anything about them. It was best that she didn't.

I thought I would try to change the subject. I said: We have no palindromes in Chinese. Having no alphabet, we can have no palindromes.

Ah, said Professor Kroll. Then you must meet our friend. The proprietor of our restaurant. *He* is a Chinese palindrome. His name is Yoy. Y-O-Y, Yoy.

8. *Beyond the Wall*

It was from Mr. Chan that I first found out about Yoy. Mr. Chan is a wonder. He knows everything. Selina's aunt—the one whose family she was staying with—worked as a cleaner in one of the office buildings in Old Bailey Street on Hong Kong side. One of Mr. Chan's neighbors was on the maintenance staff of the building.

Your sweetheart's playing you along, said Mr. Chan. She's got a fiancé in San Francisco. Green card. When her papers come through she'll go out there and marry him.

What, arranged marriage?

No. They grew up together. Their families are close. She accepted him.

When I confronted Selina she confessed immediately. She had no guile, really. I had gone to her uncle's place, gone looking for her as soon as I got off work. We walked out, along Argyle Street to the corner, then down Nathan Road. It was dark already—this was sometime in November, I suppose—but the stores and restaurants were all lit up, all bright and bustling. Yes, she had known the guy since she came to Hong Kong as a child. She'd marry him as soon as she got to the States.

You might have told me. Better still, you might have been faithful to your fiancé and not have gone out with me.

You were very insistent. How could I resist you?

If you cared about the guy, you would have resisted. If you cared about me, you would have spoken plainly to me before now. I really wonder if you care about anything.

If you will force yourself on people, you must expect disappointments.

It wasn't such a mighty battle, as I remember. I'm not afraid of disappointment. I'm not afraid of anything. I just don't like dishonesty.

It's not dishonest to be silent. I just wanted to spare your feelings.

Leave it to me to manage my feelings. Just tell me the truth.

It was basic left-brain/right-brain stuff: feeling and expediency versus reason and principle. By the time we reached Eternal Peace department store I had worked up quite a head of steam. I think it's better we just stop seeing each other, I said, and turned away from her, and walked off down to the roofed area of food stalls on Jordan Road, where I consumed a bowl of beef tripe in noodle soup and a bottle of San Miguel beer.

Well, I talked a good game, but this girl had got under my skin somehow. I held out about a week, then went to find her, to her uncle's place, straight up to the door and ringing the bell. She made no protest, but trotted out with me obligingly, and we walked down to my apartment and put Francis Yip on the cassette player and embraced in a frenzy.

It was like that with us. If you have had this kind of affair, you know all about it. If you haven't, it probably seems like a kind of madness.

Mr. Chan was pretty scathing when I told him we were back together.

She's taking you for a ride, he said over Heineken in the Saddle that Saturday evening.

Not anymore, she isn't. I mean, I know the situation.

Mr. Chan chuckled. Yes. And you think you're in control. You think she'll change her mind and stay with you. But of course she won't. Aside from anything else, she wants to go to America. You have no way to go to America. You're just a Mainland boy. No citizenship, no passport.

So I'm not only up against this guy—whatever his name is (at this point I did not know his name)—I'm up against Uncle Sam.

Check out the line on Garden Road. Everybody wants to be in America.

The U.S. consulate was on Garden Road. There was a long line there every day, stretching round the block.

Oh, America. I'll make her forget about America.

Mr. Chan laughed again at my boastfulness. You're a young guy. You don't know much. Listen: A woman is more dangerous than a tiger. You believe it?

No. That's a dumb thing to say.

Read the papers. How many stories you see about people getting killed by tigers? Not too many. But every day, every day, some guy gets killed because of a woman.

Mr. Chan was a Chinese misogynist of the old school. Happily married though, with a charming wife who seemed, as best I could judge, pretty much in control of her household.

Some days after this Selina actually showed me some pictures of Yoy. We were at her uncle's house. The family was watching TV. Selina and I were alone in the bedroom she shared with the uncle's three daughters. She brought out this photograph album. There was Yoy: a morose-looking youth with glasses on a round face. Selina flipped dully through the pages: a bored child doing homework.

So you're really going to marry this guy.

If I can get my visa.

Don't you think you should wait? You're only seventeen.

It's all settled.

You've got a mind of your own, haven't you? Well, then you can change it.

She shrugged, closing the album. It's all settled.

I may have stormed out then. I don't remember. I did that, quite a lot. Every time Yoy's name came up, I think. But I always went back, and she was always glad to see me. Pretty soon we just stopped talking about Yoy.

This kind of affair—what is it made of? There were sentimental movies—neither of us cared for the martial arts genre, then in the ascendant. There were late-night feasts at the food stalls in Yaumadei, Sunday trips into the New Territories, in spring and summer—we were together over a year—picnics on the outer islands. At the still center of it all there was the poky apartment on Temple Street, the rattle of mah-jongg tiles, Francis Yip on the cassette player.

And some Western music, too. Sometime in 1972 I heard the Beatles for the first time. I thought them very charming, and bought a pirated tape. Some others, too: the Bee Gees, Simon and Garfunkel, José Feliciano. I had never heard Western pop music before leaving China, and it easily seduced me. Indeed, the West itself was gradually, quietly folding itself around me.

Working at the bank, I was in daily contact with foreigners for the first time. I had *seen* foreigners before, of course. When I was a child the Northeast was full of Russians. Elder Brothers, they were called, and we were supposed to look up to them because they were helping us to reconstruct our country. We all had to learn Russian in school, and half the movies shown were Russian.

Actually everybody hated the Russians. In the period between the collapse of the Japanese armies at the end of World War II and the establishment of New China, the Russians had occupied the Northeast. Everyone said their occupation was much worse than the Japanese. They raped all the women they could find and stole everything to take back to Russia—whole factories, whole *industries.* My grandmother told me that in that time, the women in the Northeast used to dress up as men and dirty their faces in the hope of avoiding rape—but usually without success because the Russians raped men, too. They even raped animals, she said, and there was indeed a common expression for the Russians, spoken behind their backs of course, referring in a rather disgusting way to their supposed affinity for pigs.

After Liberation the Chairman cut a deal with Stalin, and the soldiers all left. In their place came experts to help us reconstruct. I was never close to any of these experts, but I sometimes saw them in the town. They seemed large, silent, and vaguely ill natured. Or perhaps that last is just a prejudice I took after hearing my grandmother's stories. The thing everyone said about them was that they were never sober after twelve noon.

Teacher Ouyang was the only person I knew who didn't mind the Russians. He used to say that while of course the disgraceful incidents could not be excused, we should take the long view, in which (according to him) the Russians were a modernizing force, and should be welcomed by everyone who wanted China to be modern.

Teacher Ouyang was a kind of surrogate parent to me. After my mother died he took pity on me and let me go to his house. Not really his, of course. The house was an old gentry house, the rooms set around a courtyard, everything enclosed by a high wall. In the courtyard were some rocks, which on reflection (it did not occur to me at the time) must have been set there as an artistic arrangement by the family that had owned the place before Liberation. Among the rocks was an artificial pool, full of dirty rainwater. The gentry family were long gone, of course—this was the mid-fifties—and each of the rooms had been assigned to a family. Teacher Ouyang and his wife had the smallest room, because they had no children. The wife was a terrible shrew—a consequence of her infecundity, perhaps—but I never saw Teacher Ouyang in an ill humor. At school he kept a well-ordered class by sheer force of personality, and by spicing his lessons with little fables which he delivered with much waggling of eyebrows and many changes of voice, and very occasionally—but with what desperate anticipation we waited for these moments!— by performing conjuring tricks with coins, pencils, playing cards, or bits of cloth. His art was so pure as to be transparent, but I see now that he was in fact an extraordinarily gifted teacher who took his work very seriously. He told us this himself in one of his fables, though of course we had not ears to hear.

There was once a crooked doctor. He would take money from people, then give them false medicine. Sometimes the medicine was poisonous and the patient died.

In the natural course of things the doctor himself left this world at last and found himself standing in judgment before Lord Yan-Wang, the emperor of hell. It is difficult to imagine any crimes worse than yours, said Lord Yan-Wang. When people were suffering and helpless they placed their trust in you and paid you with silver and gold. You repaid them with poison and death. Eighteenth level! [In our old Taoist religion there were eighteen levels in hell, the deepest levels for the worst sinners.]

Well, there was the poor doctor—though of course we should not feel *very* much compassion for him—down on the eighteenth level, resting up between tortures, crying out in remorse for his evil life, when he heard a knocking from below. Then very faintly he heard a voice coming up from beneath the floor of his dungeon: *Who are you? What crime did you commit to be immured so deep in hell?* The doctor was astonished. He had never heard that there were more than eighteen levels in hell; yet here, apparently, was a nineteenth level! Placing his mouth close to the floor he called down: I was a false doctor! But what great crime did you commit, that you have been banished to a level so deep it has never been known to men? Came the answer: *False teacher!*

For two or three years—from my ninth year to my eleventh, I think—Teacher Ouyang was the closest person in the world to me. I had Younger Sister and Grandmother, of course; but Younger Sister was only a kid, without understanding, and

Grandmother, though I loved her dearly, was dull witted and ignorant, her brains addled by decades of drudgery. Teacher Ouyang was the clear shining window into the larger world, the world of knowledge, that every child needs at that age, but all too few find. He had books—including one on botany with *color illustrations.* He let me look through his books as I pleased, answering my questions, sometimes reading a favorite passage out loud, making all the different voices. He would carry out little demonstrations of scientific principles—oh! hundreds of them!—using the most commonplace objects: an eyeglass lens, a dish of water, a Ping-Pong ball, a razor blade. Once he got a sheet of fine tissue paper from somewhere, and rolled it to a cylinder, and stood it on the floor, and put a match to it. *Phwoot!* It disappeared in a flash—but its membranous gray corpse, instead of collapsing onto the floor, took off and floated evenly, deliberately up on its own thermal, perfectly vertical, almost to the ceiling. Teacher Ouyang clapped and chuckled with pleasure that his experiment had performed so well, then submitted meekly, winking at me occasionally and causing a five-fen coin to walk across his knuckles, to a ten-minute harangue from Xanthippe, who had been saving the tissue paper for something *important.* I have since tried this one myself, several times, but never made it work.

Though a pedagogical genius of the first mark, I do not think Teacher Ouyang was much of an intellectual. His literary knowledge did not extend far beyond the classic novels and poetry, and some foreign books in translation—he had *The Three Musketeers, Treasure Island, The Last of the Mohicans, The Time Machine,* and *Bleak House* (whose Chinese title— *Huang-liang zhi Wu*—while as exact as a translation can be, makes it sound like a ghost story, so that I dared not look into it). He was rather the kind of person who delights in wonders, antinomies, lists, odd facts, and popular expositions of scientific subjects. The flying saucer dementia that seized

America in the early fifties somehow became known to him, and he had me scurrying home through the twilight streets with my eyes cast down in terror lest I should glimpse in the sooty air above me a hovering disk with lights flashing round its rim. (The Chairman's China was by no means as hermetically closed to foreign ideas as Americans supposed. I have heard an eminent TV newsperson say that the landing of men on the moon lay unknown to Chinese people for years. Not so: I myself, laboring as a peasant on a remote production brigade near the Mongolian border, knew of it—and even heard the astronauts' names, somewhat garbled—within the week.)

Well, it was from Teacher Ouyang that I first learned of the larger world. It was he who first threw open that window for me. To the degree that I have been able to escape from the prison of self, it was he who first showed me where to direct my steps. Such true understanding as I have I owe to him, and to President Coolidge. In the infinite vanity of adolescence I came to feel that I had outgrown him, and I left off visiting his house, and moved to the upper school, where he did not teach, and learned with only the merest pang during my first semester away at college that he had died of pneumonia, followed after a few days—to the utter amazement of everyone who had ever seen them together—by his wife, from inconsolable grief. May heaven bless them both, and grant them a quiet corner in paradise, with the *Guinness Book of World Records*—Celestial Jumbo edition—in a Chinese translation.

When I went to college I saw real foreigners. Not just Russians, I mean. Our country was at that time advertising herself as a friend of the oppressed colonial and ex-colonial peoples of Africa and Asia, so that all our institutions of higher education had Third Worlders on campus. My college had Arabs, Pakistanis, and Black Africans.

The Pakistanis were a thin, nervous lot, who always seemed to be in a hurry to get from one place to another. Several of them turned out to have TB and had to be shipped off to sanatoriums. The Arabs mostly just slept. The Africans were noisy and rambunctious, always trying to organize dances, which were forbidden most of the time. Not just for the Africans, for everybody. Back then, in the sixties and seventies, you could take the political temperature of China to a fraction of a degree from the attitude toward dancing. I don't know why: it was something the leaders were obsessed with. Because the prime minister was a good dancer and the Chairman a poor one, someone once told me—as good an explanation as any for what happens in China.

There was trouble with the Africans. There was an accusation—whether true or not, I don't know—that some of them had been pestering Chinese girls. Some Chinese boys broke the windows in the block where the foreign students lived, to show anger about the Africans. The authorities at the college took this very seriously. Three or four of the Chinese students were expelled. For the Africans, some whores were provided, so that they could have sex with Chinese girls whenever they wanted to.

We weren't supposed to know this. It was supposed to be a big secret. The authorities even sent a bus to take the Africans to the place where the whores were kept. The driver of the bus gossiped, and soon everybody knew. Once they knew we knew, the authorities feared that the Chinese students would become even more indignant, so they had a special meeting for us. In the meeting they explained that Africans had an uncontrollable sex drive, and if they couldn't have plenty of sex they went mad. Since it was impractical to bring women from Africa for them to have sex with, there was nothing for it but to let them have access to some low-class Chinese women. The authorities would see that the women came to no harm, and provide them with birth control and so on, and pay them, so there was really nothing to get indignant about. These were our brother revolutionaries from the Third World, and we had to show consideration to them, however odd their ways might seem to us.

In my third year at college, just before the Great Cultural Revolution broke out, I actually made friends with one of these Africans. His name, at any rate in Chinese, was A-bu. He came from Mali. He was very beautiful—physically, I mean. He had small, well-proportioned features, a perfectly black matte skin, and a globe of fine tight-curling hair. His body was slim and delicate, like a girl's. His hands, I remember, were particularly expressive, with long agile fingers and palms of surprising pink.

We were not supposed to mix with the foreign students, but I got into conversation with A-bu while walking in the college orchard, where students went to rehearse their lessons, pacing up and down reciting from their books. He was very sad. He had already been in the country three years, and longed for his home. He said that Mali was a beautiful country, lush and fertile. I have since read that it is in fact covered by the Sahara Desert. Well, I guess homesickness had warped his judgment.

A-bu was, in fact, lonely and melancholy. He had nothing in common with the other Africans, he said. This startled me, as I thought Africa was all of a piece. No, he said, the different peoples of Africa were as remote from one another in outlook and culture as a Japanese from a Malay, or a Sicilian from a Finn.

After two or three conversations I felt sufficiently familiar to ask him about the uncontrollable sex drive. He said this was nonsense. The Africans were just bored, and trying to be friendly. When the authorities first told them they could use whores, they were insulted, and most refused to have anything to do with it. Then gradually more and more of them gave in, and now there were quite lively parties at the place where the whores were kept—a disused army base outside the town. However, many Africans, including A-bu, continued to refuse as a point of pride. *Je suis celibataire!* he said, laughing, then translated it for me into Chinese, the language we conversed in.

I liked A-bu very much, for his gentle melancholy wit, for his intelligence (his Chinese was flawless—the best I have ever heard a foreigner speak even to this day), and, I confess it, for his beauty. Nothing happened between us, of course. You couldn't even think about things like that in China in the sixties. Well, I couldn't, or at any rate didn't. I went home for the summer and he went to Peking to visit some fellow countrymen. Soon after we came back the Great Cultural Revolution struck and the foreign students were all sent home. I often wonder what happened to A-bu. But his importance in my life was this: he inoculated me permanently against any notion that geography or race tell you anything interesting or important about a person's character.

So from the very beginning in Hong Kong I dealt with foreigners on equal terms. Our writer Lu Xun said that we Chinese are forever either despising foreigners as uncultured barbarians or else on our knees worshiping them as masters of science and democracy. Well, I have never done either of those things. I take people as I find them, Chinese or foreign, white, black, yellow, or tan.

Not that I don't recognize differences in national style. Hong Kongers used to say: If you work for an American boss, you're in heaven. A British or even a Japanese boss will do. But to work for a Chinese boss—that's the pits. This was broadly true, I think. To go from working in Chinese factories to an American bank was to pass from darkness to light.

I particularly liked the American managers, several of whom I was in daily contact with. They didn't bother about face at all. In China, in every part of our life, relations between the superior and his subordinates are very highly colored: the superior should be haughty and distant, the subordinate should grovel. With the Americans there was nothing like that. They looked you straight in the eye, gave a direct expression— a smile or a frown—to show their emotion, and said whatever was on their minds.

Or tried to. I was distressed to discover how much trouble I had with spoken English. I had decided to leave China when I was sent to the countryside, after the army broke up the Red Guards. Once I had decided to leave, I knew I must learn English. I had learned none in school, only Russian. But it was very difficult to learn English in a remote production brigade in northeast China. There were three radios in the brigade, but they were all in public places, and listening to foreign stations was illegal, anyway. The county capital had a bookstore, but it was a poor place, full of Party stuff and childish adventure stories. There were, of course, no English-speaking foreigners within five hundred miles.

Then one day in the county capital I was browsing among a pile of junk a peddler had on display on the sidewalk, and found an English-Chinese dictionary. I took it back to the brigade with me and began to memorize it.

To memorize a dictionary seemed to me a very obvious way to learn a language. A month later (I had reached *amalgam*) I saw the futility of it. I went back to the street peddler. He had no other foreign books, but promised to hold them for me when he did. After that I went to him every month, or as often as I could get a ride into the capital. He was a very ignorant fellow. He could barely read Chinese, and of course could not discriminate between one foreign language and another. Most of the books he kept for me were Russian or Korean. Once in a while there was something in Bulgarian, Hungarian, or Vietnamese. But everything comes to him who waits. One blistering cold December day he hailed me from inside his mass of fur and padding, and liberated one hand from his sleeves long enough to pass me a very battered, soiled *David Copperfield*.

That was how I learned English: I memorized *David Copperfield*. I have stopped telling my American friends this because they do not believe it. The only way to prove it would be to recite the whole book, which, alas, I can no longer do. But I could do it once, and Ding knows—any Chinese person will know—that it is not only possible, but a common way for Chinese people to approach any field of study. As a matter of fact, I knew another Mainland boy in Hong Kong who had indeed memorized an English-Chinese dictionary. You could start him with any English word, and he would proceed from there doggedly through the alphabet with words and definitions until everyone present screamed for him to stop.

Americans are astounded by this because their lives are so full. There is so much to do with their spare time, they cannot conceive of setting aside three or four thousand hours to memorize a book. But in China in the late sixties there was nothing else to do. The boredom of life in a village in northeast China during the Great Cultural Revolution cannot be described. Especially in winter. The winter up there is five months long. I mean, the ground is frozen like iron for five months. The peasants have nothing to do. They sit around playing cards. When that palls, they occupy themselves with drinking and fornicating. The peasant women, who for the most part did not play cards, were always looking for someone to fornicate with. Northeastern peasant women are the most promiscuous I have seen anywhere—and I have lived in New York City. I really don't know how they figured out which children belonged to whom.

I did not follow this sport very much myself, because the peasant women were all, without exception, hideously ugly. Still, I must have had relations with thirty or forty women in that brigade out of sheer boredom. Whenever I needed some relief, I could always find it—usually in an hour or less. So even the fornication, though it was always there when you wanted it, did not make any great demands on one's time. Since I do not care to drink myself into a stupor day after day, I was left with *David Copperfield.*

Well, there are worse ways to occupy one's thoughts. If you memorize a book that size, you must spend most of your waking hours reciting great slabs of it to yourself. It is really rather a good way to fill up your time, and I don't at all regret having done it. Reflect on your own thoughts—the commonplace thoughts that make up the largest part of your mental activity. Are they useful to you? Are you proud of them? Dr. Johnson said that if he were to divide his life into three parts, two of them would be filled with shocking thoughts. Which of us is any different?

As well as lacking the time or stamina to memorize a long novel, Americans would doubt the usefulness of such an exercise. In this, as in most other things, they are right. The guy who had memorized the dictionary in fact spoke very poor English. Similarly, when I began to come into daily contact with foreigners, I discovered that while I had a most comprehensive knowledge of the drawing-room manners, courtship customs, and moral code of Canterbury clerks and Yarmouth fishermen in the early nineteenth century, the Americans I was dealing with could not understand a word I said.

I started from scratch with a systematic course of study. I divided my course into two parts: theory and practice. Then I divided each part into four further parts. Theory I divided into phonetics, grammar, vocabulary, and usage. Practice I divided into reading, writing, speaking, and listening. I kept a careful log of the time devoted to each of these eight disciplines, so that all would have equal weight.

I suppose that study is a very individual matter, and that what suits one person may not be appropriate for another. Still, the results of my own system speak for themselves. On the telephone I am taken for a native American (or occasionally for an Australian—I articulate some of my vowels a millimeter too far back). I am coauthor, with Boris, of *Credit Control and Risk Management in a Derivatives Trading Environment,* of which I corrected all the proofs myself, without assistance. *Investment Banker* magazine described the book as "definitive." My articles and book reviews have appeared in numerous publications, always written without assistance, without any so-called polishing by other hands.

It is a pity that more Chinese people do not put themselves through this kind of discipline. Ding, for example. While her vocabulary and grammar are both very good, her pronunciation leaves much to be desired. She often leaves a plosive unfinished at the end of a word—coming out of a word like *cup,* for example, with her lips pressed tight together. (This method of articulation, common in our southern dialects, is described as *applosive* by Professor Riesz-Nagy; but this rather attractive word—disaster at the cider mill—seems not to have found favor with either *Webster's New Twentieth-Century Dictionary* or the *OED.*) She has never mastered nasal or lateral plosion, pronouncing *cotton* and *bottle* as *co-tun, bo-tul.* When I first knew her she would pay close attention each time I tried to correct these faults. Now she makes a joke of it, calling me a dusty old pedant. My English serves its purpose, she says. I'm not going to chase perfection.

Possibly she is right. Only it distresses me to think that our children might make fun of her for her accent. Once, at Meng's house, I heard his wife chide one of the children for something. Meng's children are both ABC—American-born Chinese. The kid played back what she had said, right back at her, with precisely her awful accent, then added: Why don't you learn to talk properly? The kid was wrong, of course. If my own kids ever do such a thing, I will punish them.

But although you can punish them for saying it, you can't punish them for thinking it. Respect of children for parents is absolutely fundamental, and anything that weakens it is to be avoided or corrected. There, now: a little nugget of weapons-grade Confucianism. Well, perhaps I *am* a pedant. In the matter of filial piety, certainly, I cleave to the old notions. I suppose this is easy for me, having no parents myself. I have never been able to enter into other people's negative feelings about their parents. I would give a limb to have one minute with either of mine. Once, in an almanac in Hong Kong, I read the *Twenty-four Acts of Filial Piety,* a hortatory text from the old times. I could not see anything remarkable in any of them—not even in the tale of young Jin-er, whose father, according to the attending physician, would either recover from his illness or not, depending on whether his stool tasted bitter or sweet, a test our hero (brows V'ed in earnest concentration in the accompanying line drawing as he sampled a spoonful from the bedpan, the physician's hands raised in a cat's cradle of reverent astonishment) was glad to perform.

Perhaps I should begin to cultivate one of those long wispy white beards. But I have lived some, I have not led a bookish life. I have watched helpless as my mother died. I have been a peasant, a soldier, a factory worker, and an intellectual. I have swum for my freedom, I have said farewell forever to a girl I loved beyond all reason. More: I have fought in a battle, I have killed a man—or at any rate, tried to. I have even committed rape—a thing I recall reluctantly, and with deepest shame. May Heaven forgive me for that.

Well, my pedant's cap came to me not from a life spent in libraries and lecture halls, but after suffering borne and suffering inflicted. I can wear it with dignity and humility, as it should be worn, not with the empty arrogance of the merely credentialed.

9. *Fourfold Peace*

Yoy! For days following Boris's dinner the name ricocheted around in my head like the little metal ball in one of those arcade games. How many Yoys could there be in America?

Selina's Yoy had lived in San Francisco. It would be satisfying to say: That was why I came to the East Coast, to be as far away from her as possible. Untrue, though. The bank sent me over and fixed up my visa, and their back-office work is all done from New York. I had no choice about it. Once in the States, I schemed for a while to get a trip out west, to our San Francisco office; but no plausible reason came up, or something else always got in the way, and then I met Ding, and Selina Yoy, as she presumably now was, shriveled to a small, hard, bitter memory.

Once I had decided to marry Ding I knew I must erase even the few dusty traces of Selina that remained. Ding, though in all other respects of a sweet and equable temperament, is jealous in the extreme, and her jealousy knows no boundaries of time or space. I was not unprepared for this—you can generally take this situation for granted with a Chinese woman—and took evasive action when it seemed to be called for. She did a certain amount of probing before we were married.

Had I had other affairs?

Of course. No use denying it. I was already forty years old. What kind of man would I be if I hadn't had any affairs?

Yes, but *how serious were they?*

Oh, not serious.

What, none of them?

No. None. Just *hun ri-zi*—passing the time.

Ding herself was a virgin when I married her. I asked her about it frankly in the later stages of our courtship. Are you a virgin? I asked. Yes, I am, she replied proudly, and I knew her well enough at this point not to doubt her word. I cannot say that I would not have married her otherwise; but I am sufficiently of my culture and generation to value a woman's virginity as a great prize. She knew, of course, that I was not a virgin, though she had never asked me. It would be unnatural, and unhealthy, for a man of my age to be without sexual experience.

Of course, this is a double standard. So what? I cannot understand these complaints about a double standard. You may as well say that it is a double standard that men impregnate and women parturiate. All human sexuality is founded on a double standard. I am not much in sympathy with this great modern project to make everything equal to everything else. Or rather: I know it all too well, having been a soldier—literally a fighting soldier—in one of that movement's most intense episodes, and I have seen with my own eyes what it all leads to.

On another occasion: Did I think a person could be in love— *really* in love—more than once?

I was incautious enough to say that I thought it depended on the person.

Two, three: Could *you* be?

No, no, no, of course I did not think I could be. Was *sure* I could not be. But her eyes stayed fixed on me for some time, watching my color. Obviously I passed the test.

Was this dishonest of me? Yes, of course it was. But believe me, with a Chinese woman there was no alternative. If I had confessed to her that I had endured an intense and erotic affair fifteen years previously, she would not have married me. I wanted very much for Ding to marry me.

Love was her main concern, but even sex disturbed her to some degree. She knew, of course, that I had had a sex life before meeting her, but to actually hear anything about it caused her great pain. Once, shortly after we were married, there was something on the TV about prostitution. I am sure, she said, you have had some direct experience of prostitutes. She said it lightly, and I played the ball back in the same spirit. Yes, indeed, I replied—though never in America, only in the Far East (where, as she and I both knew, attitudes to this particular branch of commerce are very much more relaxed).

She burst into tears at once, and it took me all evening to restore harmony.

For quite a long time after we were married I was haunted by the fear that I might address Ding by Selina's name in error. The fear grew and developed fronds and involutions, like a fractal. I began to fear that I might become so obsessed with not letting slip that name that the obsession itself might bring it out—as in the childhood conundrum, When you see a donkey don't think about his tail, the injunction itself, by its very existence, guaranteeing its own violation.

For this reason I deliberately took to using American terms of endearment when addressing Ding: darling, honey, baby, sweetheart—avoiding names altogether. For some reason I have never fathomed, this seems exceedingly unnatural to a Chinese. We call our husbands and wives by name, sometimes in a diminutive form, or address each other as Mother and Father (in the manner of the Coolidges, indeed, who were Momma and Poppa to each other), or—though generally only in the third person—as Old Woman and Old Man (or Old Bean in Cantonese—don't ask me why). Ding herself has never called me by anything but my name. At least, this was true until very recently, when Hetty began making little *ba-ba-ba* sounds. *Ba-ba* means daddy in Chinese, though also, in a different tone, doo-doo. We took the more filial interpretation, and now Ding has taken to echoing the infant, calling me Ba or Ba-ba. But I have kept on resolutely with honey and darling, and this not only served the initial purpose of helping to expunge the Other Name, but made me think more tenderly of my wife, in an American way.

Yet in spite of all this caution, I had reason to think that Ding somehow grasped that something happened in Hong Kong. Perhaps because I had so assiduously avoided saying anything about my Hong Kong years. I always skipped neatly over it, or round it, whenever the subject came up.

She had even, I fancied, developed something of an animus against Hong Kong itself. Most Chinese are happy to see that city return to the bosom of the motherland, but her enthusiasm was somewhat beyond the bounds of normal patriotism. When there was anything on the TV news about this she would sit forward on her chair, murmuring approval, or say things like, Yes, it's time they learned to behave like real

Chinese people. She professed to detest the Cantonese language, and spoke very scathingly of Cantonese Americans.

As a matter of fact Ding speaks Cantonese well enough. Not to the extent of knowing all the little side roads and rutted tracks of the language, as I do, but quite well enough to understand and to be understood. When she first came to the States she earned money on the side by working in the jewelry stores in Canal Street, down in Manhattan's old Chinatown. They are all Cantonese down there, of course, and she had no choice but to use the language. But when she mentions that part of her life it is to berate the grasping, tax-dodging merchants and their whining, lisping speech.

I am wise enough to say nothing when these topics turn up. I am temperamentally in sympathy with the Cantonese and the marvelous city they have created, but have sense enough not to let it show.

The only trace of my Hong Kong life still extant is Mr. Chan. We have stayed in touch through all these years. We exchange cards and phone calls at Lunar New Year, letters perhaps two or three times a year, and occasionally I call him from my office, or he calls me. When he calls me he is generally drunk, and very sentimental, but I don't mind. He is nearly seventy now, though he still works for his living. His boys are all doing well—the youngest has just got his Ph.D. With the boys all gone the tiny apartment on the hills above Aberdeen must seem very still. Evenings I know Mr. Chan sits by the TV with his wife, drinking *yuk-bing-sue* till he falls asleep, or picks up the phone to call an old friend. Dear old Chan.

> We shall drink together again
> Freed of all passion
> When we meet,
> Far beyond the River of Stars.

Yuk-bing-sue is Cantonese vodka. You can also use it to strip the rust off bolts.

To tell the truth, I should have preferred Ding not to know that Chan wrote to me. However, our mailman comes at midday, so Ding takes in the mail and there is nothing I can do about this. I was sorry about the whole situation, but I had to preserve the harmony of my marriage. Really I should have liked to invite Chan here to stay with us, but I did not know how Ding would react. It was an experiment I preferred not to conduct. Although I had not said this frankly to him, I think he understood. Mr. Chan understands everything.

Yet who can understand this? That that dry husk, lying twenty years in dust and silence at a far corner of the attic, should suddenly sprout a bright poisonous flower? Yoy! Yoy! Had they moved to the East Coast? *Could it be them?* Are these the San Francisco Yoys? Or some collateral branch? The Boston Yoys? As one might have said, as the Late George Apley might have said: the Boston Lowells.

Newspaper reporter to Calvin Coolidge: Mr. President, are you related to the Boston Coolidges at all?

Coolidge: They say no.

By this time I was very intimate with Mr. Coolidge. I knew of his birthplace: a tiny mountain hamlet in backcountry Vermont. I had been introduced to his family: stolid Yankee farming types—closemouthed, close pursed, unimaginative. I had pursued him through childhood and adolescence into Amherst College, where, after two years solitude, he emerged at last from his shell to become the class wit. I had watched his remarkably methodical climb up the ladder of public service: city councilman, city solicitor, state representative, mayor, state senator, lieutenant governor, governor, vice-president,

president. I had read all the Coolidge biographies and memorials available from the New York Branch Library system. I had read Coolidge abused by Mr. Mencken, mocked by Mr. White, patronized by Mr. Schlesinger, psychoanalyzed by Mr. Bradford, calmly set in his place by Mr. McCoy, and canonized by Mr. Fuess. Let me tell you, when I have these enthusiasms I stop at nothing.

The only thing I had been unable to determine was: Could he whistle? That original note in *Facts about the Presidents* had, for all its irreverence, proven accurate on all other points of actual fact: but Mr. Fuess spoke of Coolidge in the White House *whistling up his dogs.* How could he whistle up his dogs if he couldn't whistle? It seems absurd for a grown man to fret over such details, but I like to get everything right.

The biographies yielded some satisfying numerological data. Mr. Coolidge was born on July the Fourth—the only president with that distinction—and died on Twelfth Night. He had died, in fact, sixty years to the day before my own sweet Hetty was born; and he had been born in the same year as my own maternal grandfather. I like to discover these odd, random resonances.

I have a single, very dim memory of Grandfather, who was already in his seventies when I was born. The memory is of his boots. He had a pair of thick felt boots, like a Mongolian—to see him through the northeastern winter, I suppose. In fact these kinds of boots are not uncommon in Manchuria. I suppose it was only that Grandfather's were the first I had seen. I must have been very small. I can remember nothing else about Grandfather, only his boots.

My grandfather was raised in Shandong Province, the home place of Confucius. His people were gentry. At least I believe this was the case. In my childhood we had Class Struggle and any hint of gentry origins could get you killed, so my grandmother kept quiet about it, and I have only inferred the facts from some indirect evidence.

In any case Grandfather's people soon lost their position. The dynasty had been on the throne more than two centuries and, as always happens, was beginning to collapse under its own weight. There were disorders everywhere. To escape them my grandfather's people fled across the Bo Sea to Port Arthur, then trekked north into Manchuria looking for tranquillity and cheap land. I do not think they found them—or, if they did, my poor mother did not inherit any.

My mother died when I was eight years old. In theory she died from TB, for which there was no medicine at that time in China, or at any rate none that answered my mother's condition. I believe that in fact she died from prolonged grief. She loved my father very dearly. When she died she was holding in her right hand a letter my father had written to her, the last words she ever had from him. I knew the letter well. It was written in bluish pencil on a rough brown paper. Together with her, I had read it or heard it read ten thousand times.

My father had written the letter in a town called Siping— Fourfold Peace. It is a railroad town in central Manchuria. He was waiting for a train to take his unit to Korea. The letter was full of revolutionary and patriotic rhetoric, of course ("We shall teach the imperialists a lesson!"), but we all understood that that was required of him. In between those arid slogans was great tenderness. He was even bold enough to say at one point how much he missed us. At the very end of the letter he said: "Hug the little ones for me—my little sparrow and my little rabbit. Show them these kisses and tell them they come from Ba-ba." This was followed by a line of X marks, supposed to be kisses. The little sparrow was my sister, because she had skinny legs. I was the rabbit, because my ears were somewhat too large.

How I wish I had that letter! My grandmother kept it after Mother died, but it got lost somehow in the Cultural Revolution. Perhaps she destroyed it for fear that it was too well written, or not revolutionary enough. Or perhaps it was just mislaid when she fled her home for a while. There was fighting in our district and people sometimes had to run for their lives, even if they weren't directly involved with one side or the other.

An even greater grief to me is that no picture of my mother has survived, except for the one printed on my most inward heart. I should dearly love to see her face again, even if it were only a poor chemical image.

Mr. Coolidge was somewhat luckier than myself in the matter of mementos. He too lost his mother when a boy—also, it seems, from TB. He describes the matter with characteristic brevity in his autobiography.

> When she knew that her end was near she called us children to her bedside, where we knelt down to receive her final parting blessing. In an hour she was gone. It was her thirty-ninth birthday. I was twelve years old. We laid her away in the blustering snows of March. The greatest grief that can come to a boy came to me. Life was never to seem the same again.

Reading this, my eyes filled with tears. The whole scene came to me—with no effort at all, since I had been there. The cold death chamber, winter wind scraping and whining outside. The rickety table beside the *kang:* oil lamp, bloodstained rag from the last hemorrhage, sputum cup. The smell of inadequate acts of hygiene by a body too frail to move. The terrible death-glow of a last-stage consumptive—skin like fine paper with a furnace raging on the other side. Mother slipping into delirium, silently mouthing Father's name. My sister and myself, too awestruck to weep. Grandmother, her dear peasant face already drawn in grief, sitting patient at the foot of the bed mumbling sutras: *A-mi-tuo-fa, A-mi-tuo-fa, A-mi-tuo-fa*. The nails of the fingers holding the letter as blue as the crude pencil that had made the characters. I see it again, I see it again, everything so clear.

But Mr. Coolidge had the consolation of photographs, one of which he carried with him in a locket for the rest of his life. Another stood on the desk in whichever office he occupied, including that of the president. I envy Mr. Coolidge that. More, though, I envy him the mortuary practices of his time and place.

> Five years and forty-one years almost to a day my sister and my father followed her. It always seemed to me that the boy I lost was her image. They all rest together on the sheltered hillside among five generations of the Coolidge family.

How very satisfactory it must be to know one has a definite resting place! And that one will share it with one's own. My own poor mother was cremated, probably (I learned this some years later from a fellow Red Guard who had once been a crematorium worker) without even the dignity of a wooden box. Wood is scarce in China. So is land: until recently only the most important of leaders were permitted a burial. For people like us there was not even a Garden of Rest where the ashes might be scattered. I do not know where my mother's remains rest. Perhaps that is just as well. Her life was so poor, so unfortunate, it is certain that her ghost will seek some recompense from the living. Of my love for my mother I need not speak. Who does not love his mother? Yet I do not wish to meet her ghost.

In the matter of sisters I was hardly more fortunate than Mr. Coolidge. Little Abigail Coolidge died in 1890 from appendicitis. My own sister survived into adulthood, but married a man who insisted she have nothing to do with me, an injunction she seems to have yielded to without protest. He was strong for the Gang of Four in the seventies, when I was in Hong Kong. When the Gang of Four fell he somehow avoided persecution and went into business. I later heard that he and my sister had become very rich, at least by Chinese standards, and controlled the wholesale market in personal computers across northeast China. At the time I became involved with Mr. Coolidge I had had no direct contact with them for twenty years. This was now only indolence on my part—I bore no resentment toward my sister. I always said if I went back to China I should probably look her up. Blood is thicker than water. You cannot nurse a grudge against your sister for twenty years.

Infatuation, apparently, is more durable.

Yoy! I hardly knew myself how deeply I had been stirred by hearing that name. It was Ding who showed me.

We were playing Scrabble one evening a few days after Boris's dinner. I was drawing an excellent mix of vowels and consonants, and had built up some confidence in a win. I set down SERVE, the s modifying Ding's TRAP to STRAP. She extended SERVE to RESERVE, a feeble move by her usual standards. I trumped with a P to make PRESERVE, with PRAISE going downward—a very skillful move.

Ding went into deep concentration, flicking her eyes from her rack to the board.

PRESERVE brought to mind *pickle,* and I told her about the remark by Miss Alice Roosevelt about Mr. Coolidge's having been weaned on a pickle. Ding didn't get it, so I had to fill in some background.

It was the New England business, you see. It was a *type,* which young people in the twenties thought very quaint.

Quaint, repeated Ding thoughtfully. I could see her putting the word onto her mental stack, ready in the event she drew the Q, which had not yet made an appearance.

New Englanders were supposed to be very close, I went on. Stingy and taciturn. Do you know this word, *taciturn?*

Yes. You used it the other evening at Boris's house. Reaching out, she set IGIL under the V.

Mr. Coolidge was famously taciturn. There was an occasion when he had to perform a ceremonial breaking of earth for a tree planting in Washington.

Breaking of earth?

Yes. Just start the digging, you know? It's a thing presidents have to do. Some relic of primitive religious beliefs, probably. Like the emperor plowing the first furrow in old China. Or the czar blessing the Neva. I extended the VIGIL to VIGILANT.

All right.

Well, he did what was necessary and stood back. There was a very awkward silence. At last the master of ceremonies came forward: Won't you say a few words, Mr. President? And Mr. Coolidge looked down at his spadeful of soil and said: That's a mighty fine fishworm.

Ding didn't get this, or at any rate didn't laugh. That is a *very* few words, she said, with a considered gravity that actually made me smile. And as she was speaking she was setting down E at the end of VIGILANT, then proceeding with Q, U, A, and L. The Q fell on a double letter, and EQUAL reached to the triple word score in the corner.

Eighty-five said Ding, who calculates her score before setting down the pieces.

Eighty-five? Surely not. I pulled the letters aside a little and counted. Yes, eighty-five.

VIGILANTE is okay, isn't it? The Park Slope Vigilante. (She was referring to a recent news story.) I don't think they print it in italics.

Of course it's all right. I suspected her of rubbing it in. From a commanding lead, I was suddenly forty points behind. But I suppressed my irritation. I know she likes this game, and I am proud she has such an extensive vocabulary. Thanks to my encouragement, of course.

Now she hurled her dart.

You have been rather taciturn lately, she said. Since Boris's party.

This remark threw me into confusion. I knew, of course, that Ding observed my moods very closely. She is, after all, my wife. But I had not thought my agitation so visible. I was flustered, and could think of nothing to say. From

109

embarrassment I bent my head over my rack of letters, hoping my face was not changing color.

We have had some serious problems at work, I said at last. With these Emerging Markets securities.

Then it will do us good to get away for a couple of days.

Us? Why *us?* Should she not have said: It will do *you* good . . . ? But I realized the ice was very thin at this spot, and said nothing. We had fixed up a long weekend in Vermont, to see the fall foliage and visit Mr. Coolidge's native place. But here was an opportunity to divert the talk onto a safer path. I had not told Ding about Mr. Ruggles the actor.

Rebecca, the lady who seemed to be in charge of the birthplace, had told me that an actor from Boston who specialized in impersonating Mr. Coolidge would be at the birthplace on a certain weekend, doing his performance in the church. I particularly wanted to see that, and had booked for that weekend. The actor, whose name was Ruggles, was himself a New Englander, and had made a minuscule career out of one-man shows featuring famous New Englanders— Governor Winthrop, John Adams, Daniel Webster, and so on.

I told Ding about the actor.

I don't understand how you can have a play with only one person in it, said Ding.

Well, to be sure, I don't think you could have a very *long* play. But perhaps an hour or so, done by a skillful actor, could bring the subject vividly to mind, and offer fresh insights into his character. As a matter of fact, there is an actress who sometimes performs with him, as Mrs. Coolidge.

From what you have told me of Mr. Coolidge, I don't see how you could get an hour's worth of material from him, even with his wife included.

I understand this fellow makes some use of Mr. Coolidge's letters and autobiography, as well as his speeches. It's your turn, honey, I prompted, relieved that she did not seem inclined to pursue her previous train of thought. Employing a blank piece I had been fortunate enough to draw, I had turned STRAP into STRAPPING while telling her about Mr. Ruggles the actor, attaining triple word for thirty-three points, my triumph dimmed only a little by the wasteful necessity of placing the blank on a double letter square. It was a good move, and I had some hopes to recover the situation after Ding's devastating eighty-five.

Sounds boring, said Ding frankly. She furrowed her brows for a moment, then at once relaxed them and set down WATCHING along the bottom—another triple word. Sixty, she said, and um fifty for using all my letters, right? So, a hundred and ten.

My hopes all fled. In Western-style martial arts I believe this is called the old one-two. But I am proud of her, I am proud of her.

10.   Poor Flesh

My military career was very short and not very glorious. The Red Guards were put out of business at last by the army. In the Northeast this was often a messy procedure.

Huang Jen and I had gone back to the Northeast, to our hometown, and his father, who was prominent on the Revolutionary Committee of the local paint factory, had got us jobs there. I was working in the bank, oddly enough (in China at that time, a large factory was like a miniature welfare state, with schools, clinics, banks, libraries, and so on). Huang Jen was on something called the Design Committee, though don't ask me what there is to design in a paint factory. Colors, I suppose.

In fact, nobody was doing much work. People still had the fever for making revolution. Some of the people, anyway. I myself had lost my faith, but didn't quite realize it yet. I was revolutionary from inertia.

Those who didn't want to make revolution tried to form a committee of their own—they had the nerve to call it the Revolutionary Study Group—but they had a hard time of it because the Revolutionary Committee wouldn't let them meet in any of the factory buildings. Then we got wind that they were meeting in the local army base, and had army support. Well, next time they turned up at the factory they were arrested. We locked them in one of the upper floors of an administrative building and beat them. One of them was beaten to death, but I believe this was an accident (to further confuse matters, her body was thrown, or possibly fell, out of an upper-floor window). Next thing we knew, there were shells dropping on us.

Pretty soon the whole town was fighting. The mayor of the town had his own faction. I had always believed him to be in the pocket of the Revolutionary Committee, but when fighting started he threw his lot in with the army. From that point it was a foregone conclusion. There were further defections, but we put up a good fight.

Of course, it was very scrappy and disorganized. Only once did I get a clear shot at anybody. I was doing lookout on the roof of one of the factory warehouses. There was a railroad sidetrack coming right up to the warehouse—also a normal arrangement for Chinese factories. An enemy unit—civilians, from the look of them—were crossing the railroad track two hundred yards away, in a clear line of sight from my position.

They were aware of the lack of cover, of course. The track was on a slightly raised embankment at that point; so they were all hunkered down under the right side of the embankment, then would run one or two at a time across the open track and dive down at the other side. I guess they were egging one another on to run.

The range was far, but the line of sight perfectly clear, and I had a good rifle. It was a *san-ling-san,* a Lee Enfield .303, an old British army piece—northeast Asia is littered with small arms of every age and provenance from a century of wars. What a fine weapon that was! If I am ever in a war again—and you can never tell, the way the world is going—I hope to have a weapon as good as that *san-ling-san.* No wonder the British were top dog for so long. It had a heavy wooden stock with a cavity for the cleaning kit (which in my case I had not got), a sliding bolt that you worked with a great black metal knob, and a kick that would break your collarbone if you didn't cradle the gun correctly. The sound it made was tremendous, though more of a thud than a bang. I had been issued just one magazine of ammunition—eight rounds—and heaven only knows how the factory had obtained even that.

Well, it was just a matter of timing—of getting off a round while one of the enemy was scurrying across the twenty-yard-wide embankment top. I squeezed off my first round when someone's head popped up, assuming he was going to make the dash, but he popped right down again. After that nobody moved for a while and I lost concentration. Two figures ran across the track before I could take aim: then another, while I was cursing myself for inattention. This other startled me so much I let off a round, going nowhere at all. As if this were a signal, a big bunch—four or five—came up and ran over the railroad tracks. It was not the ideal moment, but I had them in my sights now and fired off three rounds very fast, just firing into the bunch. One of them jumped high in the air in an odd balletic movement, an assemblé I think it is called, then came down, rolled over and over, and disappeared down the left side of the embankment. It is possible he was just diving for cover in a particularly exaggerated way, but I feel quite sure that in fact I hit him. Whether I did, and if so, whether his wound was fatal, I shall never know.

Soon after this the Revolutionary Committee split. Politics—I mean low-level politics—in China at that time was like a magnet. A magnet has a north pole and a south pole. If you try to separate them by cutting the magnet in half, you find that you have not one north pole and one south pole, but two pieces, each with a north and south pole. It was the same with us. Every unit, every committee, no matter how revolutionary, turned out to have a moderate faction and a revolutionary faction. The unit would split, and the revolutionary faction would feel they had attained greater purity . . . until they discovered that they, too, had a moderate faction. . . . The logical end of this process was a tiny faction of utterly pure revolutionaries and a swelling mass of people who were at odds with them for one reason or another. So we revolutionaries, who had been hunting down class enemies for two years, woke up to find that *we* were the class enemies!

That's what happened at the paint factory. The moderates cut a deal with the army. Part of the deal was that we Red Guards should be shipped off to the countryside. And so, after brief careers as an intellectual, a revolutionary, a worker, and a soldier, I at last became a peasant.

Still, I am pleased to have some military background, even so slight a one. Dr. Johnson said that every man feels himself inferior in the presence of a soldier. I feel inferior too, when faced with a professional soldier like Ding's father; but less so, I am sure, than one who has never fought at all. I can say, with the Roman poet (though more literally), *militavi non sine gloria*. I feel sorry for the fellow I shot, of course. But he would have shot me if he could, so I have never let my mind dwell on it. Anyway, his ghost is in Manchuria, and I have never heard that ghosts can cross the ocean.

Is military experience essential for wisdom? I do not think so. Dr. Johnson himself is a counterexample. So is President Coolidge, who likewise never served, though his father held the rank of colonel from staff work during the Civil War. No: while I have some satisfaction from recalling the crack of rifle bullets passing over my head, and the thump of the dear old *san-ling-san* against my own shoulder, I do not think I am any wiser for having fought.

The awful truth of my own case is that it was the rape that started me on the road to America, on the path to understanding. Look, it gives me no satisfaction to say this. I have an infant daughter, whom I love more than my life. But the interplay of good and evil, of fortune and misfortune under heaven, is more complex than any person can understand. I can offer no apology, only say: These are the things that happened. I know that in the fullness of time heaven will punish me, and I must bow my head meekly and accept the justice of heaven.

The rape happened like this. We were Red Guards, myself and Huang Jen, traveling around China making revolution. In a town I will call Shacheng, in south China, we put up at a local college. The students at that college had formed their own revolutionary organization and were struggling some of the faculty. We joined in these struggle sessions.

These were not the worst struggle sessions I had seen. Nobody was actually struggled to death, as was quite common in the Northeast. Though I suppose some of the people we struggled committed suicide later. That always happened, everywhere.

Well, there was one professor who was very difficult. The students at that college told us he was a big counter-revolutionary. He was a professor of history, I think. We struggled him for three or four hours one afternoon. At first he was stubborn, and it looked as though we would have to beat him. Then quite suddenly his nerve broke, and he got very scared. He knelt down when we told him to, said, Yes, yes when we called him a traitor and a criminal, and bowed his head when we spat on him. After a while the struggle session kind of petered out and we let him go.

The leader of these college Red Guards was a fellow named Yu. He was big and strong, with a square handsome face. His father was in the army, so he had always eaten well and been able to intimidate others. The other students were a little scared of him, and followed his lead.

Well, the morning after we had struggled the professor, one of Yu's minions came to our dormitory and told us this professor was going to be struggled again. The previous day's struggle had not been vigorous enough. Although he'd bowed his head to us, the guy was still a counterrevolutionary in his heart, he still had Bad Thinking. Furthermore, he had Bourgeois Things in his house, which we ought to destroy. He couldn't possibly reform his Bad Thinking and sincerely repent his crimes against the common people while he had Bourgeois Things in his house.

We all went to his house, a tumbledown one-story brick building off at one side of the college grounds. There was a little front garden with a low wall around it. The professor, or someone in his family, had planted vegetables in the front garden. We pulled up all the vegetables and stomped on them. Then we shouted for the professor to come out so that we could confront him with his crimes. Somewhat to my surprise, he did come out, closing the door behind him. He stood there in the doorway while we shouted at him. He didn't look scared now, though I suppose he must have been. He seemed to be trying to appease us. Yes, Yes, he said to every accusation. Yes, I am a criminal, Yes, I have Bad Thinking. You young people must show me the right way. Help me to reform. Yes, Yes.

Our leader, the one called Yu, said, You have Bourgeois Things. Now I thought the professor looked a little scared. Yes, Yes, he said, it's true, I do have such things.

They should be destroyed, said the leader.

Yes, Yes, said the professor, they should be destroyed. I'll bring them all out here and you can destroy them.

The students all jeered. Do you think we trust you to bring them all out? *We'll* bring them out.

Yu reached out and grabbed his sleeve, to pull him out of the doorway. Instead of letting it happen, the professor pulled away. He spread-eagled himself in the doorway, his arms pressed firm against the jambs. His face showed grim determination. Of course, this made us mad. Some students pulled him away and kicked open the door.

It was true, he had Bourgeois Things. He had a gramophone and a stack of records—the big old 78 rpm type. We threw the gramophone to the floor and kicked it to pieces. Then we smashed all the records—passing them around from one to the other so that everyone had a chance to smash some, hurling them down on the concrete floor. I don't know what kind of records they were. We didn't read the labels. I remember seeing Russian characters on one of the labels, so I suppose it was Western classical music.

The professor also had a wife and a daughter. They were in a separate room at the back, holding on to each other in terror. Nobody bothered much with them at first. We were too busy smashing things.

There was a small glass-fronted bookcase: we smashed that, too, smashed it to splinters, and pulled out all the books and tried to tear them up. Some of them were well bound and wouldn't tear, so we just pulled out handfuls of pages and scattered them round. Also in the bookcase were some framed photographs. I suppose they were the professor's parents or teachers. We threw these down and stomped them into the mess on the floor. Now everywhere you walked in that house your feet crunched on splinters of glass or wood or vinyl.

I do believe—I do hope—I felt some shame about the books. I certainly recall that the professor's bookcase brought Teacher Ouyang to mind. Teacher Ouyang had a little structure he kept his books on. You could hardly dignify it with the name bookcase; it was just some flat pieces of wood nailed together to make a rack—two side pieces and three or four shelves. I wonder what happened to Teacher Ouyang's books? I thank heaven, at least, that he died before the Cultural Revolution.

There were Bourgeois Things everywhere in the professor's house. On the walls were some character scrolls in glass-fronted frames—of course, they didn't last long. Meanwhile, Yu and some of the other students, seeing that we were running out of Bourgeois Things, had gone into the back rooms. Shacheng was south of the *kang* line—the boundary between north and south China, north of which people sleep on a *kang,* which is to say a brick bed heated from beneath with burning straw. This house had no *kang.* The professor and his family slept on beds—not unusual for the region, in middle-class households, but to me slightly exotic.

These beds had quilts and horsehair mattresses. The beds might have been normal, but mattresses were quite a luxury in China at that time, especially in a poverty-stricken place like Shacheng. They were, in point of fact, Bourgeois Things, so the students ripped them up. Well, ripping up one of the mattresses, they found something hidden away. Yu came out carrying it. It was a silk-backed picture scroll, a real painting: some sprigs of blossom, in the style of Zheng Banqiao. Perhaps it actually was a Zheng Banqiao—it looked very rich and fine. Well, this boy Yu came storming out of the back room waving this scroll around, screaming: Look at this shit! Look at this bourgeois shit! Down with the counter-revolutionary scum that worship this foreign shit! Actually, the thing was entirely Chinese. This Shacheng was a poor place, the students an ignorant crowd. Or perhaps this Yu was just carried away with all the excitement.

The professor had been trying to get back into his living room. He was at the door: but every time he took a step in, the students at the door pushed him out, jeering at him. But when he saw the picture scroll being waved about, he suddenly went wild. Flailing his arms at those around him, he somehow got back into the room. It's Chinese, he said. It's not a foreign thing, it's Chinese! Part of our national heritage! Oh, please, please—it's Chinese! Look at it! Can't you *see?* It's Chinese!

Yu pursed his lips. Just because it's Chinese, you think it can't be counterrevolutionary? *You're* Chinese, aren't you? And *you're* a counterrevolutionary!

We all laughed and cheered at this. The leader gave the professor a lecture about Bad Thinking and Bourgeois Things, shouting at him, shaking the picture scroll at him. We all joined in the shouting. It was developing into a real struggle meeting. We started spitting on the professor, made him get down on his knees, down among the shards of vinyl and glass and the splinters of wood and scraps of torn books. But the professor was not like the previous day, with his head bowed. He was looking at the picture. He never took his eyes off it. As the leader harangued him, waving the scroll around, the professor's eyes just followed it, to and fro, to and fro.

We tried to get the professor to spit on the picture, pushing it at his face, shouting, Spit! Spit! But he wouldn't. Someone brought in a bamboo carrying pole from the yard and started beating him on the back and shoulders. At last he fell down on the floor. But at once he got up on one elbow, to fix his eyes on the picture again. It was very creepy, the way he wouldn't take his eyes off that picture.

We tried to tear up the picture. However, it was backed by some extraordinarily strong kind of silk that you couldn't tear with your hands. So we burned it, right in front of him. When it started to burn, the professor dropped his head at last. We pulled it up, to make him look at the burning scroll, but he wouldn't open his eyes. And although the eyes were closed, they were weeping, tears pouring down his face.

He had somehow made us mad, refusing to condemn the picture, refusing to look while it burned. We were angry. I, personally, was angry. I can remember my anger clearly. Now the leader, Yu, called for the professor's wife and daughter to be brought forward. We all started shouting at them. Not really struggling them—it wasn't as organized as that. We were just mad at them. The Chairman had saved our country from slavery and all the horrors of the Old Society. We loved him. We really did—I can clearly remember loving him, with all my heart. Now a counterrevolutionary clique was trying to destroy our Chairman and everything he had built. These creeps, these shits, these cow ghosts and snake spirits, were trying to pull down our Chairman and bring back the Old Society, in which we should all be slaves again. It made us mad.

The mother was a plain, dumpy woman of forty or so. The daughter was beautiful. She was about sixteen, I guess—a high-school girl, except that the high schools had all been closed. She was plainly terrified, afraid to look any of us in the eye. I noticed that the students were concentrating their fury on her, pretty much ignoring the mother. Yu especially was shouting at her, pushing his big handsome face down at her.

At this point something turned. I don't know what it was, except that we all turned with it. We were still shouting revolutionary curses, but you could see in people's eyes that they didn't know what they were saying. Something else had taken over. Yu started pulling at the girl's clothes, shouting something like: Let's make her a revolutionary! The students around the girl started pulling at her, too. Her mother tried to stop them, then her father, who had got up from the floor somehow. The student with the bamboo pole clubbed them down, striking at the head now. Thud thud thud thud on their heads. By the time this had been done, the girl had been taken to the back room.

The back room would only hold six or eight students. There was a wood-frame bed in it, and a little dresser. The dresser was all in splinters, of course, but the bed was intact. The mattress had been shredded, but not the quilt. It was laid across the bed, and the girl thrown on top of it.

Crowding around the onlookers at the door, I could see the girl on the bed. They had pulled all her clothes off. Yu was on top of her. The others—*we* others—were all cheering him on. The ludicrous thing was that even as he was raping the girl he was shouting revolutionary slogans. To rebel is justified! he was shouting. Make revolution to the end! Well, it is ludicrous in retrospect. At the time, it was infinitely exciting.

When he finished, another one got on right away. Soon everybody in the room had taken a turn. Those of us watching from the doorway had become very excited. We all wanted to rape the girl. We pushed in trying to get in position so we could rape the girl. I myself climbed over the bed while one of the students was rogering away at her. I almost fell on them, the girl with her arms flung out in a cross, the boy with constellations of bright red pimples on his buttocks, pumping away.

Suddenly it was my turn. Big Chai, Big Chai, go, go, go! They shouted at me. A few moments before, watching the others raping her, I had been very aroused; but now I knew I could do nothing. The girl was lying on her back on the bed. Her eyes were closed, but you could see she wasn't unconscious. Her skin was pale, possessed of an extraordinary creamy translucence which I have never seen elsewhere, and which gave her body a strange, vulnerable beauty. Her legs were open, and I could see her private parts. It was the first time I had ever seen a girl's private parts. I was surprised at how hairy and complicated they were. They were covered with a mixture of blood and white slime, and her thighs and belly glistened wet, and the quilt between her legs was wet and slimy and bloodstained. It was disgusting. Hateful and disgusting. I lost all feeling for what we had been doing in an instant. It was just filthy and disgusting and shameful. And I felt sorry for the girl. Terribly, terribly sorry for her.

Not sorry enough to go against my peers, of course. I knelt down over the girl and took out my organ, holding it so that no one could see how small and limp it was. Then I lay on the girl and pretended to rape her. Just going through the motions. I kept my head down to the side of hers, so that if she opened her eyes I wouldn't be caught by them.

Lying there, pumping away at nothing, I saw it all clearly. It was as if I had suddenly gone from drunk to sober. There had been something about these Shacheng students, something about their determination to go after this particular professor, something more than revolutionary ardor. Now I saw it. They had wanted to rape his daughter. Perhaps not all of them, perhaps just Yu and one or two of the other leaders—enough to whip up the rest of us.

And then I had an inspiration. (Still pumping, still stretched out over that poor girl's thin ivory-toned body.) *The whole of the Great Cultural Revolution was like this!* It was nothing to do with saving the Chairman. The leaders of our country were possessed of a kind of lust—to destroy their enemies, to triumph in some factional quarrel. They had whipped up all this revolutionary passion to cover their real desires. Their aim was not to save the revolution, to establish social justice, or to bring a new life to the common people: their aim was to rape the prettiest girl in the school.

Well, it probably doesn't sound like a very brilliant insight at this distance in time. But to a naive young student in China in 1967, it was Revelation. I stopped being a Red Guard at that precise point. I probably stopped being Chinese in some way. Talking with people of my generation, most of us had some moment of truth like that. Before it, our country's leaders were dedicated revolutionaries, their shoulders to the wheel of history, sacrificing themselves for the good of the common people. After it, they were just a bunch of gangsters.

There was much more. So much goes through your mind in these moments of insight! Later you try to reconstruct it all, in the order it occurred to you, but you never quite can. Or if you can, it just seems trite and platitudinous because, after all, you have since internalized it so well. Still it changes you fundamentally, and you are never the same.

I saw how squalid China was—morally squalid, I mean. I had thought that we were—that *I was*—full of principle. Now I saw that there was no principle at all. It was all a sham, all a power play. And I knew that things were arranged differently elsewhere.

Don't ask me how I knew that. All I had ever been told about the world outside China was the Party clichés. All I knew about America was centered around a phrase we heard over and over again: the darkness and oppression of bourgeois society. I didn't know anything about the Constitution, about laws, about justice. I didn't know that America had had its own revolution. I could name only one president: *Yue-han-sun,* President Johnson (Lyndon, of course, not Andrew), who was trying to put down the national liberation struggle of the brave people of Vietnam. Of how he had come to be president, I had no idea. I suppose I supposed the capitalists had put him there.

Still, at that moment, simulating the act of violation, I knew there was a better place, with a better way of governing people, a way that took some account of actual people's actual lives. At that point China lost me, and it was foredoomed that I would become an American. Still, it seems mysterious to me that, on no evidence at all, *I knew that there was a better place.* Li Bai had the same intuition, though in a different context:

> Peach blossoms float on the water.
> There is another world, better than this one.

Some months later, in a railway carriage, I spoke to Huang Jen about the rape. Did he regret it? I asked. Yes, he said, and I could see it was true. What we did was bad. We should have to pay for it in our futures, or in a next life. I wondered what had become of the girl. Oh, said Huang Jen, she probably killed herself from shame.

Apart from my own involvement—which, in spite of the insight it brought me, I have always regretted—I should not make too much of this incident. Far worse things were going on in China at that time: cannibalism, public torture, mass killings, starvation.

Now I see again the pellucid whiteness of that girl's poor flesh. Americans are sometimes surprised to learn how important skin color is in China. We have traditionally considered pale skin to be beautiful and high class. Since this idea extends back over some three thousand years, it has become self-validating. I mean, high-class men selected pale women to mate with, and so by a straightforward process of genetic selection the upper classes became pale. This is why you see peasant women working in the fields under a hot sun with every inch of skin covered—long pants, long sleeves, broad hat. They don't want the sun to make their skin any darker than it is.

Ding has pale skin. Not so pale as the professor's daughter, not actually white, but a sort of creamy color, very smooth and unmarked. It thrills me to touch her skin—even now, after several years of marriage, I find it thrilling. My own skin is rather dark; but Hetty has turned out light skinned, like Ding. In fact she is quite pink, like a Western baby. Perhaps it is wrong of me, but I cannot help being pleased by this.

Selina had dark skin, and it was a sore trial to her. She always wished to be pale. Though in fact her skin was good. Not as good as Ding's, but clear and smooth. Not like those peasant women in the Northeast, with pores you could grow bean sprouts in.

I remember once eating dim sum with Selina in a restaurant in Kowloon when a Hong Kong movie star came in. Of course, everyone turned to look. Selina's eyes followed this woman as she crossed the restaurant with her retinue of minders to a private room at one side. *Ai-ya!* murmured Selina to herself. *Gam leung! Fei-fei baak-baak!* So beautiful! Fat and white! Poor Selina was skinny and dark, and hated herself for it. She was an old-fashioned girl.

11. Fragrant Dust

Plymouth Notch was about as small as a place can be: half a dozen houses, a church, a store, two huge barns. And a visitors' center, for the whole village had been placed in a state of preservation. There was a special visitors' parking lot, with several cars and campers in it already. We parked, got out, and installed Hetty in the backpack I use for carrying her when we take trips.

I was especially keen to see the performance by Mr. Ruggles, the Coolidge impersonator. With a view to determining the exact time of the performance, we went first to the church. Rebecca, the curatrix of the Coolidge Foundation, had explained that their offices were in the church basement.

Sure enough, there we found her: a plump, cheerful woman of forty or so. Welcome to Vermont. Welcome to the Notch. We sure did pick a good day for it. The colors were just at their peak. That sure was a cute baby.

I asked about the performance.

Oh, she was so sorry. It was this new federal law, the Disabilities Act. The church didn't have wheelchair access was the thing of it. So they couldn't hold performances in it. They would have to get a ramp built. It was so silly. And such a shame for the visitors! Mr. Ruggles was so good. Like President Coolidge come back to life! But they couldn't break the law, did we see? They had just found out about it Thursday from their attorney. Just in time to call off Mr. Ruggles. He came up from Boston, where he lived. Had we seen the visitors' center?

I was seriously disappointed. I love any kind of performance, and had been eagerly anticipating Mr. Ruggles's. We left the church and walked down the village's only street to a small restaurant. The restaurant (we learned from our guidebook) had actually been the childhood home of President Coolidge's mother, who had been married to John Coolidge in the front sitting room in 1868. At this point it emerged that Hetty needed changing.

Let's go behind the house, said Ding.

Behind the house was a field, falling away to open meadows, which rose again to a collection of farm buildings four hundred yards away. There were meadows all around, giving way to trees on the lower slopes of the mountains. This was living agriculture, apparently: a tractor was working in one of the further meadows.

It was a bright fall day, the sky cloudless. We had indeed found the colors at their peak, the mountainsides all blazing with crimson and gold. The tractor hummed in the distance, some voices could be heard from the visitors' center, but otherwise there was no sound. I turned slowly through 360 degrees, taking it all in. This place was sensationally beautiful.

Ding was finishing up with Hetty, there on the grass. Look! I said when her eyes were free. Look around! It's so beautiful. Somewhat to my surprise, I spoke in Chinese.

Ding stood up, leaving Hetty to right herself. There was smooth grass all around, the infant could come to no harm.

Ding turned on an axis as I had done, shading her eyes against the sun when she came to that direction.

Shan chuan jing hua, she said. This is a classical idiom, *the pure essence of mountain streams,* used to describe a person who rises to greatness from rustic origins. I envy your Mr. Coolidge, she added. To be born in such a place.

This is a somewhat un-Chinese thing to say. It is a measure of how Americanized we have become that we should both be charmed by this place and its surroundings. Most modern Chinese—especially those, like me, who were sent down to the countryside in the Cultural Revolution—harbor a deep impression of the poverty and barrenness of country life. Our ideals, our dreams, are of bright city lights and throngs of people. That is why Hong Kong seemed like a paradise to me. Yet this is actually a modern way of thinking, superficial in us—an aspect of the inferiority complex we Chinese have been nursing for a hundred years. Traditional Chinese poetry and art are almost entirely devoted to nature and rustic themes. Here, in the beauty and serenity of this tiny Vermont hamlet, our souls were quite at home.

We found a resting place for Hetty's diaper, then went into the restaurant. They were serving lunch, but we had eaten a late breakfast before leaving Ludlow, so we sat only for a cup of tea. Hetty, from the depths of her padded winter jacket, surveyed the place with dull infant curiosity.

President Coolidge's mother grew up in this house, I said.

What kind of person was she? Ding wanted to know.

I told her I hardly knew. Nobody knew much about Victoria Josephine Moor. I think she was an invalid for as long as Mr. Coolidge knew her. One wonders why Mr. John Coolidge married her. He himself was a real countryman, healthy as an ox and skilled in all country arts. To be sure, you could not really say he was spoiled for choice. The pool of eligible women was not very large. Still, there were several dozen families within a couple of hours' buggy ride: yet his first wife, Miss Moor, was a neighbor, her house a few yards from his own, and his second, Miss Brown, was another neighbor, a few yards farther on. Some poverty of imagination there. It could hardly be sloth: all the books agreed that life on the rocky hillsides of Vermont could be sustained at all only by unceasing labor.

(Imagination was, indeed, not their strong suit, these New Englanders. The president's father bore the given name John, his grandfather Calvin. He himself was named John Calvin; and when his wife produced two boys, he named them John and Calvin.)

I tried to summon up the spirit of Miss Moor, sitting there in her front room. I recollected the description of her in Mr. Coolidge's autobiography.

> She bore the name of two Empresses, Victoria Josephine. She was of a very light and fair complexion with a rich growth of brown hair that had a glint of gold in it. . . .

But she made no appearance. Like all Chinese people, I believe in ghosts. But according to our way of thinking, ghosts only hang around if they have a grievance. One who has died a peaceful death will not bother the living, but will proceed cheerfully on to his next life. There is no sign of any grievance in Mr. Coolidge's account, yet I wonder if he told all he knew. If a woman is a permanent invalid, she will sometimes be a great annoyance to those she lives with, however kind they may be, however little she may wish to impose on them. The healthy can never keep themselves for long in sympathy with the sick. And life in 1870s rural Vermont was tedious for a woman at the best of times—an endless round of chores and childbearing. If Victoria Josephine had died with resentment in her heart, her spirit would surely be haunting this place. Though it would probably not show itself with so many people around. I wondered if there was any polite way to ask Rebecca about a haunting.

We toured the visitors' center and the barn. What I had thought was another barn turned out to be a cheese factory. We bought some of their cheese—the garlic flavor, both Ding and I being fond of garlic.

The village store was still in business. When we got back to it, it was crowded. A busload of tourists had arrived and they were swarming everywhere: Californians, old women with taut, sun-dried faces, speaking in that peculiar trace-of-southern accent that very old West Coasters have. *Mah Lord, will you just lurk at this, Jennifer!* The store had been kept, so far as possible, in its 1923 condition. There was a wood stove in the center of the room. In odd corners were stacked farm implements and obsolete domestic contrivances—butter churns, apple corers. Distributed among the postcards and Coolidgeana on the counters were fragments of 1923 civilization: buttonhooks, collar studs, lamp trimmers, a stereopticon, a tin plate advertisement for Moxie, old-style matches in a wooden box:

SALAMANDER

PATENT SAFETY MATCH

40 count

and a picture of a lizard.

I knew Moxie from reading Mencken. On his first day as president, Mr. Coolidge left the village to go to Washington.

Waiting for the transportation to be organized, he stopped at the store. Sarsaparilla or Moxie? Moxie, replied the president, and fished a nickel out of his change purse.

I told Ding this story, and we ordered a Moxie. It arrived in a very up-to-date can with a ring pull, somewhat to my disappointment. I drank it anyway. It tasted like Chinese medicine, with a great deal of sugar added. Ding drank some, but grimaced. Then we tried it on Hetty, with entirely negative results.

Behind the store was the birthplace, a wood-built annex of bare, poky rooms. We gawked at the bed in which Mr. Coolidge was born, 121 years and some months prior to our arrival. The bed, which was not overlarge, nearly filled its tiny room.

These people were *peasants*, said Ding, whispering in Chinese.

It sounds odd to Chinese ears. We do not think of America as having peasants. We absorb all the stuff in our school textbooks, of course—the darkness and oppression of bourgeois society, and so on—but when it gets down to details the oppressees seem always to be urban, or black. Not peasants. And lurking behind all that was the unspoken, prearticulate suspicion—which seems to travel in the air like spores, without assistance from any of the normal means for transmitting information from brain to brain—that America was, in fact, the Peach Blossom Country, a place in which anyone could have a good life, free of officials, hunger, and movements. Not a place where one would find peasants.

Yet here they are, or at any rate were. No doubt about it, they were peasants. Middle peasants, in the case of the Coolidges, with more than the bare minimum of furniture: but still living from the land, snowbound in winter, homemade implements, earth privies, minimal education or doctoring. No landlords, of course—these people held their own land.

It occurred to me, in fact, that the Coolidges were at very much the same level as the Chairman's family; and the village, in its location and aspect, was not unlike Shaoshan, the great despot's native place. I mentioned this to Ding as we crossed from the birthplace to the homestead. I never went to Shaoshan, but Ding visited there once with a school party. It is in the next province to her own.

Yes, said Ding. Just the same. Allowing for culture difference, exactly the same. But in America, the chairs were more comfortable.

I ought to have visited Shaoshan myself. A visit to the Chairman's home place was part of the Red Guard thing. Most of them went, I think. I don't recall how I missed out. I don't mind, though. It would have been an anticlimax, because I had already, early in my Red Guard career, seen the Chairman himself. This was in Peking, of course, at a rally in Tiananmen Square. There were about a million of us in the square, screaming and waving the *Little Red Book*. All the leaders had come out on the reviewing stand above Heavenly Peace Gate—all but the Chairman. The whole thing was superbly staged, with a terrific buildup of tension. The Communists could always put on a good show. At last the Chairman himself appeared, walking slowly along in front of the other leaders, who of course were all applauding him. When he got to the central spot he turned and waved to us. The Red Guards went meshuga. Tears were pouring from their eyes, they were jumping up and down and screeching for all they were worth: Long live Chairman Mao! Long live Chairman Mao! Well, I suppose I was, too. But I have that kind of ability to keep part of my brain cool and rational even when drunk, even in the throes of direst passion. Looking at the Chairman, I was thinking: He's not red at all. We had been told that the Chairman's face shone like the sun, and in our songs we called him the red red sun in our hearts; but I saw now—the distance was very great, but I could see him clearly—that he was actually rather pasty. The first disappointment of my revolutionary career.

In Mr. Ruggles's absence the homestead was to be the high point of our visit, so I had saved it until last. The elder Coolidge moved his family to this larger house, across the street from the birthplace, when the president was four. It was here that everything happened. Here Victoria Josephine died, and little Abigail, too. Here Mr. Coolidge, as vice-president, was on vacation in 1923 when President Harding was struck down by an embolism in San Francisco. The news reached Vermont around midnight. For want of accommodation at Plymouth, the vice-president's entourage were lodging at a town some miles away. They raced over the unlit country roads, a carful of reporters in hot pursuit, and roused the family, and Mr. Coolidge was sworn in as president by his own father—a notary public—in his own living room, by the light of a kerosene lamp. After which, with perfect Coolidgean sangfroid, he went back to bed.

While we were buying tickets for the homestead Rebecca came out. I greeted her, and took the opportunity to ask about ghosts.

Ghosts? She smiled, somewhat nervously. Americans, I find, have not much belief in ghosts.

Mr. Coolidge's mother died here. Also his sister and his father. All in the same room. I indicated the interior of the homestead. I just wondered if there had been any strange incidents.

134

Rebecca shook her head slowly. No, I'm sure there has been nothing of that kind. Though someone once described this as a ghost landscape.

Ghost landscape?

Why, yes. Take a walk up in the hills here. You won't get far without you see a cellar hole, or a broken-down wall. Used to be thick with farms, this district. But it's poor land, poor land. When the lads came back from the Civil War, after they'd seen the good land out west, they didn't want to stay here. They up and left. Whole district just emptied out.

So who lives here now?

Oh, retired folk. There's the ski business. And some farming, still. She indicated the fields beyond the village.

I don't believe it, said Ding, when Rebecca had gone. I'm sure there are ghosts. They probably come out at night, when the whole place is deserted. We're not going to stay very late, are we?

Oh, come on, honey. There's no reason for any ghost to bear a grudge against us. Anyway, these were mild people, country people. I don't think they had much opportunity to be wicked.

I don't know. It seems to me there is a ghost somewhere near us.

To reassure her I held her hand walking through the homestead—and succeeded, I think, for when we came to the privy with its twin wooden seats, she giggled, putting her free hand to her mouth from modesty. Should be the *Congressional Record*, I said, indicating the Sears Roebuck catalog hanging conveniently at one side, and she giggled again, squeezing herself against me. Some of the California girls had come up, and we shuffled with them through the Coolidges' laundry and kitchen to the main room, which Mr. Coolidge called the sitting room. Of course we were not allowed into the room. A little viewing box had been cut into one side where you could stand and see into the room. Mr. William Allen White had been very scathing about the Coolidges' furniture—"the worst of the seventies," etc. To me it looked just fine, cozy and harmonious, sunlight streaming in through net curtains. I let the Californians in after me, then went back after they had gone, to savor the sunlit homely shrine, quiet center of the Coolidge system, where Coolidges lived, and died, and were sworn in, and sat stunned in grief—father with a paper, son with a book—through the winter of 1890 after little Abigail died, leaving them alone in a womanless house, wood smoke leaking from the stove, eight-foot drifts against the barn, the clock ticking slow and the wind whining down from Salt Ash Mountain. I stood there lost in imagining until Ding came back to fetch me.

Leaving the Notch, we turned off the road to visit the cemetery, following directions we had taken from Rebecca. It stands away on its own, out of sight of the village along a shaded lane. The graves are all scattered over a little knoll. I parked and switched off the engine.

Please, let's not stay here long.

Ding has even less tolerance for ghosts than I have.

You don't have to get out, honey. I just want to see the president's grave.

Yes. I'll stay in the car. Hetty needs a bottle. Quite unexpectedly, she leaned over and kissed my cheek. This is unusual in Ding, unless she has been drinking.

I got out of the car and climbed up onto the knoll, walking at random among the stones. The place has been a cemetery for two hundred years, since the first white men came here. Some of the stones are as old as that. I wandered among them, looking for the president. There was a Coolidge here and there, but all from the last century.

After a while I sat down on the grass to reflect and take in the atmosphere of the place. I did not feel scared at all, though it was very quiet—so quiet I could actually hear leaves falling. The sky was bright and clear.

Inevitably my thoughts drifted back to that other cemetery, the first time out with Selina, when we had courted among the gravestones on the hillside above Aberdeen, looking down at the harbor and across to Duck Tongue Island. She was so shy, so diffident. Scared, I thought at the time; but actually she was not scared. Of what should she be scared? She was not even a virgin. It was just a woman's act; the way a well-brought-up Cantonese girl should behave on a first date, with the eyes of the dead watching from ten thousand tombstones (by grace of a technique for transferring a photographic image of the deceased onto the surface of the stone—very popular in Hong Kong, though not used at all in backcountry Vermont). But her later feelings for me were not an act, not an act. Nobody could act like that.

For a while after she left Hong Kong I toyed with a theory which I thought explained her behavior. The theory was called cultivation of melancholy. Its premise was that Selina was a sort of masochist (Western pop-psych articles were starting to appear translated in the Hong Kong magazines) who drew satisfaction from the manufacture of sadness. Certainly she reveled in weepy movies, in dreamy romance novels from Taiwan—all loss, grief, and deprivation—and in the sappier side of our race's vast and marvelous poetic tradition. As a matter of fact, I know her favorite poem: it was Du Mu's "Garden of the Golden Valley":

> Past glories scattered, fragrant dust.
> Still water, grass, all unconcerned.
> Wind from the east; a bird cries at the setting sun.
> A petal falls, a girl falls from a high tower.

The allusion in the last line being to a virtuous woman who jumped to her death to avoid marriage with a brute, in some previous dynasty, in the place whose ruins are inspiring the poet. Selina saw Du Mu's name (Dou Muk in Cantonese) in a collection of literary essays I was idling with in bed one day in the Temple Street apartment. Then she recited the poem right off.

It's my favorite. We read it in school, in *Three Hundred Poems of the Tang Dynasty,* do you have that book in the Mainland? It made me cry. I cried right there in class, although I didn't even know the story of Luk-jue. I just knew it was something very sad.

We talked about poetry for a while, then fell into familiar games that ended, always, with an embrace. Afterward I lay on my back, Selina on her side cradled in my arm. Presently I felt her thin shoulders trembling, wetness on my breast.

A-lei! A-lei! What is it? You're crying!

The girl, I was thinking about the girl. Luk-jue, the girl in the poem. I'm sorry, it's stupid of me. But it was so sad, so sad.

Never mind, never mind. It was a long time ago.

But so sad.

Never mind, A-lei. Never mind. Long time ago.

In the frame of mind I was in now—perhaps because I had spent all day peering at preserved things, the humdrum artifacts of a century ago, elevated by age and the mysterious political processes of a free republic into objects of curiosity—it seemed to me that the present was no more than a poor simulacrum of the past. I thought of our sainted ancestors, stumbling backward into the future, eyes fixed on the sages of antiquity who, in turn, hankered for the upright and selfless rulers of mythology, Yao and Shun, Yu and the Yellow Emperor. We were all like that, all of us, gummed down to the past like mice in a glue trap. Selina, weeping for a girl sixteen hundred years dead. Mr. Coolidge, clutching resolutely at truths learned on a farm in this Vermont hamlet. Boris and Cyril, worshiping in a church whose rites were intended to awe and mystify illiterate muzhiks. *I have seen the czar blessing the Neva.* The Negro mutual-fund manager hearing the clatter of night riders' hooves every time a white man jostles him in the subway. Ghosts, everyone haunted by ghosts. In the Cultural Revolution we smashed everything old, everything we could find. Now, for a moment, twenty-seven years later, I remembered why.

But this I could not smash, not yet. I had to follow it, take the path Mr. Coolidge had taken, down the valley of the Connecticut to Northampton and thence to Boston. To see her, *to see her,* to close the circle, *to find out.*

But then, perhaps I could not see her. I knew nothing about her circumstances, after all. Even supposing that this Yoy was our Yoy, still she might not be in Boston. She might be divorced and living in another state. Or back in Hong Kong, or China. She might be *dead.*

It occurred to me for the first time—I am sure it was the first time—right there, after all those years, right there on that mound of earth, in the stillness under the sky, in the cold New England air, with the Yankee dead lying all around. A great deal can happen to a person in twenty years. She might have perished of disease, with my name on her lips!—like a heroine in one of those movies she so enjoyed, like my mother. (And the people round the deathbed looking at one another in bafflement—A-cheung? A-cheung? Who the hell is A-cheung? *Keui wa mat-ye?*) Or in some mechanical futility—car accident, plane crash—perhaps screaming my name to the darkness as it came rushing to envelop her. Dead!

Now I was scared. It seemed to me that a cold wind had come up that was not present before. I had irritated the ghosts somehow with my treacherous, wife-betraying thoughts, and they were stirring in their clayey cells. I got up and scurried down to the base of the knoll and walked round to the lane, my heart beating unreasonably fast. Just as I came in sight of the car down at the end of the lane, I saw the Coolidge stones, on a raised section above me. They were all together in a row: the president, Mrs. Coolidge, his father and mother, poor little Abigail, and Calvin Junior, who died in the White House, aged sixteen, at the height of the 1924 campaign, and who bore a stunning resemblance to the movie actor Mr. James Cagney, who had made Ding and me laugh so much in *Mister Roberts.* The stones were plain, only names and dates. The words "President of the United States" did not occur anywhere. Proper republican simplicity. *Here my dead lie . . .* The lines came to mind irresistibly. It was a speech Mr. Coolidge had made while president, during a visit to his home state. An impromptu speech, on the evidence, yet so lyrical Mr. Fuess printed it as free verse:

> Vermont is a state I love.
> I could not look upon the peaks of Ascutney,
> Killington, Mansfield and Equinox

Without being moved in a way
That no other scene could move me.
It was here that I first saw the light of day.
Here I received my bride.
Here my dead lie
Pillowed on the loving breast
Of our everlasting hills.

Though lacking any very formal structure, this is at least as good as most of the verses attributed to our emperors these five thousand years past, and far better than the Chairman's turgid and sentimental efforts that so blighted my own education. I stood in respect for a moment, then hastened to the car, already beginning to plan in my mind the trip to Boston, the necessary deceptions. I could get the address from our bank databases, which included all the world's telephone books.

Such a long time, said Ding, somewhat irritably. I was ready to go looking for you.

Hetty was asleep in the car seat, her little plump face resting on the sleep collar.

You're a long time dead.

What? *Shen-me ne?* What are you talking about?

You're a long time dead. It's a thing Americans say sometimes. To indicate the importance of living a full life. Because you're a long time dead.

You're crazy. Let's get out of here. Must be crawling with ghosts.

12.   Cruel Immortality

Selina got her visa in October and left for San Francisco on the twelfth of November. The day before was a Sunday, so we were together all day.

At first I was sober and supportive, passing on to her such advice about life in the West as I had been able to gather from my contacts at the bank. She responded with some concern for the preservation of my health, especially urging me to eat rice with every meal.

You must have some rice, or ten thousand to one, *maan yat,* your stomach will be upset. You northerners don't know how to eat, you with your cabbage and dumplings.

And poor Chai, the little Chai inside, was screaming, *What does this stuff matter? If my stomach explodes next Thursday you won't know! You won't care! You'll be on your goddamn honeymoon!*

We maintained control, though, until late afternoon or early evening. We were supposed to go out for a meal, but we never got around to it. Instead we lay in bed sobbing. It was she who started: silent weeping, as she had wept for the girl in the tower—then unrestrained.

A-cheung! A-cheung! Ai ai ai ai ai, A-cheung!

Well, that started me off. Soon we were both weeping uncontrollably, naked in each other's arms, on the bed, under the red quilt I had bought from a store in Shanghai Street a year before, when everything was fresh and clear and hopeful, like the beginning of a new dynasty.

It went on for a long time. At last, somehow, we dressed and went out. It was after midnight. We began walking up Nathan Road, through the buzz and vitality of the nighttime city. Selina's uncle had moved to Samseuipo some weeks previously—too far to walk now. There was a place where she could catch a minibus, up around Waterloo Road. We walked slowly in our accustomed style, arms round each other's waist, she leaning against me. There had been some idea of getting a snack on our way to the minibus station, but in the event we did not bother.

At last we came to the place of parting. She lifted her eyes to me and looked with them straight into my own. She was a girl who did not raise her eyes much. I do not recall having often looked directly into her eyes, other than in the act of love. Now the gesture held me. I stood there on the corner paralyzed with despair, life going on all around, absurdly, pitilessly, some youngsters in a group laughing, the stores all brightly lit, the world going about its stupid business with that indifference described so well in a famous poem by Mr. W. H. Auden.

Zai jian, she said. Farewell—quite unexpectedly in Mandarin. She hardly ever used Mandarin, and in point of fact did not speak it well. But all educated Cantonese think it the proper language for a grave occasion. Besides, there had been all those Mandarin pop songs to supply her with the vocabulary.

Zai mo-di . . . She broke off, and dropped her eyes. We had been weeping all day, and neither of us had any tears left. Yet still it was hard to speak. I knew what was coming, anyway. It was one of Francis Yip's songs:

> Shuo yi sheng zhen-zheng "zai jian."
> Wo zai mo-di zhu fu ni.

Say a real—a lifetime's—"farewell." Now, at the end, I wish you happiness.

I wished only to die. I thought of just turning away, running off down Nathan Road with the words unsaid forever—but I could not.

Helpless, hopeless, I could only croak: Don't go. Please don't go.

How much braver women are than men! How much better! More worthy! She looked up at me again, resolute in anguish.

. . . *wo zhu fu ni.*

And turned, and climbed into the minibus. The last I saw of her was her face at the window of the minibus, indistinct behind the reflections of the store lights, but looking at me, looking at me. The minibus drove off up Nathan Road.

It was not quite the end. Selina would never accomplish anything so neatly. The dip sent me a postcard from Norita airport—a postcard!—to tell me that she was thinking of me, and was looking forward to seeing her accursed Granny, and had thrown up on the plane but was much better now. All other considerations apart, you see, I was her only friend. I carried the fool postcard with me for years and can still see every detail of it. The front was an incompetently colorized

photograph of some architectural monstrosity in Tokyo—
convention centre in the Angloed English of the caption. An
uneven rectangle of card was missing altogether from the top
right corner: one of Mr. Chan's boys had embraced philately.
The characters of the message were decently well made but
progressively compressed in the vertical dimension toward the
bottom of the card for an effect very much like the wall of
sponge bricks pictured in *Young Person's Guide to Modern
Science* by Andrade and Huxley (*An-de-la-de yu Hu-xu-li*), the
book of Teacher Ouyang's I liked best, after the one on botany
with the color plates, the sponge bricks illustrating the various
degrees of air pressure at different levels in the earth's
atmosphere, at the bottom of which I lay supine, struggling for
breath.

The trauma of loss followed the progress of an amputation.
First, excruciating pain, which could hardly be borne. Later
only a relentless dull ache, and the twisting, fidgeting quest for
a position of minimum discomfort. At last, no sensation at all,
nothing but the hollow hopeless awareness that one once had
had a limb which now was gone.

(I have wondered often why the loss of that girl distressed me
so much. It has seemed to me that I ought to have been
stoicized by the death of both my parents in childhood, and
that any other experience of loss ought to have been
anticlimax. The answer, I think, is that my father and mother
were taken when I was too young to digest my grief, or indeed
to do anything with it. Those events are, so to speak,
unprocessed, standing there awful and changeless in the
remotest past, like those naked singularities which,
cosmologists tell us, lurk at the remotest ends of the universe.
So I have theorized, at any rate: and yet after reading the death
of Clara Copperfield I wept for a week.)

What a business it is, this love! Once it has a hold on you it will destroy your reason, your vitality—everything. There is no one who is not susceptible. Among our own emperors, who had the choice of all under heaven, it struck often, creeping into the palace like a poisonous mist, between the stone lion sentinels, through the moon gates, over the marbled courtyards, past the fountains and ginkgo trees, to seize and stifle even the Son of Heaven himself. The Xuanzong emperor of Tang, for example, the most wise and just of rulers, yielded at last to the charms of Yang Guifei, and it was only by a mutinous ultimatum, forcing him to consent to her execution, that the Imperial Guard saved the dynasty. Even further back, the Wudi emperor of Han, whose fame was so great it seems to have reached Rome, was overwhelmed and corrupted by his grief for the Lady Li. Nobody is immune from this pestilence, nobody.

Some cope better than others, of course. I pride myself that I did not impose my misery on friends and colleagues. I kept a straight face and was diligent at my work. This does not come easily to me, to any Chinese. I am familiar, of course, with the Western faith in the inscrutability of us Orientals. We do indeed think it foolish to telegraph our thoughts when engaged in worldly transactions; but in private matters we are passionate and intemperate, and Americans seem to us, in this respect, to be somewhat calculating and heartless. But I had been attending Mr. Chan's Saturday evening seminars at the Saddle for over a year now, and had absorbed some of his stoic wisdom.

> If Mount Tai collapses in front of your face,
>   don't bat an eyelid.

Mr. Chan knew how I was churning inside, and did his best by way of support. I even stayed over with his family one night, when he divined, correctly, that if left to myself I would get filthy drunk. Mr. Chan lived—and lives—in a public housing project in Aberdeen, on the south side of Hong Kong Island. His apartment is just one room, with tiny bathroom and kitchen annexes. In this room he and his wife raised three boys—good boys, all of them, now smart middle-class professionals. But at that time they were just little boys, the oldest twelve. The youngest two doubled up and I got the little one's bunk bed. It was the Lantern Festival, I remember—fifteenth day of the first lunar month. People were sitting out in the hallways of the project, sitting outside their doors gossiping while the kids ran around with little paper lanterns on sticks. Some of the lanterns were just lanterns, some were shaped like fishes or dragons. The people were sitting there in the hallways, outside their front doors, little tables beside them for food and drink, waiting for someone to stop by and gossip.

I had other friends too, of course. Old Leung—he was actually younger than I, but very worldly—would come calling, a thing he had never done before, and urge me to get out and live a little. I yielded at last, but his idea of living was to pay forty Hong Kong dollars for fifteen minutes of fellatio in the pleasure parlors of Jimsajeui. I tried it once, but Selina had taken my manhood to San Francisco with her. I could do nothing, and ended up chatting to the girl. She was from Zhongshan County, I recall, the birthplace of Dr. Sun Yat-sen, and had come to Hong Kong with all the rest of her village. They were all Nationalists and had been waiting for Chiang Kai-shek to come back. When, after twenty years, he didn't show, and the famines and movements got to be a serious nuisance, they bought a boat and sailed straight to the Colony, running up onto the beach at Repulse Bay, where everyone piled out and made a run for the city, their belongings bouncing at the end of shoulder poles, chickens squawking away in canvas bags. Those were the great days of illegal immigration.

I think the only time I lost it at work was with one of the Indians. There are a lot of Indians in Hong Kong—Indians, Pakistanis, and Sri Lankans, that is; I can never tell which is which. The Cantonese refer to them collectively as *a-cha,* which I think is the word for yes in one of their languages—at any rate, they are always saying it when talking among themselves. Well, there was an Indian in the bank's legal department—I cannot recall his name—for whom I had to make frequent deliveries. He was a sleek, plump, jolly fellow, with a fondness for jewelry, especially large garish finger rings, and opals. It happened that one day, as I was waiting by his desk for him to finish going over some documents he wanted sending, he got a phone call from San Francisco. It was a wrong number and he fussed a great deal with the caller, trying ineffectually to help identify the reason for the error. Meanwhile I had gone into a preposterous spasm of hope. *She is trying to find me! She is calling the bank! She can't stand America! Her husband is a swine! She wants to come back!*

When he hung up at last, the tears were running down my cheeks. I just couldn't help it. The fat Indian was all generous solicitude.

My dear chap! Whatever is the matter?

Still blubbering, I told him.

You poor fellow! Oh, I know just how it is! I understand precisely what you feel!

Rallying a little, I thanked him for his concern, which was clearly very genuine. Indeed, I thought he might burst into tears himself.

Had it myself, dear chap! A beautiful young Chinese girl. A virgin—yes! No use, no use. It was her family, you see? Because I am *a-cha*. He patted my knee consolingly. Your people (he went on) do not wish for their daughters to marry foreigners. Probably wise. Oh, I am sure it is wise. But, oh, how I suffered! A virgin, she was! Yes!

What happened to her? I was curious despite myself.

He waved very dramatically, to indicate perhaps a bird flying up and away, into the winter mists above the Colony.

Gone, dear fellow! Gone, all gone! Gone with the wind! Me only cruel immortality consumes!

I can still see that dear man, his plump dark face wrinkled with remembered pain, his great gesture of abandonment, his confusion of poets. Such comfort we can give to one another—even to those we barely know! This is one of the better things about human life. "I have found the world kinder than I expected, but less just," said the great Dr. Johnson in old age. Yes, yes, that is right, that is exactly right. Kinder but less just, yes.

Well, these things mend. More easily for us, perhaps, than for the Son of Heaven, for whom it must be very distressing to discover how small, after all, is the scope of his power over the misfortunes of this world.

I threw myself into study. Of English—then, early the following year, of banking, too. Our bank practiced, and still does practice, the very enlightened policy of encouraging its workers to improve themselves. They offered grants for study, and I took up some evening classes at Hong Kong University. It took five years to my bachelor's degree, four more to my master's, twelve years altogether until I came to New York; then three more till I met my sweet Ding, and married her, and five to the present day.

Twenty years: and the pain of that parting faded and shriveled, and I truly believed it had died. What fools we are! What a farce it all is! How much happier we should be unborn!

13. Long Time No See

The address was in one of the northern suburbs. A modest house, but an excellent neighborhood—the Yoys must be doing well. The place was on half an acre, at least, with trees out back, a two-car garage, and a third car in the driveway: late model, one of the midrange Nissans in deep blue or black—hard to tell in this light.

I cruised past, all the way to the end of the street, then U-turned via someone's driveway and cruised back. By the fourth pass I was beginning to wonder exactly how to proceed. I could not go cruising back and forth indefinitely. This was a suburban neighborhood, like my own in Long Island, and no doubt harbored a full complement of curtain twitchers and Neighborhood Watchers. *Officer, this car has been going up and down the street for an hour. . . .*

I pulled over, parked strategically equidistant from two houses, and switched off my engine. From here I could see the Yoys' place more or less clearly. Less, but becoming more: in my zeal, and knowing nothing about the Yoys' daily routine, I had left the hotel at six, arrived in spacious Fairlawn before seven, and the sky was still not yet fully light.

It occurred to me at once that sitting was hardly any less conspicuous than driving. Who sits in a car on a suburban street at 7:15 A.M.? Private eyes, I remembered from some magazine reading, and they carried bottles from the surgical supplies store for bladder relief. I didn't have, and the neighborhood was waking up. A dog was being walked in my rearview mirror, a couple of cars passed.

The uneasiness drove me from my own car at last. Boldly I walked along, right past the house. Well, not altogether boldly: I was on the other side of the road, and kept my head down, my chin tucked into the collar of my jacket. Someone was moving around inside the house—shadows on the curtained windows. I passed, then walked fifty yards farther on. Then— what? Pace back and forth here all day? I thought I would certainly be arrested.

I crossed over and came back on the Yoy side. I passed the house. No moving shadows now. Then—I was halfway from the house back to my car—the creak of a screen door, and the main door slammed. *Woop! Woop!* Reckless, I turned and ran back fifteen paces—and stopped.

A young man had come out of the house to the Nissan and was standing by it with the keys in his hand, to open the door and get in. The *woop-woop* was the car's security system, which the young man had alerted coming out of the house. He had been startled by the sound of my running. He was standing there by the car, with his keys hovering at the lock, looking straight at me. We were no more than twenty yards apart, and there was light enough now that I could see him clearly. I saw him quite clearly. How well he saw me, and what conclusions he was able to draw, I do not know. Not well, and none, probably, for he was, I judged, a little scared, as anyone should be when approached by a stranger, running, by the dawn's early light, on an otherwise empty street. At any rate he quickly turned from me, opened the car with some urgency, got in, and drove away at once, no warm-up, some tire burn.

But I had seen him clearly, I had seen him clearly, and there was no doubt at all, there was no doubt at all.

I drifted back to my car and sat there in a stupor. They could have arrested me at this point—I should not have cared less. I have no idea what I was thinking, nor indeed whether I was thinking at all. There is nothing to which I can compare this experience. There was anger, I am sure; and pride—he was better-looking than I had been at his age, and held himself straight, like a man. Well, he *was* a man—twenty years old, and two months at most. Yet the main thing, sitting there in the car—this I recall very well—the main thing was a kind of wonder. This was a magical occurrence, a violation of all things humdrum, a gift from the stars—like winning the lottery. It was that glow, that lunar glow of wonder, that I most distinctly remember.

It took the appearance of Selina, twenty minutes or twenty years later, to stir me. Not much of an appearance, even. She must have entered her garage direct from the house, so I had no full sight of her. The left-hand garage door went up. A car backed out—very new Buick Century in maroon or burgundy—and stopped at the end of the driveway to check the street. She looked right, then left. The right was for me, to re-create our parting so long ago and far away: her face seen indistinctly through the window of the minibus, on Nathan Road, through the window of the Buick on Laurel Drive. The symmetry established, the decades of her absence thus neatly parenthesized for annihilation, she backed into the street, straightened up, and drove away.

I deduced that she had a job, and supposed, in my unimaginative flat face way, that her routine would be like mine: drive to the railroad station, park, ride the railroad into the city. Threading through the suburban streets behind her, I developed suburban anxieties about whether the railroad was permit parking only and whether I should be able to buy a ticket on the train. In fact she drove directly into Boston, to the very center of the city, and vanished into a subterranean parking garage beneath some glum newish office buildings.

I wanted to follow, but the lot was gated, and the gatekeeper sauntered out to inspect me. This really was permit only (my anxieties are rarely fruitless, though sometimes misplaced by an hour or two, a mile or two, a civilization or two). No visitors, even—the lot was private, employees of Schacht and Pearson only.

Two cars had backed up behind me and there was some fuss about waving them round into the outward lane to get past me, before I could back up. I parked at random in the street and ran back to the lot, shouting an excuse at the gatekeeper and down into the bare concrete dimness. I saw the Buick at once, at the far end, but Selina had gone. Now the gateman was coming down the ramp after me, brandishing his portable phone in a suggestive manner. I went back and excused myself to him. Was just trying to find a friend of mine. Guess I missed him. This lot belonged to whom? Schacht and Pearson? Which was what? Department store chain (now it registered—we had one in Manhattan). This was their head office. All the accounting and administration. So all these people worked for Schacht and Pearson? Certainly. (Phone back in its holster on his belt now, this gook not dangerous.) And where was the main entrance? Round on the street, back there, first right, glass doors.

Round on the street my poor car was disappearing, assisted by a city tow truck. It took three hours and $150 to recover it. It was past noon when I presented myself at the glass doors. Beyond them was a long empty lobby, with a bank of elevators on the left at the far end. Before you got to the elevators you passed a security man at a sort of lectern affair. It was an older guy—my father's killer, possibly—black with silver hair. Neat uniform, friendly smile.

Whom did you wish to see, sir?

I want to see Mrs. Yoy.

Got to sign the book. He pushed it at me. Have you a business card, sir? Thank you. It's the fifth floor. He walked out to get an elevator for me.

The fifth floor was a receptionist—a dumpy girl, also black—behind a desk, corridors leading off to each side, distant noises of office bustle—a telephone ringing, the repetitive *ng-ts* of a copy machine. I asked for Mrs. Yoy.

Do you have an appointment, sir?

No, I don't.

I don't know if she'll see you without an appointment.

Please, just call her.

Well, I can call her secretary.

Her secretary! Selina—my skinny, vague, helpless teenage sweetheart—had a secretary!

And your name, sir? Reaching for the phone.

Joy. Mr. Joy Tin-cheung from Hong Kong. I wrote it down for her, in English letters of course. From Hong Kong, tell her. Temple Street, tell her Temple Street.

She dialed and spoke. Mr. Joy from Hong Kong. Company is Temple Street. Joy, J-O-Y, then Tin T-I-N and then . . . No. Yes. No. Temple Street. Temple. Street. Yes. No. Don't know. Hold on (hand over mouthpiece). Are you a rep?

No, no. I'm not a rep. Honest to God.

He says no. No. Don't think so. Yes. Is she? All right, I'll tell him.

Mrs. Yoy was tied up. Not for the first time! I wanted to shriek—we had played many games. But I nodded patiently. Would I care to wait?

I sat. The magazines were dull—fashion, men's fashion, children's fashion, *Marketing Week.* The fluorescent glare got oppressive. People came and went, from one corridor to the other. The copy machine whined, the receptionist smiled encouragingly, colors began to drain away under the glare. It seemed a rough-and-ready sort of office for such a big concern. Perhaps I had been spoiled by too many years on Wall Street. All that wood paneling, those mock Queen Anne side tables.

She appeared quite suddenly, from the right-hand corridor. I struggled up awkwardly from the too low couch, tiny hot white meteors drifting insolently across my retinas.

Selina.

Mr. Joy.

She was dressed to go out, it seemed, wearing a smart fur-collared jacket, carrying a small brown leather pocketbook. Beneath the jacket, knee-length tightish skirt, panty hose, low heels. Her face was rounder than I remembered, her figure—

as much of it as I could see—fuller, but still trim. Legs excellent. Her hair, which she had always worn long and straight, was now permed. But it was the way she carried herself that was most different, that most struck me. A professional lady. No more the downcast eyes, she now looked at me straight, as she had done only once before, in a previous dynasty, about to board a minibus to the Future.

There was no sign of shock. To be sure, she had had time to prepare herself. Yet creating the moment in my imagination on the long drive up to Boston, I had foreseen her mouth fall open O! and a hand—the fingers arching back almost unnaturally (an art she shared with Ding) flying up to cover it: tips of fingers against upper lip. No: she looked at me levelly, very calm, as if she had been expecting this for twenty years, for every instant of twenty years.

A-cheung. Her tone was plain, conversational. *Hou loi mou gin.*

Long time no see.

If anything, I was more confused and uncomfortable than she. This I had really not expected. Selina—my Selina—was a shy eighteen-year-old, a demure Hong Kong girl, raised mostly by women whose own attitudes and expectations had been formed in the Old Society, in which—until 1949!—it was entirely legal for a gentleman to kill his wife if she displeased him. Now, here was this . . . *woman*, this *American* woman: fortyish, but trim and attractive, stylish clothes, head up, the equal of anybody.

I had never been so awkward with a woman. She let me walk with her, seeming not to mind. I wanted so much to put her arm round my waist, and mine about hers, and stroll as we had strolled along Nathan Road so many evenings; but I dared not. Any notions I had had about sweeping her off her feet evaporated rather fast. I was, in fact, tagging along with her, by her leave, until we reached the restaurant she had been heading for. By which time it had been established, in exchanges I cannot now reconstruct, that I had come to Boston from New York on business, seen her by chance going into her office building, and decided to call on her.

I felt I just had to see you, I said, seated in the restaurant.

Oh, you *haaaaaad* to see me. She was mocking me, drawing out the vowel in a low throaty pitch, the contour falling then rising. Suddenly something very important came up and you *haaaaaad* to see me.

Selina, you don't seem surprised at all. It's almost as though you were expecting me.

Mmm. She opened the menu and scrutinized it. I always thought I'd see you again.

Did you dream about me, Selina?

This jolted her a little. She looked up from the menu, straight at me—so direct!—eyebrows slightly raised. Then down, back to the menu. Yes. Sometimes. How about you?

Often. This was not strictly true. I had dreamed about her fairly regularly for three or four years, then less and less. I thought I had had at most four or five Selina dreams since getting married—average one per annum, say.

The waiter who had seated us came back with our drinks— beer for me, soda for Selina. Then he hovered. I picked up the menu and ordered at random. The place was Italian, I noticed for the first time. Selina ordered and the waiter left.

Do you like Italian food, Selina?

Mmm, is okay. Not as good Chinese.

As Chinese, honey. Not as good *as* Chinese. Your English really needs some work.

This gave me the upper hand momentarily. She actually dropped her eyes. How sensitive we all are about our English!

As Chinese. *As* Chinese. But, you know, my . . . (still looking down) . . . my husband . . . Got the Chinese restaurant. So, I go out time (her English now breaking down completely) don't want to eat the Chinese. Always go . . . some other country food. She looked up. Her eyes were full of tears. Oh, A-cheung! And she stood up, grabbed for her pocketbook, and ran to the ladies' room.

The restaurant was not busy. It was upmarket without being grand: about midway between Naugahyde booths and the dessert trolley. There was piped music, though very faint and respectably operatic, and we had been asked, on being seated, if we wanted a cocktail. On the other hand, there were cloths on the tables, decent silverware with a separate salad fork, and specialties *di giorno* chalked up on a little blackboard by the kitchen door. How reactionary it is, this restaurant business! The idea seems to be that we are all yearning to act out the high life of seventy years ago: being fussed over by tailcoated flunkies, eating and drinking in accordance with elaborate sumptuary codes. Cocktail!—a word which now survives only in restaurants, or in the homes of the aged like Walter and Abby. The tipping business—noblesse oblige, as if you were rich and the waiter were poor, when in fact you are both perfectly middle class, and it would make just as much sense for him to tip you. The whole thing irks me, and I generally avoid restaurants outside business hours. There is the Red Guard still in me. We used to march into restaurants, shout a few revolutionary slogans, hear a few shouted back, and get fed for nothing, or for chits from the local revolutionary committee (look, China was the country that *invented* bureaucracy). Ah, my youth.

Selina had still not reappeared when our food arrived. It occurred to me momentarily that she might have fled—slipping out through the bathroom window like a character in a movie; but her coat was on the back of the chair, and it did not look like the kind of coat one would abandon.

A Selina dream came to mind—from talking about dreams, I suppose. This dream, which had recurred a dozen times in the years after she left Hong Kong, was based on something that actually happened. We had gone with Mr. Chan to check out a posh new Japanese department store in North Point. The store had a large women's section with changing rooms—an innovation in the Colony at that time. Selina had gone into the changing rooms with an armful of clothes, while Mr. Chan and I stood around spare, as men do when women shop. After a while, bored, Mr. Chan had gone off to look at some other area. I may have wandered briefly myself, though not far. Time went on. Chan came back. Where's your girlfriend? I said I thought she was still in the changing rooms. How can she take so long? We waited longer, and I fell into an unreasoned panic. *She had left. Something had happened to her.* At last I got one of the sales assistants to go into the changing rooms to root her out. Selina, who feared and hated any kind of public embarrassment, was furious. What did I think had happened to her? I don't know what I thought. She was lost; she was dead; she had run away from me; she had been spirited away by ghosts; Chang E, the moon lady, alerted by her moon name, had carried her off to that cold palace in the sky. I have no idea what I thought, but whatever it was I dream-thought it again and again in the months after she left, the panic and insecurity still the same, though dream-translated into a variety of improbable locales: the library at my college, the bank's huge neon-lit climate-controlled computer room, the Piranesioid railroad station at Fourfold Peace which I had passed through on my first trip to the South, which my father had passed through on his last trip, to Infinity.

Now she came trotting between the tables, perfectly composed, pocketbook held under her arm (the Chinese verb *xie*—our language, in most respects as bare and poor as the stripped loess hillsides of the old heartland, boasts a sensational profusion of carry words, and I—and, for all I know, every other Chinese person—savor a tiny thrill each time I select precisely the right one).

The food arrived as she was seating herself. For the gentleman, eggplant parmigiana. And for the lady, angel-hair pasta with clam sauce. The portions were small, the flavor slight. To tell the truth I do not care much for restaurant food. I always come away feeling disappointed. I have got used to Ding's food, and nothing else seems as good.

Is your wife a good cook? Selina possessed considerable telepathic powers.

How do you know I have a wife?

Of course have a wife. How can be not have a wife? Handsome guy like you.

I could have decided to become an old bachelor. After you broke my heart.

161

She snickered. Not you. I know.

How about you, Mrs. Yoy?

We-e-e-ell. She tilted her head a little to one side, as if calculating. Got a husband. Three children.

Boys? Girls? Ages? I was watching her closely, while trying not to look as if I were. But she was unembarrassed.

Twenty, and, mmm, eighteen, and fifteen. Boy, girl, girl. You?

He was her only boy! *Our* only boy! *My* only boy! But I did not want her to know I had seen him. I maintained my appearance of nonchalant inquiry.

I have a little girl, ten months.

Her eyebrows went up, genuine surprise. You wait so long? How long been married?

Six years.

So when you got married, already more than forty.

Yes.

Is too late.

I don't know. A wise man said: Those who marry late are better pleased with their children, those who marry early with each other.

What wise man?

Samuel Johnson. An Englishman.

*English*man? *Pei!* What do they know? You shouldn't wait so long. Is not healthy. I'm sure you had many girlfriends.

Not really.

She was quite animated now. My Selina, the old Selina, but more self-assured.

How about your wife? I think she's American.

No, she's Chinese.

ABC?

No, born in China. Sei-chuen girl.

How old?

Thirty.

Pretty?

Yes. Very pretty.

Prettier me?

Prettier *than* me, Selina. How can you live in America for twenty years and still speak such crappy English?

Thaaaan me. Prettier *thaaaaaaaan* me. Is she?

Yes. Prettier than you.

This did not altogether please her. She looked down at her food. I'm glad you got a pretty young wife, she said, after a moment's consideration.

How's your husband's business?

Is good. The Harvard professors, they all come to his
restaurant.

And how is your husband's enthusiasm? How often does he
embrace you? This I did not say. But I was beginning to heat
up from being with her. She was not the eighteen-year-old
who had left me, of course. There was more on the hips and
thighs—anything is more than nothing—and a not unpleasing
plumpness about the face. But I had seen the nape of her neck
when helping off her coat, and the slimness of her arms and
shoulders, and smelled her perfume; and now, watching her
eat, seeing the moistness of her mouth, her small even teeth,
her slender fingers, now the old Adam woke and I was hot for
her, crazy for her. I wondered if she had a lover—then, boldly,
asked her right out.

She sputtered on a mouthful of pasta and lowered her sweet
lips almost to the plate to release surplus strands.

Chisin lei! Of course not. Wiping her chin.

But I know you are a working woman. There must be guys
around you at work. And you're still very pretty, Selina.

She liked that (dabbing her lips with a napkin now) and
flicked me a glance of appreciation. Fruits.

I'm sorry?

Most the guys I work with are fruits. She giggled. You know.
Fruits.

Sure I know. What kind of work is it?

Buyer. For Schacht and Pearson. Where you came. Big department store. Buy the clothes.

Schacht and Pearson, I know. We have one in New York.

Yes. I go there.

You go to New York?

Yes. Every month once, sometimes twice.

To Manhattan?

Yes, Manhattan.

Where do you stay?

Stay Midtown Pavilion. Hotel. Madison Avenue.

She came to New York! Once a month! Sometimes twice! Stayed in midtown! In a hotel! Joy, hope, and anticipation roared and surged in my head. Somehow I held myself steady. Easy, easy.

Selina.

Mmm?

Perhaps . . . I wanted it to be tentative, put to her diffidently, with reluctance and some shame, even as my blood seethed with lust. Perhaps I could see you. When you're in New York.

Long pause. I let it hang there, watching as she finished her pasta and set down the fork (by the side of the plate—not yet fully Americanized after all). Now she did not lift her eyes.

I don't know.

Just . . . have dinner together. In a restaurant. Like this.

Maybe . . . is not so good. Still not looking up.

Why not? We are old friends, aren't we? We've never fallen out with each other. Never any bitterness between us. Why shouldn't we have dinner together, if you come to New York?

Now at last the eyes—a little too bright, tears waiting on station.

I don't know. Oh, A-cheung . . . She lapsed into Cantonese . . . It's upset me so, seeing you like this. I really don't know what to make of it. All these years, I have thought of you so much. Sometimes, when I was by myself, I wept, thinking of our sweet hours together. Truly—perhaps you won't believe me, but it's true. But, you know—just as I told you in Hong Kong—our love was of the kind that can have no result. It was just a brief, precious dream—that's all. I wanted so much to go to America, and you couldn't go. I wanted so much to go—to see my grandmother. Yes, and to be married. I wanted to be married, to be a wife, to have children. I had to choose, so I chose those things. You understood that, didn't you? What happened between us was only a dream, a sweet sweet dream. And now, now when I see you here, that dream wasn't a dream. It was real. Oh, I knew, I knew, I knew this moment would come. I always knew. Now it's come. Now I can't go on saying that was just a dream.

Can't reality be just as beautiful as a dream?

She frowned at me, as if I had said something irredeemably stupid. Of course not. Dream is dream. Reality is reality.

Love is love.

For some reason, some inexplicable woman reason, that was a bull's-eye. She dropped her head and grabbed for the pocket-book—too late, and half a dozen large bright tears fell on the table, on her plate and the tablecloth, before (groping blindly) she had extracted a little carry pack of paper tissues.

A-cheung! A-cheung!

I got up, went round the table, and half knelt, my arm round her shoulders.

I'm sorry, A-lei, I'm sorry. I really was sorry, too. Holding her like that, her weeping head on my shoulder, feeling her narrow rib cage trembling beneath the sweater, smelling her hair (actually her shampoo, I suppose—it was a peculiar nutty smell), I was filled with pity and remorse—lust trotting along close behind, of course. I'm sorry. It was wrong of me.

She straightened up, pulling away from me.

I go ladies' room, she said in English. You pay check. Then we go.

Right. I got the check settled and was waiting by the door, her coat over my arm, when she came out. I held the coat for her. Before putting her arms into the coat she shrugged the sleeves of her sweater down to trap them under her fingertips—a maneuver I remembered from that other dynasty. So many things to remember!

Jau-le. We stepped out into the street air, colder than it had seemed coming in. *Then we go.* Go where? I rolled the dice.

I'm staying in a hotel. We could go to my room and talk.

Bad move! No, she said much too quickly. No.

I only meant to talk.

No. I go back my office.

I'm sorry.

Never mind.

I didn't mean.

Is okay.

I was devastated. I had spoiled everything with my too forward approach. Now there were, what? a hundred yards to the office, then I should never see her again. I thought at that point about our son, the first time this particular act of treachery crossed my mind, but dismissed it at once. At this point I was still relatively sane. Yet nothing else came to mind, I could think of no way to recover the situation, and the distance was closing—sixty yards, fifty.

Selina.

M?

When . . . when you come to New York, may I see you?

(Forty, thirty.) I don't know.

Please. Just tell me when you're coming. We'll have dinner somewhere. Somewhere nice.

Maybe . . . (twenty, fifteen) . . . is not right.

168

Why not? Old friends, that's all. Just old friends, having dinner together.

She stopped. We had reached the door.

Old friends.

Yes. Just old friends, that's it.

Now she looked right up at me, directly, calmly, and for the first time with some of the old tenderness.

Old friends.

Yes, yes. Old friends. *Lou pangyau.*

Okay. She turned to the door.

Selina! Selina! When will you come? How shall I get in touch with you?

She paused at the door. I guess you have business number.

Yes, yes, I have. Wait. I produced another business card from an interior pocket. Here. Please, call me. But when will you come?

Next Wednesday. Evening time. Wait my call. I will call you.

I'll wait. I had positioned myself at the door. Now, everything settled, I pushed it open for her. She slipped past me—trailing some last stray molecules of her perfume—then turned back.

You'll wait for my call? In Cantonese now, within earshot of the security man.

Yes, my heart. I will wait for your call.

She paused for a couple of beats, just looking at me. Much tenderness now. I fell in love with her, in love in love in love with her, all over again.

See you then, Mr. Joy.

See you, Selina.

I think I could have kissed her then, but did not. She went to the elevators. The old black security guy tap-danced . . . no, I have made that up, he merely *walked* out from his desk to hold one open for her. She turned to glance once more at me before stepping inside. When the door had closed Mr. Bojangles went back to his desk, but not before rolling a benign understanding smile down the length of the lobby to me. *I've been there, buddy. I know what it's like.* I let the door go and stepped away, thinking: Courtesy Walt Disney Productions.

14.   Harmony Disturbed

Jip ran to the door to greet me when I got back on Wednesday evening. Ding was in the kitchen, Hetty crawling around among her toys in the living room. I greeted and kissed, then went upstairs to unpack my bag. When I came down Hetty was upright, circumnavigating the coffee table, holding on to it with one hand and falling frequently, making the sort of froggy croaking sound she generates when concentrating on some pleasurable task.

I went into the kitchen and sat at the table. Jip put up his paws to be shaken and panted appreciatively into my face. His mentality is that he exists to guard and protect us, and that our well-being is consequential on his efforts. It is, therefore, a mystery to him how we can be absent from him for several days and yet survive. When, after such an absence, he sees us again, he is filled with joy that Providence has somehow spared us.

Soon she will be walking, I said, referring to Hetty.

Yes. How was your library?

My cover story had been that I was going to Northampton to investigate the Coolidge collection at their Forbes Library. And truly, after parting from Selina and doing some perfunctory sight-seeing in Boston, I had driven over to Northampton and spent a pleasant day and a half browsing in the Forbes. I had seen some of the president's personal letters, and heard his voice for the first time. (By no means the duckspeak his enemies mocked. Nor, I believe, was it really true that he pronounced the word *cow* with four syllables.)

Most interesting, I replied. They had recordings of Mr. Coolidge's speeches, and many photographs I had not seen before. A splendid collection.

Jip is not my first dog. There was another, named—or misnamed—Lucky, when I was a child. He was small and did not eat much, which was important, since we were a zero-income family, sustained only by my father's pension and Grandmother's occasional work as a seamstress. In fact, I don't know how he stayed alive on the scraps we gave him.

Stay alive he did, though, until the year when there was a movement against dogs. We tried to keep him in the house out of sight, but the neighbors all knew about him and someone told the Public Security Bureau. They came round one morning early, before school, and clubbed poor Lucky to death in the kitchen. I tried to stop them but I was just a skinny kid, and they swatted me aside, laughing as they did their work. It is a vivid scene to me because I really loved that dog, and after my mother died I lived in fear that everything I loved would be taken from me. The PSB men were brutal and clumsy. With a little dog like that, one blow would have done the job; but Lucky got into a corner and it's hard to take a swing at something huddled in a corner. At last they dragged him out and flattened his poor head in the middle of our kitchen, my sister shrieking, Grandmother scolding them, and left, still laughing.

Afterward Granny sold Lucky for meat. Why not? He was healthy—I mean, the meat wouldn't be diseased—and dog meat is a delicacy in northeast Asia. In that way, said Grandmother, he paid us back for all the scraps. Later—it seems to have been years later, but I really have no grasp of the chronology here—I found one of Lucky's teeth among a stack of coal dust briquettes in the corner. I washed the tooth and kept it, carrying it around with me for years, until my first year at college, in fact. Then I decided I was indulging in bourgeois sentimentality and got rid of it somehow; I don't remember the details.

Now we live in America, where even a dog has rights. Nobody will harm our Jip. This dog was Ding's idea. Our house came with a white American Gothic picket fence round the backyard, and Ding's first comment was that we could get a dog and let him run free in the yard. We went to the North Shore Animal League one morning. We arrived too late for all the cute puppies, but in one of the cages was this small, unkempt heap of fur, lying with his head on his paws looking very sorry for himself. His card was marked AR, which is to say Adopted Then Returned, which might be taken to mean he had some unattractive personality quirks, or possibly just that someone was allergic to him. At any rate, the AR business had sent the poor creature's self-esteem to rock bottom. When we had them take him from the cage for us and put him on a leash, he could hardly be bothered to walk. Poor little creature, said Ding, and my heart went out to this fellow orphan, and we took him home. After some research in library books Ding, who likes to get everything into categories, declared him to be Tibetan terrier. In fact, he is just a mutt.

It took Jip some time to feel secure with us. Whoever had charge of him previously had trained him well, so he was not a problem. He was just very nervous, overanxious to please. By firm, loving care Ding gradually accustomed him to us. Now he is the best, happiest dog you could wish for.

He pooped in the garden this morning, said Ding. Because I couldn't walk him.

Couldn't wait till Daddy got home? We try to walk him once every day, so that he can poop away from home. We are very responsible, and always scoop. But when I am away, Ding doesn't like to leave Hetty, so unless a neighbor can be enlisted as baby-sitter Jip isn't walked.

I found it in the back, behind the garage. Gave him a smack.

Jip knew very well what we were talking about. He hung his head, watching me from under his eyebrows with doggy apprehension to see how bad it was.

Wagging my finger at him I uttered a Chinese idiom: If you don't want people to know you did something, don't do it. But somehow I screwed it up, pronouncing the connecting word in Cantonese, *cheui-fei*, instead of Mandarin, *chu-fei*. Presumably this was subterranean guilt—*cheui* (though in a different tone) being the second syllable of Selina's given name. I knew my error at once, and felt myself beginning to blush. I thought perhaps Ding might not notice; then I saw that she had frozen in place, scraping a carrot over the waste bin.

Cheui-fei? Why *cheui-fei?* Very calm and even, but with something underneath.

Cantonese. Sorry. I took dinner last night at a Cantonese restaurant in Northampton. I was talking to them.

Ding had not turned to face me. Now she began slowly scraping again. Slowly, thoughtfully. I picked up the mail and began looking through it.

I guess you like to talk Cantonese.

Huh?

Reminds you of your time in Hong Kong.

No. It's just that they were Cantonese people. I was being polite, that's all.

There was a long silence. Scrape, scrape. Something classical was playing on the radio. Hetty crawled in. Grateful for the distraction, I picked her up and talked some baby talk at her.

I sometimes wonder how you passed your time in Hong Kong, said Ding, apparently unwilling to let it go.

I studied. You know that. How else could I get from bank messenger to VP?

You didn't study all the time. Scrape, scrape.

Come on, honey. I've already told you about that. There was nothing serious.

Hetty, who is acutely sensitive to tones of voice, was watching us silently.

Scrape, scrape. Ding finished her scraping and stood upright to set a pan on the range.

So many years and nothing serious.

At this point it could have got very nasty, but the telephone saved me. It was Mrs. Meng. Ding took it and got into a long conversation in Chinese about the pros and cons of insurance, which she is mainly con. I lifted Hetty onto my hip and crept upstairs, breathing softly.

I don't know what was going through Ding's mind, and dared not ask for fear of betraying myself. There was no way she could know about Selina, and it was not unusual for me to be away for a day or two—though this had been the first time since Hetty was born.

Whatever it was, the next day she was really upset, with good cause. When I got home from work, soon after seven, Ding was not in the kitchen at all, but in the living room. She was sitting on the sofa watching a TV show, the TV much too loud. Her eyes were red, as if from weeping. I was immediately concerned, and went over to her before removing my overcoat.

Darling, what's the matter? I got the remote control and turned down the TV.

Is nothing, nothing. She did not look at me.

Oh, come on, honey. I took her hands. What is it? The hands were cold.

My teacher, my old teacher. Who was very kind to me. She has died.

I struggled to recall the teacher. I thought Ding had indeed said something, early in our marriage, about a teacher who had shown her some special kindness, but I couldn't remember the details.

Was that Teacher Zhao? In your middle school?

No, no. Teacher Ma. My mother called this morning and told me. It makes me so sad. I had no chance to see her again before she died.

Ding still had her eyes on the TV, and did not incline toward me. I said some soothing words in Chinese. I thought she might begin weeping, but she did not. Indeed, she recovered quickly. When I suggested she need not cook, that we could order in, she said no, not necessary, she would cook, and went to the kitchen.

When we went up to bed I wanted to hold her in my arms to console her. However, she lay down with her back to me, indicating no wish to be held. This was odd, but not altogether unwelcome. My outlook was dominated by the coming tryst with Selina, at this point only six days away. I wanted to conserve my *qi* so that I would be vigorous for her. If I took Ding in my arms, I was not sure that I could restrain myself from entering her; and if I entered her, I did not think I could control my *qi*. So I whispered a tender good-night (to which she made no reply) and turned on my side away from her.

Thinking about it during next morning's commute, it seemed odder and odder. If she had had such a strong sentimental attachment to one of her teachers, surely in six years of intimacy I should have heard more of it? She had certainly heard plenty from me about Teacher Ouyang. Not even knowing what I was suspicious of, yet hating myself for it anyway, I called China from my office. Her mother picked up.

Mother-in-law, I heard that Wife's old teacher died.

Yes.

I forget the name. Was it Teacher Zhao?

177

No, no. Ma, Ma Yihong. She was very kind to her in middle school.

I'm sorry.

People must die. It can't be helped.

We exchanged some pleasantries, then I hung up. I really should not have been so suspicious. It was my own guilt, of course. The wicked flee when none pursueth. Or, as we say in Chinese: The man with a clear conscience has no fear of a ghost knocking on the door.

I had just hung up on Mother-in-law and was turning to deal with some E-mail when Chan called. It was around midnight in Hong Kong, and he was pretty drunk. I suppose he had been sitting in the apartment with his wife watching TV and drinking *yuk-bing-sue*. Dear old Chan. He was, in fact, barely coherent.

How's the one indoors? was his first question. I said Ding was very well.

Mistress Ding is a good woman, he said, referring to her by her maiden name in that archaic way Cantonese people have. You are a lucky guy.

I said that I was entirely cognizant of my good fortune. Then I asked after Mrs. Chan and the boys.

Same as before. Nothing new.

There was a long pause; then we both tried to speak together, and stumbled over each other in the time lag. I thought he was saying something about cheating.

What? What? What about cheating?

I said, don't cheat on the one indoors.

Don't worry, Mr. Chan. I'll take good care of the one indoors. One woman is quite enough for me. The one indoors! I had slipped into his idiom.

I'm telling you. You listen.

I humored him. Mr. Chan waxes philosophical when he's drunk.

Then, suddenly: That one you were making hot cakes with, back when we first knew each other. The Toi-san girl, the one who took you for a ride. Named—what?

Gwok. Gwok Lei-cheui.

Right. You ever see her since?

No. She went to the States in seventy-two. Married a guy called Yoy. In San Francisco. No, I never saw her again. Of course not. Why would I see her? San Francisco is three thousand miles away.

She try to get in touch with you?

No. What, after so many years? No, of course not. Absolutely not.

Another long pause. I let this one ride.

Okay, I'm going to bed now.

All right, Mr. Chan. Always good to hear you.

Take care of the one indoors. Take care of your marriage.

Sure. You too.

The call left me feeling glum. I wanted to see old Chan again, to sit and drink with him. Not *yuk-bing-sue*—he only drinks that when he's alone. A few cold beers, some bar snacks, the way it used to be in the Saddle, so many years ago. Death in life, the days that are no more.

Ding recovered herself and was quite composed all weekend, though somewhat distant. There were only two uncomfortable moments. One was on Saturday night. I generally embrace Ding on Saturday night, but I was still intent on conserving my *qi*. However, when we were in bed she came into my arms, clearly wanting to be embraced. I kissed her and held her, but made no advance. After a few minutes she pulled away, and turned onto her back.

Seems you don't have the mood for *tongfang* lately.

It comes and goes.

It's been two weeks. Since Vermont.

Women always know! I said that what with the pressure at work, and researching Mr. Coolidge, I had very little energy.

I'm sure you had more energy when you were in Hong Kong.

Of course I did. I was twenty years younger.

We lay there in the darkness, both on our backs. I was tense as a bowstring, waiting for the other shoe to drop. But after a

moment or two Ding began massaging her eyes and temples—
an exercise she does to prevent wrinkling. I took this to signify
the close of the conversation. Cautiously I turned on my side
away from her and soon fell asleep.

The other bad moment came the next day. Ding made a fire in
the evening, our first of the season. This is something she does
very well. I brought in wood for her and she built a fine
balanced structure in the fireplace: two large logs on the grate,
thicker branches all around, twigs and kindling in all the
interstices. She is really a genius at this. Normally, once the
structure is complete, she puts a match to it, then
demonstrates her prowess by stepping away and letting it burn
without further attention. This evening, however, she
remained hunkered by the fireplace, squatting on her heels,
prodding spasmodically at the logs with the poker, staring into
the flames.

I think it's just fine, honey, I ventured after a while. Doesn't
need any more attention.

She stabbed at the logs a couple of times, as if from defiance,
then got up and went into the kitchen. Time to wake Hetty,
she said, without turning or looking at me.

Hetty takes a nap in the afternoon. It is understood that at
weekends I will take some of the load off Ding by waking the
child, feeding her, getting her to sleep, and changing her
diapers.

Hetty was actually awake when I went up, standing holding on
to the side of her crib, grinning at my approach. Picking her
up, I perceived at once that her diaper was full. Setting her
back in the crib, I went to fetch warm water from the bathroom. Then I changed her on her mat, on the floor. We have
never used a changing table for fear of the infant falling. Hetty

was wonderfully cooperative—she is a very good baby—holding her little ankles up so that I could wash her fundament.

It is a commonplace thought, often expressed in both Chinese and English, that a man can never look upon the face of his sleeping son without calling to mind that day which must come, when the son looks down on the father's own face more permanently stilled. Similarly, I wonder if there has even been a father who, leaning over his infant daughter to attend to her hygiene, has not imagined forward to that moment when she will receive some stranger man in a similar position. Sex and death, the great eternals. I fixed the diaper, buttoned her up, and carried her downstairs.

At some point in these proceedings old Abby had come over, entering by the side door into the kitchen, where Ding was beginning preparations for dinner. Coming round the bend in the stairs I heard Abby's voice.

. . . for that international call the other day. You can settle up with me—

Oh! Here comes the princess! Ding cut her off, turning to bestow on Hetty her first smile of the day. Hetty smiled back, full display of all seven teeth. Abby had her hand over her mouth, as if she had just yawned.

I set the child carefully on the floor in front of Abby, who took her little hands and goo-gooed at her. Abby is a kind old soul. Because of the dearth of infants here, Hetty is the neighborhood baby, and all the older women drop by when they feel like a dandle.

I asked Abby if she had got candy in for Halloween, the following weekend.

Hardly worth it. The parents won't let them out, said Abby. Scared what will happen to them. What a pass we have come to.

You should do as we doing in China, said Ding. Smash the criminals to pieces. You too sentimental about criminals. TV and exercise machines! Shoot them all, like we do.

This was something near to an outburst, and most uncharacteristic of Ding. Of course, the absurd and irrational concern Americans feel toward criminals is a source of wonder, and of anger, to all Oriental peoples. We cannot understand it. In China, criminals are put to hard labor and beaten if they misbehave. Serious criminals are killed. When I was a child it was done in public. We schoolchildren were marched across to the town sports stadium to see the executions. The criminals were paraded in front of the people and made to listen to a denunciation of their crimes. Then they were shot in the head. Sometimes, if the bullet traveled a certain way, the brains would jump out. The older kids used to say that a really skillful executioner could make the criminal's face explode in a terrific shower of blood, teeth, and eyeballs, but I never saw that. We kids found it all very fascinating, of course. The adults, who had lived through too many horrors, looked away. However, nobody felt sorry for the criminals. They were just getting what they deserved. They stopped shooting the criminals in public in the early sixties. Now they are just humiliated, then taken away for shooting in some closed place.

You will never find a Chinese person who disagrees with these methods. However, neither Ding nor myself is a U.S. citizen. We both have green cards and could apply for citizenship if we wanted to, but we have never thought it worth the trouble. Not being citizens ourselves we never criticize American life in front of those who are, however scathing we may be in private. It would be like going to somebody's house as a guest and finding fault with their furniture. I don't say that other Chinese people might not be so uncouth—the Mengs, for example. It is only that we, by mutual agreement, never make open criticism of our adopted country. Yet here was Ding coming out with this stuff about criminals. Furthermore, I could not help but notice that her English was under some strain, regressing to Dinglish.

I guess each country has its own way of doing things, I said, to cleanse the air a little.

Well, I'd best be going, said Abby.

When she had gone I went to Ding and put my arm round her waist. Are you all right, honey?

My stomach a little upset.

I suppressed the urge to correct her English. Ding's stomach is the weak point in an otherwise robust constitution. She suffers from gas pains sometimes, and had an episode of colitis soon after we were married.

We can order in if you don't want to cook.

No. It's okay.

Really. Why don't you go lie down?

It's okay.

What was that Abby said, about an international call?

Yes. When I was in her house the other day, I called Teacher Ma's family. For . . . what is that word?

Condolence.

Yes. Condolence.

Why didn't you call from here?

I don't know. I was there. I was upset. Abby said it was all right. I'll settle up with her when her bill comes.

Hetty, sitting splay-legged on the floor, was watching these exchanges with the apprehensive look an infant has when the customary order of its tiny world is disturbed. I took her into the living room and read *Pat the Bunny* to restore her faith in the harmony of the universe. *Pat the Bunny* is her favorite book. Of course she cannot read, nor even understand the words; but the book has little built-in objects to touch—some fur, Velcro strips, a frog that jumps out of the page. The main thing is for her to get used to holding a book and turning the pages.

Normally we go up to bed together. This night, however, Ding stayed downstairs, saying she wanted to watch a late movie. I lay in bed for a long time, thinking of what was to happen on Wednesday. I got into a rather intense erotic fantasy, imagining Selina's body, somewhat plump but firm and smooth—a mature woman, a wife and mother. Mellow fruitfulness. I wondered how it would be between us after all these years, and whether I would be too nervous to acquit myself properly. I thought I would not be, that I could easily rekindle our old intimacy, once alone with her.

I was still awake when Ding came up, after midnight. She undressed quietly, without switching on the light, and slipped into bed beside me, her back toward me. Her behavior was really out of the ordinary. It occurred to me that she might be pregnant again. There had been some oddities in her first pregnancy, though nothing I could recall as disturbing as these recent moods. Perhaps it is different each time. And there was that business about Teacher Ma, of course. Naturally she was upset. Perhaps it was the two things acting together.

15. Four Knows Yeung

Mrs. Yoy will be down momentarily.

Mrs. Yoy! I could not get used to this. Not skinny, horny little
Selina, my private feral A-lei, a waif somehow strayed from the
land of fairies, but Mrs. Yoy, lady of standing in her
community, patron of posh hotels, buyer for a big department
store, a matron. At the same time, to hear her spoken of in this
way was indescribably aphrodisiac. Mrs. Yoy, respectable
married lady, mother of three children, whose most secret
parts had presumably been rifled, what? two thousand times
by a man I had never seen. Instead of being irritated by the
front desk clerk's misusage I at once began mentally parsing
and eroticizing it: Mrs. Yoy will be taking her clothes off
momentarily. Mrs. Yoy will be in your arms momentarily.
Mrs. Yoy will . . .

She appeared at last, wearing slacks and a ski jacket. She
looked straight at me but did not smile.

Okay. Let's go. Speaking English.

Go where? I thought perhaps we might have dinner here.

Go Rockefeller Center. She turned. I followed. Out into East
Fifty-first Street.

You want to eat at Rockefeller Center?

I want *skating* at Rockefeller Center. But we can eat there, too.

This was entirely new and altogether unexpected. It took me a moment or two to grasp her meaning. Of course: the open-air ice rink at Rock Center. I had stopped by there a couple of times, when in midtown, to watch the skaters.

When did you learn to skate? I had caught up with her now. We were walking west on Fifty-first Street.

After we move to Boston. There is a place in Boston I like go there. But Rockefeller Center is much better. When I come New York in winter, always go Rockefeller Center.

So! In all these years, while I was in my office downtown, she had been four miles away, skating on the ice at Rock Center! Perhaps she had been there on one of my occasional trips to midtown. Perhaps we had missed each other by yards. What a comedy life is!

The rink is on the lower level, but open to the sky. You can stand in the plaza at street level, lean against the railing, and look down at the skaters. Metal flagpoles are set around the railing on three sides, with flags of all the nations. It is very pleasant to stand there in the chill autumn air, the halyards rattling against the flagpoles, watching the skaters whirling and spinning below.

We went down some steps to the rink office. Here Selina hired a locker and some skates. I sat on the bench with her as she fixed her skates.

Size four, I said.

You remember.

I remember everything.

Her ankles were slim and naked beneath loose woolen socks. There were tiny oval discolorations on them which I also remembered: scars from her childhood in the village, left by leeches or some biting insect. I watched her lacing her boots, trying to hold every image. Slim dark ankles and wrists.

You sure you don't want skate?

I really can't.

You can try.

No. I am too old to make a fool of myself.

She smiled at me for the first time this day, quite tenderly—standing now, a little uncertainly, on her blades.

Never too old for that.

I stood at the side of the rink for a while, watching her. She was by no means a skilled skater. She did not attempt any reverses or spins, nothing of that sort. Her balance was good, though, and she sailed confidently round and round, maintaining an even speed under the impassive gaze of a large gold-painted statue at the far side of the rink. The statue represented a naked boy—with some minimal drapery—flying through the air, holding aloft in one hand what looked like a pineapple, the whole thing most beautifully gilded, like a Buddha.

After a while, when it seemed as if my ice princess would be content to glide forever round her frozen circuit, I climbed the steps to inspect the statue from above. An inscription on the wall behind told me that this was Prometheus, who stole fire from the sun, and was punished by the gods for his audacity. Oddly enough, he is well known in China. Pu-luo-mi-xiu-si, we call him, transliterating in that clumsy, illogical way we have. He is, or was, held up to the youth of China as a model of self-sacrifice for the common good. The pineapple, I now realized, was intended to be a handful of fire. Prometheus's gaze was directed downward, at the skaters on the rink.

I stood for some time at the upper railing, watching Selina make her slow circumgyrations, listening to the halyards snapping and rattling against the flagpoles. Then I got tired of the rather sharp wind—we were in the year's first cold spell—and went down to the rink level again. There was a restaurant going round three sides of the rink, with floor-to-ceiling glass walls overlooking the ice. Inside it was lit up, and not very full. It looked inviting.

I'm going into the restaurant, I called out to Selina next time she passed. She smiled, okayed, and sailed on. I went inside and got a seat right by the glass, looking out across the ice.

From this position I could watch the skaters in comfort. The glass between them and me seemed to be soundproof—at any rate, I could hear nothing from the rink. This gave the movements of the skaters a somewhat dreamlike quality. Round and round, always anticlockwise. (Is that a rule? Does everyone follow the lead of the first person on the ice? Is it the Coriolis effect? Or what?) The ice was quite crowded now. There must have been forty or more people out there. They floated past in silence, some laughing soundlessly, others—like Selina—serene in their effortless motion. Seen here, from their own level, the various speeds and radii of the skaters generated random patterns of clumping and dispersing, and I could not help but think of our great classic novel *Three Kingdoms*:

Of all under heaven it has been said:
What was once united must divide,
What was once divided must unite.

My waitress came two or three times, but seemed not to mind
my putting her off. The place was not crowded, and I suppose
she knew I had a companion outside. I fell into a trance state,
watching the skaters.

Did you find the duke of Jau? Selina addressed me in
Cantonese.

A? No, I couldn't find him.

I know you were really looking for *Miss* Jau, that slut. She
seated herself opposite me, the rink at her left. She was
flushed—apples in her cheeks, as Americans say—and smiling
now. I thought I could smell her, very faintly. Not her
perfume: *her,* her body, her essence, her juices. The ski jacket
was gone, revealing a plain sweater in a sort of burgundy
color, showing her breasts nicely.

I have to explain this duke of Jau stuff. He was in charge of the
imperial government, oh, three thousand years ago—about
the time the Achaeans were camping out on the plain in front
of Troy. Confucius, who lived some centuries later, looked
back to him as the model of a ruler. Once, when the sage was
feeling a bit down, he said: I am much decayed, for a long time
I haven't seen the duke of Jau in my dreams. The remark got
into the classics and was bandied about by the literati of the
Old Society, who liked to use arcane references that common
folk couldn't understand. This one got away from them and
percolated down to ordinary working people like Selina's
uncle, who used to send his kids off to bed with the
injunction: Go look for the duke of Jau. I thought it quaint,
and a bit affected, when I first heard him say it. This kind of

thing has long since disappeared from Mainland usage—but the Cantonese are very conservative linguistically. (The ancient poems still rhyme in Cantonese, but not in Mandarin.) Anyway, Selina and I had incorporated it into our own private language, and in the hothouse of amorous idleness the ancient cliché had blossomed into a whole clan of Jaus—shrewish old Mrs. Jau, cute, seductive Miss Jau, even (if I recall correctly) a Jau dog and a coop full of Jau chickens.

You look very beautiful, I said more or less involuntarily, in English.

Pleased, but a little embarrassed, she dropped her eyes. I'm hungry, she said. Have you ordered?

Somewhat to my surprise she went Italian again—fettuccine Alfredo. I ordered a fish dish with a side salad.

Would you like some wine?

M, no. Soda. Wine no good for me. You don't remember?

I remember. Selina was a blusher, I now recalled. I ordered a beer for myself, 7UP for her. The waitress tripped away, and there was a moment of awkwardness.

Do you stay in that hotel because it's near Rockefeller Center?

Yes. Also, is Chinese.

What?

Owner. Is Chinese. Hong Kong guy. Mr. Hou Wing-gei.

Really? Now you mention it, the desk clerk was Chinese.

Yes. They hire lot of Chinese people.

From where we sat we were looking straight across the rink at Prometheus. Selina, perhaps to avoid my eyes, was gazing in his direction.

Do you know who he is?

Without turning her head: Rockefeller, I guess.

I laughed quite loud, thinking of poor shriveled old John D. in his straw boater, stripped to the buff, up there in place of the golden boy. No, honey, not Rockefeller. Let's take it one step at a time. What's he holding in his hand?

She squinted across at Prometheus. Looks like . . . I don't know the English. *Goulaigei.*

I didn't know the Cantonese word. You mean pineapple?

Now at last she turned back to me to click with mock irritation. *Pineapple?* Ai-ai-ai, Mr. Joy, you have forgotten all your Cantonese. Pineapple is *bolo.* Don't you remember, the time we went to Cheung-jau Island, and eat pineapple in the marketplace? And you complained because they put salt on it?

And you told me the salt protects your mouth from being cut by the pineapple? I still don't believe it. . . .

This was wonderful—somehow we had got to Let's Remember. Of course, I had to spoil it.

. . . And later we found that place among the rocks. Do you remember, Selina? The rocks so white and smooth? That little clear pool you found, with a tiny fish in it that you couldn't catch. And we went into the water together. And afterward, right there on the rocks—right there on the white rocks, kneeling down . . . Do you remember? Oh, Selina, do you remember?

She colored slightly, and dropped her head. I saw that the moment was lost. But how delicious it had been!

Was a long time ago, she said at last, addressing her silverware.

We're still alive, aren't we?

She raised her eyes. I had been leaning forward to speak. My hands were out in front of me on the table. Suddenly, wonderfully, as she looked straight at me, she reached out and covered my right hand with her left. Her wedding ring was a simple gold band. On the no-name finger.

Is different now. She spoke softly.

I'm not different. *You're* not different. I can see you're not. We can make it the same.

No. We can't.

Don't you want to try?

Long pause. Squeezing my hand now.

I don't know what I want. What do *you* want, Mr. Joy?

I want to be twenty-five years old! To have no commitments or obligations! To work from one paycheck to the next, in a city where everyone else is doing the same! To be free! To be irresponsible! To be *young young young!*

This was Little Chai talking, inside. Of course I did not say it. But, after all, what *did* I want?

I want you, I said—and at once thought how lame it sounded. It obviously sounded lame to her, too: she turned away again, back to Prometheus, withdrawing her hand.

The food arrived. We began eating in silence. As always, I compared the food unfavorably with Ding's food. Yes—*there* was one thing I wanted: not to lose Ding. Nor my sweet plump pink little Hetty. Tasting the dull American food, I felt sure of that. Then what? To have an affair? Which would end how, exactly?

You already had me. This was Selina, still looking over at Prometheus. She had gone back into Cantonese. You had me for one year. That's our secret thing, a gift to us from heaven. We can treasure it in our hearts until we die. But it has no *result*. She turned to me. Don't you understand that? It was a passing thing, like childhood, like a movie. It could never have a *result*. She dropped her eyes. That's not our fate. Not mine, not yours.

Oh, come on, Selina. Don't give me this pop song bullshit. Don't give me fate and result. We make our own fates, by our own actions. The results are whatever they are. You can't say: Oh, this will have no result. You can't say: Oh, this is not my fate. You're talking like a peasant.

She developed a faint smile, twirling fettuccine with her fork. A-cheung, I was born a peasant. Can't I be true to my origins?

You were born in the country, but not a peasant. Your father was a schoolteacher. He stood up to the Communists, so they destroyed him. How was that his fate? It was because of what he did. *Chose* to do.

Was fated to do.

You're talking nonsense. Nobody believes that stuff anymore. All that stuff belongs to the Old Society. Fate, destiny, submit to heaven, *A-mi-tuo-fa*. I suppose you got all that stuff from your grandmother.

Selina's grandmother had been very dear to her. She had gone to the States with Selina's aunt a few months before I met Selina, admitted in some kind of refugee category. Midway through our affair in Hong Kong Selina had written to Granny to tell her about me, and got a firm veto from the old sow by return post. Though I had not seen the letter I could imagine all too well the general line of argument.

A Mainland boy? Not from our county? Not even from our *province?* You're crazy! How will you communicate with him? When we have already made an agreement with that nice Mr. Yoy, whose uncle owns five restaurants! Five! In San Francisco! How much face shall we have here in San Francisco if we break our agreement? How do you think people will speak of us? Of you? You told me yourself how much you like Mr. Yoy. His family even let you stay over, before he left Hong Kong. That means you've already given him the Favor, whether or not you opened your hole for him. Don't you understand? Don't you understand anything? . . .

Granny died in seventy-eight, said Selina quietly, in English.

I lied some words of condolence. It was a mistake to have mentioned her grandmother. It had thrown her into sadness. We forked glumly at our food for a while.

It's only . . . I wanted desperately to generalize the talk, away from Granny, away from her origins, her family. . . . I believe in free will.

196

But of course generalization is always a mistake with women. They can't think in generalities. Everything is personal and particular. There have been no great female mathematicians. I pressed on anyway, in English to give it more force.

This is America, the land of free will. Nobody here believes in fate or destiny. I don't agree with this determinism, this Calvinistic outlook.

She squinted. *What?* What outlook?

Not what, whose. Mr. Calvin's.

Calvin Klein?

No, honey, not Calvin Klein. *Mr.* Calvin, Mr. John Calvin, I think. He was a philosopher, a Christian philosopher. He taught that whether you go to heaven or not is decided before you're born. You can't do anything about it.

If *Mr.* Calvin, how come got a Calvin first name Klein last name?

It's a first name *now.* Matter of fact there was a president, Mr. Calvin Coolidge.

American president?

Sure. Number thirty.

His people liked this philosopher guy, Mr. Calvin?

I guess so.

But you said Americans don't like this philosophy, don't believe.

197

She was no dummkopf, Selina. Could argue the head off a chicken when she wanted to.

Oh, I don't know, Selina. It doesn't matter. What matters is, your life is yours to make. You make it as you go along, you! By your own free will.

She digested this rather startling intelligence. Then, back in Cantonese: Does your wife know about me?

Know what about you?

Know anything.

No. No, she doesn't know anything at all.

She nodded. That's good. My husband, too. Doesn't know anything. So, just like I said, that was our own secret thing. Nobody else knows. Granny knew, but now she is gone to the Yellow Spring. Now nobody knows about us. So let's just keep the secret buried deep in our hearts.

Mr. Chan knows.

Mr. Chan? Squinting again, summoning up remote, blurred memories. That one, lived in Aberdeen? Always telling you dirty jokes?

You got him.

You two are still in touch?

We write to each other. Sometimes talk on the phone.

After so many years? Wa! That's really an old friend. How do you know he didn't say anything to your wife?

He doesn't talk to my wife, except to say hello. He's a wise man. He wouldn't say anything.

Maybe he told her secretly, without you knowing.

If she knew about you, I'd be dead. She would kill me.

Selina snickered. Sounds like a jealous woman.

Yes. And what about your husband?

The same.

Really?

Yes. His temper's very bad. And he has guns, because of his business. He'll shoot me if he finds out.

I smiled over at her. It's exciting, isn't it?

Exciting, maybe. But not smart.

Oh, come on. How's my little friend? I inquired in English.

She flushed dramatically, all the way down into her sweater. Ai! A-cheung! You are so bad. Talking about these things in a public place.

Nobody knows what I'm talking about.

If you want to talk dirty, talk Chinese.

I want to fuck you, I said in her language.

No, no.

Come on. I stood up. We had finished eating. I beckoned for the waitress. Where's your jacket?

By the door. Ai! Elbows on the table, she covered her face in her hands. We are crazy!

Then let's be crazy. You can't be sane all the time.

No, no.

I paid the check in cash, with a colossal tip, then went round to Selina and lifted gently at her elbow. Beyond the window the skaters swirled and span.

Come on, A-lei. Let's go back to our dream, just for a short time.

> What was once united must divide,
> What was once divided must unite.

She rose slowly, not looking at me. I took her by the hand and led her over to the coats. We rode the little elevator up to street level. Out in the street I got my arm round her waist, and hers round mine, and we strolled again as we had strolled so long ago, in another age, in a distant place, in a dream, in Peach Blossom Country.

It was the Irish that spoiled it. To get back to the hotel we had to pass in front of St. Paddy's Cathedral. The big front doors were closed against the October wind; but as we approached, one of the wickets set into the left-hand door opened from inside and two elderly occidental women stepped out. Seeing this, Selina uncoupled herself from me, skipped up the steps, and disappeared through the wicket before it closed. I hastened to follow her.

The cathedral was almost empty, only three or four worshipers visible in the pews away down toward the front, making some solitary devotions. Selina was in an alcove at the left of the entrance, where candles were burning on a little stepped metal framework. She had taken a candle and was lighting it from one of the others.

For my grandmother, she explained when I came up. I often light a candle for her.

Repressing thwarted lust, I thought I had better play along.

It's a nice thought, Selina. But I didn't know you'd become a Christian.

Setting the candle in a sconce, she bowed her head and templed her hands—the palms flat together like a Buddhist, not closed over each other Taoist style. This lasted only a few seconds, then she stepped back and genuflected.

Not really. My husband, he is. Sometimes I go with him. Really, it's too complicated for me. But Jesus loves everybody, you know. She smiled sweetly at me, and I glimpsed the mother in her. Three times a mother! First with my son— engendered of my body, seed of my martyred father, of my ancestors—then twice more: the midnight alarms, the chiding and encouraging, the hoping and worrying, the pride and disappointment. For a moment she seemed much older than me.

All right. Can we go now?

Making no answer she turned away and walked to the aisle. Here, quite expertly, she took some water, crossed herself, and genuflected again.

Selina.

Sh. Not so loud. Come sit down.

I sat with her on a hard pew in the back row, frustration starting to burn in my stomach.

I thought we were going to your hotel.

No. It's not right.

Oh, come on, Selina. As you said, just like before, it's our private thing. Nobody will know.

She smiled at me again—that very mature smile, mother to child. She was sitting so demurely, her hands in her lap. The way you sit in church, I suppose. What do I know? I think religion is a crock, if you want to know the truth. *When times are good you don't burn joss; when times are hard you kiss Buddha's foot.* That's what we say in China, and it sums up my attitude. Religion's just a crutch for the weak, for people who can't face life.

Nobody will know? Ai, Mr. Joy, are you really Chinese? Don't you remember Four Knows Yeung?

Four Knows Yeung was an official in the Ming dynasty. He was honest—a circumstance so remarkable in China that he was made a god. The story about him is that one night someone came to offer him a bribe. Yeung refused to take it. Oh, come on, said the petitioner. The night is dark. Who will know? The magistrate replied: Heaven will know, earth will know, you will know, and I will know! Four Knows Yeung. I tell you, we flat faces have an answer for everything.

I thought you wanted to.

Of course I want to. Do you think I don't want to? But we are mature people. We can't just do what we want to. We must try to do what is right.

I want you. I need you. I love you. How can it be wrong?

Ts! Now *you* talk like a pop song! What do you want me to explain to you? Which point don't you understand? That a wife should be faithful to her husband? That a mother has responsibility for her children? Why don't we just do it in the street, like dogs?

Why not? We've done it everywhere else.

That was a long time ago, before we grew up.

Selina, married women take lovers all the time, without harming their marriages. There's nothing uncivilized about it. Look at the high civilizations of Europe, the people who built these places. I indicated the cathedral. They didn't think it was any great crime for a woman to have a lover. And you can't say they weren't civilized. They even had a word for it: *cicisbeo*, a married woman's lover.

Chi chi—what? She wrinkled her nose, as if the word smelled bad.

Never mind. It's a very sophisticated word, for a sophisticated idea. And what about our own ancestors? What about Pun Gam-lin? What about Cheun Ho-hing in *Red Chamber Dream*? Weren't they civilized? You can be civilized without being . . . puritanical.

We had been speaking in Cantonese. However, there is no word in our language for *puritanical*, so I had just used the English. She got it, though, and dwelled on it for a moment or two. Then she reached over, took my hand, and placed it between hers, in her lap.

A-cheung, I'm sorry. I know I have disappointed you. Please forgive me. I'm only saying that we are not children now. We can't behave as we behaved back then. I can't, you can't. Now we are adults. Life has different stages, and each stage has its own rules. Actually, we are middle-aged people. We have traveled different paths, but I think we have both learned many things we did not know twenty years ago. Haven't we?

I've learned that life is not endless. And that you're a long time dead.

She smiled at me, that indulgent smile again. A-cheung, there is another life beyond this one. Perhaps in that other life we can be together. Perhaps that's our fate.

I could feel her slipping away from me. This damn cathedral! Filling her head with all this metaphysics! All this garbage about other lives, other worlds! I stood up.

Won't you come with me, Selina? To be happy, as we were happy before?

She looked away, down to the front, to the altar. There was a priest there now, a tall stooped fellow in a black robe, fiddling with something in front of the altar. Phil O'Caption. A celibate—*je suis celibataire.* I was annoyed with Selina now, now it was all lust. How do men conquer this thing? What a wonderful thing it must be, to be celibate! Such freedom!

Not now. Not this time. I need time to think.

You've already had ten days.

She stood up. I have a family. I have a job. There is not much time to think in ten days.

We edged out into the aisle.

Selina, please.

A-cheung, look at you. You are begging for sex. It's not very dignified. Not very manly.

She had me defeated, and I knew it. Surrounded, unhorsed, disarmed, her lance aimed steady at my heart.

All right. How much time do you need?

How can I know? Until I feel sure. One way or the other.

This is so . . . mathematical. So calculating. It shouldn't be like this, Selina. It should be wild, spontaneous, random. Not . . . trigonometry.

We were standing in the open space inside the entrance now. She took both my hands in both of hers and looked up at me. So sweet, so earnest, so tender.

A-cheung, I am still the same person you knew in Hong Kong. If we have an affair, you won't find it short on spontaneity. You won't complain it isn't wild. It is the decision that needs care, not the act.

How will I know? When will I know?

I'll come to New York again at the end of this month. Two weeks from now, November tenth. I'll call you. Just like today.

Two weeks! How can I wait two weeks?

So sweet, so sweet. In the churchly gloom of that place, her eyes glowed bright.

You waited twenty years, didn't you?

And then—marvelous, miraculous, the merest motion of that lance, piercing my heart forever, impaling and transfixing me, peach blossom swirling in the spiky cathedral dimness—she set her hands on each side of my face, drew me down, and kissed me. And if she had then told me our next meeting was to be on the floor of the Mariana Trench, I would have gone away meekly and hocked my house to buy a submersible.

16. Dream Season

Golden Gate supermarket was, as usual, a mob scene. It seems
we Chinese can only be happy when we are jammed together
in a crush, trampling on one another's feet, jabbing our elbows
into one another's ribs. China herself is genuinely crowded,
and there is no help for it; but here in America we could surely
practice more spacious ways, if we chose. No, every time you
go shopping, there it is—the heaving, bobbing, grunting sea of
black-haired people, bringing to life that peculiarly Chinese
adjective, our ultimate term of praise for any human
gathering: *re-nao,* hot and noisy.

(Golden Gate! The onomastic poverty of our starved, stunted
language! Is there a Chinese supermarket somewhere that is
not called either Golden Gate or Dragon Gate? And a citizen
of the Mainland who declined to buy anything with the brand
name Panda, or Great Wall, or Phoenix would save himself a
very great deal of money, before dying of inanition.)

Ding navigated through the aisles with the cart, myself
plodding behind, Hetty in the backpack. But now Hetty's little
arms were long enough to reach out and knock things from
the shelves, unless you kept to dead center, which of course
with all the milling flat faces was impossible. Before we'd gone
twenty yards she had wiped out a pack of dried noodles, a
whole stack of canned bamboo shoots, and—though here my
own brilliant fielding saved us from a ghastly mess and
possible lifetime banishment from Golden Gate's scented

aisles—a jar of sesame paste. I peeled off and went down to the lower area, where nonfood goods are sold. This was much emptier and quieter. I strolled at peace among the rice cookers and microwaves, the skillets and spatulas, coming to rest at last in the section I like best: the *oggetti religiosi*.

Golden Gate has a particularly fine selection of devotional aids. Mostly for the grannies, of course: younger Chinese people don't believe in anything except money. Though there is money there, too, if you want it: hell money, for burning, wrapped up in blocks, each bill bearing an image of Lord Yan-Wang, the emperor of hell.

It's not the hell money I like to look at, though. Nor the red-painted wall shrines wired up with red bulbs, nor the great fat candles embossed with sutras, the little red paste-up doorway blessings—Chinese mezuzahs!—packs of incense or jars of lucky sticks. What I like to see is the gods, the little porcelain figures of our gods. Shou Xing, God of Longevity, with his bulbous forehead like a Martian; Guan Yin, Goddess of Compassion, Who Hears the Cries of the World; Duke Guan, God of War and Literature, with his mighty halberd; Cai Shen, God of Wealth. Cai Shen wears the uniform of an imperial bureaucrat. How else do you get rich, except by working for the government? Imperial China was a lot like New York City. We used to say: When a man becomes an official, even his dogs and chickens will go to heaven.

As a matter of fact, Cai Shen is also Duke Guan. War, literature, wealth—this guy had quite a portfolio. He was a real person, name of Guan Yu, one of three sworn friends—the Peach Garden Comrades—who struggled together to revivify the disintegrating Han dynasty, back in the second century A.D. On these shelves in Golden Gate there are pictures showing all three of them. The other two are also gods, or at any rate demigods—I'm not too clear about their places in the pantheon. Certainly neither has the stature of the duke. One was a belligerent drunkard, the other (if you want my opinion) a bit of a wuss. At any rate their efforts failed, and after the Han our country fell into a long period—five hundred years!—of division, occupation, and chaos before the Glorious Tang raised our civilization to heights it has never since attained, nor even approached. The unfortunate people who lived through those dark times looked back wistfully on the Han and deified those who tried to save it. We northerners still call ourselves the Han people, in fact. So here they are, these three patriots, all decked out in lurid primary colors, on the shelves of a supermarket in Queens, on a continent they didn't know existed, in a world they could not have imagined.

I nodded at the duke. Old friend, old friend. He scowled back, pointing straight at me with his halberd, as he had on Double Tenth, out on the patio at Compassion Boat Temple, on the hillside above Chuen Wan, when I climbed with Selina up through the villages to our first coupling on Big Hat Mountain.

Now—oddly, inconsequentially, and I believe for the first time—I recalled the dog. Higher up the hillside, where the human settlements thinned out, the people kept dogs to guard their property. We got into somebody's yard by mistake and their dog took after us. This was not your Long Island suburban mutt: this was up-country Hong Kong, way back before everyone got jobs as commodity traders, and the dog was an emissary from Lord Yan-Wang, truly a hound of hell— big, dun, mean, the inner tissues of his mouth a startling crimson. I was much more scared than Selina—perhaps that is why I suppressed the memory. I ran for the fence and vaulted clean over it. My unflappable mistress turned and strolled back out through the gate, back onto the path up the hillside to her fate, to who knows what consequences for future generations. There was that quality about her, something masculine really—deliberate even in retreat, refusing to be panicked, staring down the world and all its absurd threats. Including, as events will prove, mine.

This Saturday—it was the thirtieth, three days after Rockefeller Center—was a doubleheader. After the shopping we were to call on the Mengs. We and the Mengs take turns calling on each other. Why, I really don't know. Inertia, I suppose; and the reluctance to give offense by breaking off an undemanding relationship.

With the shopping taking longer than we thought, we were somewhat late arriving at the Mengs. Other guests were already there. The Mengs have a wider social life than we do, perhaps. All Chinese, of course. All Mainlanders, in fact. The district where the Mengs live has only recently gone Chinese. The Chinatown in Manhattan was always there. Queens— starting with Jackson Heights—started to be sinified after the immigration laws were liberalized in the sixties, when the Old Bachelors of Mott Street turned out not to be bachelors at all. They brought over their Chinese wives (who not infrequently found themselves sharing a house with the old boy's American mistress), then the sons and daughters, grandsons and granddaughters, and filled up Jackson Heights with them. Then the Taiwanese came in, colonizing Flushing and Elmhurst. Now, since the policy changes of the early eighties, here come the Mainlanders, bad teeth and cheap shoes, buying into the narrow jerry-built houses, passing their driving tests at the ninth attempt, cursing the *heigui*, fiddling their taxes, flirting with Christianity.

I knew only two of these people from previous acquaintance. Their name was Hao, and they had been lecturers at the college Meng went to in northeast China. They had got out of China somehow and taken jobs as housekeepers to a movie star out in Southampton. The movie star owned several other houses, of course, and was only in Southampton for a few weeks in the summer, so the Haos were mainly just house-sitters. Not bad work if you can get it. Better than teaching college in China, anyway. They were a nice couple. We liked them. Their kids were in China, old enough to take care of themselves, so the Haos were enjoying carefree lives for the first time—their youth having been wiped out, of course, by the movements. They were happy, cheerful, and imaginative, and were probably enjoying some sort of second honeymoon in this, their Peach Blossom Country.

Apart from the Haos there was a woman I did not know, a recent arrival from the Mainland apparently, with a little girl; and a tall guy with Buddy Holly glasses, some kind of scholar. The woman wanted to be called Rong-rong, which sounded to me like the name a peasant might give to his favorite pig. The man was introduced to us as Dr. Wang, a researcher from Qinghua University on some sort of exchange assignment at Columbia.

We freed Hetty from the backpack and let her crawl around. Everybody clucked over her. Mrs. Meng's mother put us through a long questionnaire about Hetty's health, feeding habits, sleeping patterns, bowel movements, and so on. The little girl started teaching her patty-cake. Then Meng and his mother went off to the kitchen to cook.

I asked Hao about his master. Oh, said Hao laughing, we shan't see him until the spring. He doesn't go to Southampton in the winter.

So you have the house to yourself for six months?

House, beach, pool. He laughed again, gaily. TV, VCR, car. I shall do more painting.

Hao is an amateur artist, rather a good one. We have a painting of his—a scene from *Red Chamber Dream*—and also a character scroll of Li Qingzhao's *Dream Season:*

> Thin rain but a wild wind last night.
> Slumber deep yet still the worse for drink.
> A query for the maid who draws the curtains.
> "The crab-apple blossom's just as before," she replies.
> How can that be? How can that be?
> The green must be plentiful, the red very sparse!

The character scroll hangs in my study, where I am writing this petty memoir. It is very skillfully done, the angry incredulity of the mistress (*Zhi fou? Zhi fou?*) emphasized by a subtle but definite boldness of stroke in the verticals—a *slashing* quality—chiding that maid forever for her deceit— which no doubt was well intentioned, or at worst just thoughtless sloth. Poor Li Qingzhao! She shared the scholarly, antiquarian interests of her husband; but they had to flee from an invasion by the horrid Jin barbarians, and he died suddenly and unexpectedly (*zu*), and she was left alone and helpless, with only her ink block and writing brush for consolation. No more drinking parties, no more maid, no more curtains, no more blossom, the sweet middle-class life all soiled and torn and dead. This was in the Sung dynasty, nine hundred years ago. So many years, so many lives, so much misery, without end or beginning. My poor country, my poor poor country!

But it's a summer house, isn't it? Is there any heating for the winter?

Oh, yes. If no heating, the water pipes would burst. We're very comfortable.

How about you? I asked Mrs. Hao. What do you do to fill the time?

Translation. I am translating Edith Wharton. She is hardly known in China. I can introduce her to the Chinese people. *Ethan Frome* is ideal for our countrymen. Rural poverty, thwarted desire, no social life, not much cultural context— very accessible. Then I shall do the society novels. First *The Age of Innocence,* my favorite.

About what? enquired Dr. Wang politely.

About a man who tries to go astray with a woman. But his relatives—his female relatives, mostly—get him back on the straight and narrow. Without him knowing, of course.

Do you really think a woman can outfox a man in that way? I asked, smiling over at Ding. Ding smiled right back at me.

Oh, I don't know. Mrs. Hao giggled. The man is not very bright. But it's a beautiful book. Will need annotating for Chinese readers, of course. Oh! a lot of annotating! This may be my life's work! She laughed again. Then she and her husband both laughed, looking fondly at each other, relishing their good fortune.

I was glad for them. I could imagine what kind of lives they'd had. Lecturing in a cow college for twenty bucks a month, the students asleep at their desks (not much point studying—the ones with connections will get all the good jobs). Political study every Wednesday afternoon, some semiliterate branch secretary trying to read the latest gibberish editorial from *People's Daily* while the bolder spirits in the back row play cards. Kissing up to that same branch secretary for permission to visit another province where your mother is dying of cancer (the branch secretary blows his nose on his fingers, wipes the

result on his shoe, and says, We'll consider, We'll consider. . . .)
Having your health destroyed by bad food, bad ventilation,
filthy hospitals, and ignorant doctors. Stumbling through the
frozen mud of Manchurian winter to scramble for a ration of
moldy cabbage. Getting dragged to struggle meetings, made to
insult and deny your family, your friends, your dearest beliefs
at the command of teenage bigots like . . . well, like me. Then
reform and prosperity—for the nimble footed and well
connected. Not for you, not ever for you. The Haos clearly had
no intention of going back to China.

Of course, said the scholar, Dr. Wang, you have no security of
employment.

Ts! Who cares? We had security of employment all our lives in
China, and what good did it do us? The hell with security.
They both laughed again. They were holding hands, this late-
fiftyish couple—sitting on the sofa holding hands, in America.
Much more green than red, both of them, but peaceful at last.
Dream Season.

I thought Dr. Wang did not altogether approve of this
response, but he said nothing. We fell into the usual émigré
talk: the latest fads in quack medicine, everybody's
immigration status, the sentimentality, gullibility,
shamelessness, and obesity of Americans, the right length of
visit for relatives from the motherland. Three of us had read
the latest book by America's pet Chinese-American novelist,
and we had good sport with that for a while. Chinese-
American means American, of course; the authoress in
question knows China like I know Patagonia, like the imbecile
in green hat and jacket on St. Patrick's Day knows Ireland, like
the dashikied lout selling anti-Semitic pamphlets at the rap
concert knows Africa. You are Americans, for heaven's sake,
indistinguishable from each other to my eyes: citizens of the
most remote, most secure, most self-sufficient nation that ever

was, and your birthright and privilege is to know little and care less about the Old World and its mad millennial vendettas. Mr. Coolidge left the States only twice: to Montreal for his honeymoon (they got bored and cut it short) and to Cuba on a battleship, to make a speech. The man was a true American. He even had some Indian blood—a thing he was exceedingly proud of. In his autobiography he does not mention foreign affairs at all.

And then she says . . . (Mrs. Hao was nearly incoherent with laughter at this point) . . . that her Mainland relatives wrote letters in up-and-down script!

Everybody laughed. Ding aired our private theory that the celebrated novelist has in fact no Chinese ancestry at all, but is just a smart Jewish kid from Scarsdale, epicanthic folds courtesy of Dr. Schwartz the cosmetic surgeon.

You could be right, said Mr. Hao. How long is it since anyone wrote a personal letter up and down?

I said I thought Kang Youwei was probably the last one.

Dr. Wang's eyebrows went up.

Are you familiar with Kang Youwei's writings?

I made a study of him, when I was at college.

Ah. One of the more interesting reformers of the last dynasty.

Yes, I thought so. And his opinions so far as our country's problems were concerned were mostly correct.

Meng laughed. You can't be serious. What, bring back the emperor system?

215

Certainly. It was the only system we had. Why discard it?

Oh, that's silly, said Mrs. Meng. The emperor system was very feudal and corrupt. Our country needs a modern system.

So modernize it. You don't have to throw it out. Japan has been very successful, hasn't it? Yet they kept their emperor system. Look at Britain. Look at the Scandinavian countries. They all have their old kings and queens, and it doesn't seem to have held them back. Britain was the first country to modernize, under their traditional monarchical system, and they defeated us in several wars.

But now they are very weak, pointed out Dr. Wang.

Because they've taken up socialism. And weak or not, their society is more stable than ours. Look at us! Look at China! We are a civilization without a country. Our leaders prosper by eating one another. Our citizens believe in nothing, nothing. None of us believes in anything. We are just vegetables. Just lumps of flesh, chasing money. China is a dish of loose sand.

This last phrase is a kind of idiom, coined by Dr. Sun Yat-sen a hundred years ago.

My husband is very negative about our country, I'm afraid. This was Ding, who had been watching me with quiet amusement. She has heard it all before, of course.

How can you not be negative? It's a disaster area. Aren't we all glad to be out?

I don't know. This was the woman Rong-rong. My parents came over for a visit earlier this year. They were better dressed than I am. After three months they'd had enough of America and went home. They said themselves, there was nothing they can get here that they can't get there, usually cheaper.

That's nonsense. What, they can get a car? They can get a house with a garage? They can get a doctor if they're sick, a lawyer if they're wronged, a priest if they're distressed? They can get justice? They can get liberty? Of course they can't. Anyway, I was speaking of spiritual things, not the material situation. This is a country of free men, ruling themselves. Americans don't believe (I was translating on the fly from one of Mr. Coolidge's speeches) that one part of the human race was born saddled and shod, the other part booted and spurred to ride them.

Dr. Wang was smiling in a superior way. Don't they? They are making a dictatorship right now, as we watch. Every year they give more and more power to their government. Not grudgingly—willingly. Eagerly. People don't want freedom. They want to be governed. General liberty is not really very popular. Only a few people want liberty. There were a few people like that in Europe, three hundred years ago. They left and came to America. For a while everybody in America was talking about liberty, liberty. It was a self-selected group. But now, after a few generations, Americans are just like anybody else. They want to be slaves. You recall Lu Xun's remark about our people?

"We Chinese have alternated between two states: either we have been slaves, or we have been yearning for someone to come and enslave us."

Right. But it's nothing particularly Chinese. The ancient Greeks loved freedom, but they yielded rather easily to Alexander's oriental monarchy. Rome was a republic of free men, but they turned themselves over to emperors and officials as soon as the idea presented itself. And who loved freedom more than the English? Yet—as you yourself said—they are socialist now, the government controlling most of the national life.

I agree with Dr. Wang, said Mrs. Meng. People want a government that takes care of them, with Father and Mother officials. They don't want democracy. It doesn't work. Look at all this crime, all this corruption. It's a stupid system. People prefer a government that takes care of them. They don't want to have to do everything for themselves.

This very interesting talk was interrupted by a new arrival. It was a middle-aged guy who, though we were all talking Chinese, introduced himself by the English name Sammy. I picked up from his accent that he was Cantonese. So did Ding, who, to my utter amazement, addressed him in his own dialect, asking him if he was from Hong Kong.

Sammy said yes, he was. Been in the States more than twenty years, though.

My husband used to live in Hong Kong, said Ding, still talking Cantonese. He's still in touch with some old friends from that time. She looked at me encouragingly, as if urging me to get into the conversation. However, I was struck dumb, being still astounded at hearing my wife speak Cantonese, a language she has always professed to despise.

Sammy has a restaurant on East Broadway, said Meng, who had come back in from the kitchen to introduce Sammy.

East Broadway is in Chinatown—the old Chinatown, in Manhattan. The man's owning a restaurant there was actually pretty impressive. Chinatown property is very expensive. To get a place in a location like that, and equip it, and pay the key money, and keep the Triads at bay, you need to gross a couple of million a year and have damn good connections. However, it cut no ice in this company. The word *restaurant* gets about the same welcome from the new generation of Chinese as *bale of cotton* might in a gathering of educated young Negroes.

It was Sammy who introduced me to that doctor I told you about, added Mrs. Meng. The one in Pell Street who treated my asthma.

What, the hypnotist? I was glad to close out further opportunities for talk about Hong Kong. Did he cure you?

Not really. But I had to stop seeing him. The medicine—the one that makes you suggestible—was upsetting my digestion. I was constipated. My stools were very dry and hot.

A pity, said Sammy, talking Mandarin with us now. He's really a wonderful doctor. Hua Tuo reborn!

Driving home, I said I had been under the impression Ding didn't care to speak Cantonese.

Oh, she said, sometimes I like to. I have no prejudice against the Cantonese. Some of them are very understanding, very helpful.

What about all those penny-pinching storekeepers in Canal Street you used to complain about?

That was when I worked for them. It's true, they're not the greatest people to work for. But as friends they're okay.

How would you know? You don't have any Cantonese friends.

M, at college there was one. And look at you and your Mr. Chan. Still friends, after so many years.

She said nothing else for a while. Then, out of the blue: I should like to have a Cantonese friend.

I couldn't make head or tail of this, and let it be. We drove the Northern State Parkway in silence, except for Hetty gurgling at the scenery. At home, with Hetty put to bed, we sat drinking wine and eating some quite excellent American cookies Mrs. Hao had baked. I made another effort at *Letters, Lectures and Addresses of Charles Edward Garman*.

> Now that we are on the subject of altruism, I must say a word as to its essential immorality. The term surprises you, but is not a whit too strong. If it is possible to put self and its welfare completely out of sight in order to labor solely for others, it will be equally possible to put out of sight self and its responsibilities and obligations. Unless self is the center of one's horizon and is degraded by wrong doing and ennobled by right doing, there is nothing to tie to, nothing to bind the person to the path of duty.

It was heavy going; but Dr. Garman, who taught at Amherst College in the nineties, was a great influence on Mr. Coolidge. If you want to find a man, follow his teacher, *cherchez le professeur*.

Ding went upstairs. When she came down she was wearing a nightdress. This was a new development. Ding has pajamas, which she wears during her period or if she fears she is getting a chill, but otherwise we both sleep naked. Now she stopped on the stairs to show off the nightdress to me. It was a simple thing—ankle length, short sleeves, low neckline—but very filmy, and she was clearly visible beneath it.

Do you like it?

I was doing some rapid calculations. It was ten, no eleven, days till Selina's next visit—and who could say what decisions the dumb broad might make in the meantime? That stupid business at the temple. *Cathedral.* When the glow of that kiss had faded, it left behind mostly annoyance and frustration. I had been ill-tempered when I came home Wednesday evening, and Ding herself had had an attitude about something; and home from work on Thursday we hardly spoke to each other. On Friday, however, Ding had been sunny and wifely, cooking one of my favorite dishes and chattering brightly through my moodiness, making me feel doubly guilty—guilty for my deception, and guilty for not masking it decently with a cheerful manner.

Now here she was—my wife, my companion—flushed with desire and liquor, small neat body sheathed in muslin and caged by the banister. And there was the other: unwilling, unpredictable, elsewhere. Well: Better the bird in the hand than the one in the forest.

Sunday was Halloween. Ding had made pumpkin pie from pumpkin she got out on the Island somewhere. Ding believes that food is best if she has grown it herself, acceptable when she has at least seen it growing and picked it herself, seriously inferior when bought from a store. I am not so fastidious, but I am glad for any interest she has to occupy her time. It is really not too healthy for a woman to be housebound with a child all day long. Ding at least has her vegetable garden, her canning and pickling, her trips out to the Island to pick apples, pears, peaches, pumpkins.

Halloween is a low-key affair in our neighborhood. This is an old community. There was a population surge in the forties and fifties—mostly engineers drawn in by the defense industries. Now these people are all in their seventies and eighties, like Walter and Abby. They are quiet and helpful, full of useful advice about roof shingles, sump pumps, and cesspools, but they leave the neighborhood child-poor.

Thus we had only two trick-or-treat calls all afternoon, tiny kids in costume, their parents hovering protectively down at the end of the driveway. Ding handed out candy and wished them well, smiling and waving to the one set of parents we knew.

As evening approached she made a fire. This time she did her watch-this routine, touching the scrunched-up paper in two or three places with one of the long matches we keep for this purpose, then stepping away to me, putting her arm round my waist to watch the fire burn up. We stood together watching for a while, then I went to wake Hetty from her afternoon nap. Later the three of us sat on the carpet in front of the fire and made a tower from Hetty's nested blocks.

I wonder about that doctor Meng's wife was seeing, said Ding. Giving her a drug to make her suggestible. I never heard of such a drug. And persimmon isn't astringent. Only the skin; the flesh is very sweet.

The woman's a bumpkin, I said. Talking about her goddamn turds like that in company. I wonder how Meng puts up with her. He's a smart guy, not bad looking, he could do much better.

Do you think there really can be such a medicine? asked Ding, who is not easily deflected.

I doubt it. Probably just a placebo. Do you know this word, placebo?

She did not. I explained at length—the word does not exist in Chinese—and resolved to introduce it into our next Scrabble game if possible.

The next few days were very pleasant. I had turned into a mood of fatalism about Selina and her vacillations. Not that I anticipated our Wednesday meeting with any less enthusiasm; but I had erected some defenses against further disappointment.

Ding, in the meantime, was entirely back to normal. And then some: she was, in fact, peculiarly attentive to me, in quite a new way, rather an odd way—as one might be toward a loved one about to undergo a painful operation. In her culinary endeavors she pulled out all the stops: no Vegetarian Days or Leftovers Days in that week. At night she was warm and affectionate, resting her head on my chest, her slender arms round me, but apparently not minding when at first I declined to consummate these embraces. Never mind, she said, sometimes a man just hasn't got the mood. So understanding! With the result, of course—perhaps this was her art—that I got the mood all too tumidly and could not hold back what I was trying to hoard.

What a paradox!—that we were so close, so married, in just those few days when I was plotting betrayal! We even fell back into some habits from our early married life. At that time I had used to read to her, as part of the effort to raise her standard of English. I read magazines mostly, or passages from *Gone with the Wind* and *Forever Amber*—woman-stuff that would hold her attention. Now she had to make do with some old New England writers I was exploring—Dorothy Canfield

Fisher, Margaret Deland—in my attempt to encompass altogether the world of Mr. Coolidge. I had exhausted all the primary materials I could easily get on the great president and was being forced back into circumstantial texts of this sort. Ding bore it with fortitude, and really seemed to like Mrs. Canfield's innocent little tales of Vermont country life.

Of course I found myself wondering whether perhaps I had lost my reason, to be pursuing a plump, fractious ghost from my past, when my present and future were so comfortable and assured. I cannot truthfully say that it ever crossed my mind to abandon that pursuit, but I did become resolved on a sort of containment policy—that is, whatever sort of affair developed, it would be occasional and entirely separate from my married life, and of course entirely secret from Ding.

During those few days I can say—in retrospect, perhaps somewhat overconfidently—that I recalibrated my attitude to the whole matter of marital infidelity. Ding, I realized over a game of Scrabble one evening (a game I easily won—I think I won all the games that week), was the still center about which my life turned. She was—to put the thing into Copperfieldian terms—my Agnes, while the other was my Dora.

The chemistry between us was so intimate that she grasped, without (I am sure) my doing anything to alert her, that I was anxious about the tenth. I made up a very excellent and watertight cover story about some Japanese bankers coming in to discuss Emerging Markets with us, how I should be expected to host them for a meal, take them to a show, and sit around negotiating in their hotel until late. Would most likely have to stay in town for the night . . . but this had occasionally happened before and gave her no alarm. She smiled, nodded, and wished me luck with the Japs, and even got up early to breakfast with me that morning, a thing she does not often do, and kissed me good-bye so tenderly, and said she would be waiting for me tomorrow (why should she not be?), and coming out of my driveway into the street I almost backed into old Walter, who nearly kept me from catching my train with rambling talk about property taxes, Medicare, and it was nice they'd been seeing so much of my wife this few days, notwithstanding she *did* seem to spend all her time there on the telephone.

17. *I Do Not Choose to Run*

At work that morning I had to attend a meeting. How Americans love their meetings! In this regard they resemble the Communists in China. When I was growing up in the fifties there was a ditty current among Chinese people, comparing the new government with the one we had had in the thirties and forties:

> With the Nationalists it was nothing but taxes,
> With the Communists it's nothing but meetings.

(It rhymes in Chinese.) This particular meeting was with some fools from the finance area, to decide whether we should trade certain categories of these Emerging Markets securities that were flavor of the month on Wall Street that November. (Emerging Markets is the politically correct way to say poor countries.) Actually, the firm had already decided in principle that these securities were sound, so the whole thing could have been settled with a few telephone calls—but then none of us would have felt half so important. For me the meeting created a tactical problem. Selina of course had my office number, and it was possible—though not, I thought, very likely—that she would call in the morning. Georgina, my secretary, would take the call. Georgina, though very competent in her duties, is not best known for severe restraint in the retailing of gossip, and within a matter of nanoseconds it would be known around the office that I was being left personal messages by an Oriental woman not my wife. This was more than I wanted the office to know. I could route my calls to the conference room, but this is not good form. Every trader wanting credit approval would come through, and the meeting would be unacceptably disrupted. At last I told Georgina to route through any calls *not* from the trading floor, and hoped it would work out. Back at my desk at twelve-thirty I went through the little heap of Someone Called While You Were Out slips—nothing, only traders.

I asked Georgina to order in a lunch, cleared the pile of phone calls, and settled down at my desk behind a Great Wall of documentation on the Emerging Markets stuff. Two, three o'clock—nothing. Four, five—no Selina. The telephone on my desk rings differently for in-house and outside calls: still I jumped at every ring, enduring a tiny spasm of hope for the fraction of a second it took my brain to compute the nature of the call. At five-thirty people began drifting out. When six o'clock came and went I began to sweat.

Boris stopped by, sat on my office couch, and began inveighing against the current administration in Washington.

Oh, I said, I'm sure they're doing their best for the country.

He left, trailing a little cloud of profanities. No sooner was he gone than the telephone rang—outside call! It was Ding.

You still with the Japanese guys?

They've gone off to meet with someone else. We'll take them to dinner later.

(Pause.) So you'll stay in the city tonight?

Yes.

Meridian?

This threw me. The Meridian is the hotel our bank uses when employees need to stay in town. There's a standing arrangement, I think they just keep rooms available on a retainer. I hadn't even known that Ding knew about it. I guess I fumbled the ball. It occurred to me to say, No, we're using another hotel—and I may have started to say it before realizing that she would ask: Which hotel, then?

Ah, ng, right. Meridian.

(Pause.) Okay. Then I'll see you tomorrow.

Yes, yes. Good night, honey.

You know . . . There was rather a long pause. We had been speaking English up to this point. Now, suddenly, Ding went into Chinese. Sometimes (she said) things don't go the way you want them to.

What? What are you talking about?

The Japanese guys. I mean, if your business with them isn't satisfactory. Or if perhaps they don't turn up. I just don't want you to get upset. Everything will be all right.

Why on earth would I get upset? I never get upset. What *are* you talking about?

It doesn't matter. Just come home to us soon.

Yes, yes. Good night, honey.

Good night. Hetty says good night, too.

Yes. Tell her good night from Ba-ba.

I heard Boris leaving. It occurred to me that I was the only person in the office now. Why didn't Selina call?

After a further fifteen minutes I picked up the phone and called the Midtown Pavilion.

Mrs. Yoy? No, not this week. Were they sure? They checked. Yes, sure. No reservation. *What?* She was standing me up? But didn't she have to come to New York for business?

I got the yellow pages from the shelf behind Georgina's station and started calling midtown hotels. There are rather a lot of hotels in midtown. After five or six I stopped doing this, took my bag and coat, went downstairs, and hailed a cab to Rockefeller Center.

There were few people about in the plaza. You don't get crowds at Rock Center until they've lit the Christmas tree, which happens after Thanksgiving. There were a few obvious tourists, some people much too early for the movie house on Fiftieth Street, and a sprinkling of random passersby. About twenty skaters were on the ice. There was one in a proper skater's outfit, a sky blue tutu, doing really tricky stuff, leaps and pirouettes. I thought momentarily of the man I had shot, back in China, a quarter century ago. The music murmured, the halyards rattled against the flagpoles, the skaters drifted round beneath Prometheus's impassive gaze, and Selina was not there.

After a spell of confusion and despair I took a cab back to my office. The cleaners were in by now. Their chief, an oblong Peruvian lady called Blanca, greeted me with a frown. Blanca is a control freak who expects to find the offices empty when her crew arrives and disapproves most strongly of office staff doing overtime.

Mr. Chai we not jet done jew office, she complained.

I need my office. Go away, please.

Jesús María José y todos los santos, said Blanca. She went away.

I pulled up the Yoys' telephone number on my database. Selina answered on the second ring.

I've been waiting for you. I thought you were in New York.

Yes. Sounds of a TV in the background. Cantonese—a video, probably.

What do you mean, yes? I've been sitting here *waiting* for you to call. You told me you'd be in New York.

No. No, thank you.

How about if I come up to Boston, then?

No. Okay, I'll speak to you about it tomorrow. Tomorrow morning. Click.

I was trembling from anger and frustration. I sat there staring at the telephone unit, at its stupid display. It was one of those computerized things that show the date and time. Eight fifty-four. Blanca the Inca, Atahuallpa's Revenge, flung open the door without knocking, marched right past me, and took my wastepaper bin. I suppose she felt I could not deny her that, at least. I thought I had better make some arrangements.

Have you ever tried to find a hotel room in New York at nine o'clock in the evening? I called the Meridian first, but they had nothing. What about the special arrangement? That had to be done through the firm's travel office, and preferably several days in advance. I called half a dozen others. They left an impression of general astonishment that anyone would want to just *take a room*. These things are arranged by your firm, your travel agent, your airline, your car rental company. We have become a civilization of middlemen, Mr. Ten Percent, without whom nothing can be done. At last I slept on my office couch, waiting until Blanca and her elves had left.

Selina called at nine-thirty next morning. No background noise now.

Mr. Joy please. *Chai*, Mr. Chai.

Yes.

Is me. Selina.

What the hell happened to you?

(Long pause.) Is no good, A-cheung. You know.

I waited for something else, but there wasn't anything else.

What do you mean, no good? You're in New York—*should* be in New York—I'm in New York, why shouldn't we get together?

You know why.

No. I don't. Why not? Why shouldn't I see you?

(Even longer pause.) Is not right.

Is right. Selina, I want you. I love you.

Just as I told you. So many times. This love can have no result.

I now approach the thing I most hesitate to tell, the thing for which I feel most shame. Was it blackmail? Morally speaking, there can be no doubt: yes, it was blackmail. Yet when you review these things in your mind—the way they happened— you realize how approximate and inadequate is the language of law and responsibility: intent, decision, forethought. This is not to excuse myself. If what I did next were a crime, which it ought to be, I would accept conviction and sentence without complaint. It is only that I never thought, not for a second, of doing what I did. I just went ahead and did it.

Your son, I said. He is mine, isn't he?

November 11 is Veterans Day. In my firm it is classified as partially staffed, along with Columbus Day and Dr. Martin Luther King's birthday. These are not like full-blown public holidays—July Fourth or Labor Day—but a sort of hybrid. A lot of our customers are closed, but the New York Stock Exchange is open, so we stay open, too. However, nothing much happens on these days, and at my level—vice-president—there is not much point being in the office unless you have a meeting scheduled. With anger, confusion, and guilt boiling away inside I knew I would get nothing done, so I went home.

Ding was giving Hetty lunch in the kitchen. Hetty, belted into her high chair, chuckled and waved at me, pleased to see the common order of things so agreeably disturbed. Ding paused from spooning food into the child to smile at me, eyebrows lifted in query.

Is everything all right?

Veterans Day. I took off.

Oh, good. She put down the spoon and came over to kiss me.

We have you home today then. I'm glad.

Well, I'm glad too, honey. Taking my shoes off.

Don't you notice anything?

Uh-oh. I did fast inventory. You had your hair cut.

Yes. Do you like it?

She turned full round to show me. It was a smart style, a kind
of boyish cut, the hair cut down close to the head—I don't
know the name for these things. Mrs. Coolidge had something
similar, in photographs from her middle years. Ding's
previous style was a sort of bell shape. At first glance, I thought
this one too short.

It's okay.

This was not enthusiastic enough. Her face fell a little. She
turned back to Hetty and her spoon.

Thought you'd like it.

Sure. It's okay. Maybe a little too short, that's all.

Ding brightened. I'll let it grow a little, and you tell me when
it's just right. Okay?

Sure.

I guess you're exhausted from the Japanese guys.

233

Yes, I said. We were up till late with them. They were all jet-lagged, of course, and couldn't sleep.

This was good. Some detailed invention—very authentic.

Where did you take them?

Mmm, karaoke bar in midtown. Those places are all over now.

Did you sing?

Me? No. It was Japanese stuff.

But they always have some English songs, don't they? "My Way," songs like that.

No, it was all Japanese, so far as I can remember.

She spooned in the last of Hetty's lunch. No further questions. I was aware of my own breathing. Ding makes all Hetty's food herself, mashing up rice and vegetables in the blender. She bought a jar of baby food once, but when she sampled it she declared it had no taste at all, and she would not give her child food with no taste. It has been a source of some anguish to her that, for technical reasons, she could not breast-feed.

I'm making *guo-ba* for dinner.

This is a Szechuan dish, rice made crispy by skillful overcooking, served—in our house, at any rate—with fishy delicacies. It is one of my favorites. Though I still felt raw and inflammable, I thought I should show some appreciation, so I went over and put my arms around her. She lifted her face to be kissed. After I kissed her she held me with her eyes for a moment. I know you've had a hard time, she said.

What?

With the Japanese. Just go sit down and rest. I'll take care of everything. Fix you a nice lunch. She stretched up and kissed me again. Her ears were very small and white, visible in the new hairstyle.

After lunch the telephone went. It was old Abby across the street. Is your wife there? It's real important. Ding was putting Hetty away for her afternoon nap. I called up the stairs, and she picked up in the bedroom. Coming down: I have to go see Abby. She wants some advice about houseplants.

Houseplants? She said it was real important.

When you're eighty and retired, I guess houseplants are important.

I guess so. Don't be too long. I kissed her on the lips, starting to like the new hairstyle.

But she was long. I sat in the afternoon stillness with a book: *About Time* by Mr. Jack Finney. Mr. Finney was a science fiction writer of the fifties. He wrote *The Body Snatchers*. In this other book, however, there were no extraterrestrials. It was a collection of stories about time travel. In the stories people encountered various kinds of faults or lacunae in space-time and were thrown back from the fifties, which the author seemed to dislike, into the twenties or, in one or two cases, to the nineties. In the twenties people had fun, didn't worry about the bomb, and drove picturesque cars with names like Moon Roadster. In the nineties they sat on porches a lot listening to the piano.

Time flew by till I heard Hetty stirring on the intercom. It was four-thirty. Ding had been gone three hours. I could have gone upstairs and dealt with Hetty, but I was still distressed to a degree from the previous night's disappointment and from sleeping not very well on the couch in my office. Also perhaps guilty for what I had done—though, in a way, thrilled that it had worked. Selina had agreed to come to New York the following week, though she could not say exactly when. She would call to let me know. I knew that I could win her. Win her in spite of the blackmail, not because of. She would see how right it was, once we were together.

So instead of going upstairs to deal with Hetty I called Abby's number. It was busy. I looked out through the curtains at the front window but could make out nothing in the house opposite. Damn. I set aside Mr. Finney's Arcadian fantasies and went upstairs.

Ding returned half an hour later. I'm afraid I was rather short with her. What the hell kept you?

Oh, you know. When Abby gets talking. She did not look at me, went straight to Hetty, playing in the living room.

I changed her but didn't feed her.

I'll take care of it. Still not looking at me.

The *guo-ba* dinner was not up to Ding's usual standard. I did not complain. There was something about her this evening that warned off complaint, or indeed any kind of exchange. Had I been too harsh with her for staying long with Abby? She seemed angry. I hate to leave these things untreated, and was about to say something, when the phone went. It was our video store. They had obtained a movie I had been wanting: *The Trial of Billy Mitchell*, starring Mr. Gary Cooper. It was an obscure movie. The reason I wanted it was that it was the only movie ever made that included President Coolidge among its dramatis personae. In my pursuit of Mr. Coolidge I was really scraping the barrel by this point.

Instead of tackling Ding about her sullen silence, I went to get the movie. When I came back she was more at ease, though still thoughtful. We put Hetty to bed and watched the movie. It was an old movie, the color not very good. I had wondered if perhaps the actor taking the part of President Coolidge was Mr. Ruggles, whom I had been so disappointed to miss in Vermont. No, the movie was much too old, and it was someone else, and the part anyway was very brief. *I want you to take care of this Morrow,* said the actor, and that was all we got of Coolidge, the rest of the movie being an attempt to blame him for Pearl Harbor. Since there already seemed to be general agreement that he was to blame for the Great Depression, I thought this rather hard on the man.

I had thought Ding would be bored by the movie. Indeed, she was, up to the point where we got a glimpse of Coolidge. She was once again sunk in whatever thoughts were preoccupying her, and I resolved to discover what they were before we went to bed.

Then, suddenly, an odd thing happened. The Coolidge actor spoke his line; the scene changed; I turned to pass a comment to Ding; and she had come forward to the edge of her seat, sitting bolt upright staring at the screen, her mouth slightly open, her eyes wide. The sight of her sitting like that, as if faux Coolidge had reached out from the screen and thrown a bucket of ice water over her, threw me off what I had been going to say.

Are you all right, honey?

She jerked toward me, as if waking from a dream.

237

Yes. Yes . . . Oh! I forgot to put up the side of the crib!

I would have volunteered myself, but she had darted upstairs before I could move. Later, when the movie was over, she asked if the Coolidge actor was the one who performed in Vermont.

No, no. Different guy. The movie's forty years old.

This seemed to be very fascinating to her—the first time she had ever displayed any real interest in Mr. Coolidge, other than just to humor me. I felt gratified that I had managed to ignite some enthusiasm in her for one of my own heroes. Married couples cannot expect to share everything, but they should share as much as they can.

And the guy, the one in Vermont. What was his name?

Mr. Ruggles. He only performs in Vermont. I believe he lives in Boston.

In Boston! Her excitement was really quite intense. In Boston! she repeated. Then, suddenly, she caught my eyes. She laughed—an odd, nervous, inconsequential little laugh.

It must be a nuisance for him to have to go to Vermont. From Boston.

I suppose so, was all I could think of to say to this rather strange remark. But Ding's sour mood, whatever it was, had utterly gone. She was sunny and merry. These mood changes! I began to feel sure that she was pregnant again—as, indeed, later proved to be the case.

Undressing for bed, I could see that she wanted me to embrace her. With several days to Selina, I saw no reason not to.

I worked the next day, never having had any sympathy with the theory that a Thursday off is license to take a Friday off. When I came home Ding was gone. She had left a note, written with care in her neat square characters.

> I had a call from my mother. Second Outside Cousin Gao in Washington is in trouble. I have to go down there for a couple of days. I took the Taurus. There are dried noodles in the closet opposite the refrigerator, some TV dinners in the freezer. Abby has menus from the take-out places. I'll call this evening around ten.

Second Outside Cousin Gao? I did not think I had ever heard of this person. However, Ding's family is large and diffuse and I knew that some of them were abroad.

Promptly at ten she called. Second Outside Cousin Gao's husband had left her. She was distraught. Needed some moral support. Ding would stay the weekend. Hetty was fine, enjoyed the trip.

All right. Give me the number so I can call you.

Better not. Cousin Gao is on tranquilizers, sleeps a lot. Doctor says not to disturb her. Don't worry, I'll call you.

Give me the number anyway. In case of emergency.

No, I'll call you. I'll call in the morning.

The weekend seemed very long. No Ding, no Hetty. The house so empty. I had not realized how accustomed I was to being married. I did some wiring work in the attic, blew leaves, rented another video—Jimmy Stewart in *The Spirit of St. Louis*. How fine they were, these actors of the forties and fifties.

239

There was one odd, premonitory thing. To accomplish my wiring I had to lift some floorboards in the attic. Our attic is unfinished, is in fact in the state the builder left it in 1925. However, he laid floorboards—tongue-and-groove cedar— along the center of the attic, for convenience. Well, beneath one of the floorboards, in the dusty space between ceiling joists, was the butt of a cigar. I lifted it out tenderly. A cigar— from 1925! It was so dry pieces flaked away as I touched it. I imagine it must have been left there by the builder. There was no band, so I could not determine the quality of the cigar. I left it at one side, resolving to replace it before nailing down the boards again. However, while getting in position to drill a hole to pass wire down to the wall switch, I accidentally stepped on the cigar, reducing it to dust.

Sleeping alone for the first time in this house, strange dreams came to trouble me. In one I was trying to take a daytime nap but could not for the noise of the builder banging around in the attic, and for worrying his cigar might start a fire . . . yet when I went up to speak to him the attic was empty and silent. In another I played host and travel guide to Mr. Deng Xiaoping on his first trip to Long Island. He was very affable, and I am sorry to say I brownnosed disgracefully to him. But somehow I managed to get us lost, and we ended up in Hong Kong, among the nighttime crowds on Nathan Road, where I kept trying to catch sight of Selina without letting Mr. Deng perceive that he did not have my full attention. For all my efforts he was smiling in his sleeve at me, and at last said frankly, in his coarse Szechuan accent: I know you've got us lost, but it's all right—I wanted to be in Hong Kong anyway.

Tuesday morning Ding called me at work. Would be home that evening. Everything fine, Hetty fine, see you later. She sounded exhausted. And within fifteen minutes, Selina.

Go to Midtown Pavilion Wednesday evening.

You're coming to New York?

Wednesday. Eight o'clock.

Yes, yes. But no skating, Selina. No trips to Rock Center. No cathedrals.

Sure. Okay. What you say.

I want to go to your room. Not meet in the lobby, go up to your room.

Yes. Fine. Is ten ten.

What? What is what? Ten what?

Room number. Is ten ten. *Yat-ling-yat-ling.* Impatiently.

You're kidding.

A?

Ten ten. Double ten. Don't you remember, Selina? Double Tenth, Big Hat Mountain?

You're crazy. Wednesday evening. Eight o'clock. Okay?

Okay.

By way of celebration I took a cab up to Chinatown for lunch. There's a place on Mott Street I like very much: Fujian people, the Sicilians of China, the place probably a front for a drug-smuggling operation, but they do great mussels and sea cucumber. The place was crowded, of course: a jostling crowd waiting inside the door, women with kids, old grannies in frog-buttoned jackets, office workers, one or two *guilou*—

tourists, possibly—the tables all full, waiters yelling back to the kitchen, the cashier yelling at the manager . . . all very *re-nao*—flat face heaven. Ding's new hairstyle, I noticed, was a fashion; I must have seen twenty girls cropped just the same. Coming out, in fact, walking up to Canal Street for a cab, as I passed the entrance to Pell Street I could have sworn I saw sweet Ding herself, halfway along the narrow old street, going up some steps, up a *stoop* I should say, straight into one of the doorways. Of course, it could not have been Ding. Ding was on her way back from D.C.

When I got home that evening she had just arrived. She was indeed exhausted. Had done her best with Cousin Gao. Had to make her a cash loan, two thousand, was it okay? Her family would guarantee it. I made no objection. Blood is thicker than water. Ding put Hetty to bed early and went up herself, before me. When I went up she was asleep.

I was at the Midtown Pavilion at seven-thirty next evening. The desk clerk was Chinese, from Hong Kong.

I'm sorry. There is no response from ten ten.

It's all right. I'll wait. I'm early.

Why not wait in the Garden Bar? Doors at the end, turn left. The guy's English was excellent, but like Ding he had not mastered nasal plosion. Gar-den.

The bar was (I thought) a good idea. If I hung around in the lobby I might encounter Selina coming in, offering her opportunities not to invite me up to the room. I wanted to meet her in the room, Double Ten. So auspicious!

Garden Bar—naturally there was no garden in sight (in Hong Kong once Chan and I went for drinks at a Münchner

Bierkeller up twelve floors by elevator)—was nearly empty. Only some name-tagged businesspeople at a table to one side. The bartender was another Asiatic, an older guy with greased hair. He was taking a phone call when I came in, but hung up at once with an abrupt *m-gan-yiu*—never mind—and nodded at me.

My idea was to have a couple of glasses of wine to prime myself. However, I felt uneasy about ordering wine in a bar. It seems a bit wussy. I was going to order brandy instead, though I am not really a liquor drinker, and did not feel altogether easy about this either. The bartender solved my problem.

Complimentary cocktail, sir?

Really?

Sure. Before eight o'clock.

All right. What have you got?

Anything you like. I can do anything. My specialty is Kowloon Knockout.

It sounds rather potent.

Not really. Just fruit juice, mostly. Mango, passion fruit, persimmon, and some vodka.

All right. But not too strong, please.

I sat and made small talk in Cantonese with the bartender. He was a Hong Konger—a Hakka from the New Territories—and he spoke fluent Cantonese. Gone to sea as a cook with the Royal Navy, switched to cruise lines, settled in London, restaurant work of course, got the New York job through a family connection. Green card, sixth preference, took him five years. Kowloon Knockout did not seem overstrong. I ordered another one, and only then noticed that the persimmon was leaving a rather unpleasant back taste . . . but drank the second anyway, out of politeness. The bartender took another call.

I guess you're Mr. Joy Tin-cheung.

Yes.

Your meeting's ready. Room ten ten.

I tried to pay the bartender for the second drink but he waved me away, laughing. Complimentary! Complimentary! We are both Chinese!

Double Ten was of course on the tenth floor. I rode up in the elevator with a fat Englishman, Robert Morley type, braying at a short nervous woman apparently his wife. They got off at eight, and I was alone to ten. The elevator seemed infinitely slow. *Stately,* I suppose they would have preferred it seem, in key with all the dark wood paneling and leather chairs and hunting prints—some Hong Konger's notion of the middle-class American notion of Olde Englishe solidity and style.

On the tenth floor I got lost. It was an odd sort of building. Not a hotel in the first place, I think—perhaps an apartment building. The corridors were not straight, but turned and branched in a most confusing way. It brought to mind the old *chang-lang* style of Chinese walkway, deliberately made crooked to foil ghosts and demons. I felt giddy, and began to regret the second drink. You can't trust vodka—everybody says so.

I saw 1002, and went in the direction of increasing numbers. This led at last to a dead end with a fire door, naked steps on the other side leading down. I tried to retrace my path but somehow got into the 1040s. The giddiness was giving way to a peculiar, disoriented panic. Where, where? I walked into a hotel worker in a braided uniform. Where is ten-ten? I asked him in Chinese—which was foolish, as he was an obvious Aztec. The guy squinted at me suspiciously. *Qué?*

I'm sorry. Room ten ten, *mille decem, por favor?* In the correct language phylum, at any rate.

A smile now. Back that way, sir—probably thinking, How the hell did I wind up working for flat faces? Left at the ice machine.

I was transported there instantaneously. The door flew open when I touched the handle. Immediately inside the door was a short hallway, with the bathroom on the right. The hallway opened into the room proper, which was not very large. Two steps from the door I caught the strong smell of tobacco, without having time to form an opinion about the oddness of this. Coming into the main part of the room I saw, at the other end, by the single window, the indistinct figure of a man— indistinct because hidden by a great veil of green smoke. All that was clear was that he was a smallish man, seated, one leg crossed over the other. His trousers were made of some heavy worsted fabric, the shoes old-style oxfords with a rather pointed toe, all well polished.

As I stopped in bafflement the veil of smoke parted. There before me, large as life, crisp and clear as a new dollar bill, smoking a cigar, sat the president of the United States—Mr. Calvin Coolidge!

18. The Man from Vermont

Have a cigar, said the president. He pronounced it see-*gaaaa*.

I was expecting someone else, I said.

Oh, she cried off.

Sorry?

What's the matter, young feller? Your ears ain't set opposite the holes in your head? I told you, she cried off. Ain't a-comin'. Not now, not ever. Best forget about it. Come on, have a cigar.

The president was sitting in one of the room's armchairs, on the other side by the window. On the table next to him, where normally you would expect to find a little tray with water glasses on it in cellophane prophylactics, was a flat wooden box, the hinged lid folded back to show a row of cigars, each with a red-and-gold band.

Fonseca Corona Finos de Luxe? I enquired. Twenty-one dollars the hundred? Or are these the three-cent item you gave to White House visitors?

The president made an odd, brief sound. You couldn't call it a laugh. More like a cough.

Hngh! These are the real McCoy. Certainly, I kept a can of Pittsburgh stogies for callers. People come to the White House, they generally want something they oughtn't have. Thing is, to get rid of 'em as fast as you can. But you, young feller, you've got me at my leisure. So come on, sit down. Here. He indicated the cigar box.

I could not refuse him. After going back to shut the door I stepped over to the window and took a cigar from the box. The cigar was fat and heavy.

Do I take the band off?

Please yourself. Personally, I do. What, you've never smoked a cigar before?

Matter of fact, no. I sat down and took off the band. I had a vague idea that I was supposed to bite open the rounded end of the cigar, but hesitated, never having done this before. The president leaned forward, offering me something. It was a small pocketknife.

Careful. I keep it honed sharp.

I cut the end off my cigar—a little too liberally, it seemed.

Cut the darned thing in half, why don't you. Y'only need enough of a hole to draw through. Want a holder?

He displayed the mouth end of his cigar briefly, and I saw that it was held in a white cardboard cone, attached to a quill stem. I declined: the arrangement looked complicated, and I thought I had already embarrassed myself sufficiently without signing on for further tests in cigar handling.

I returned the knife. The president offered a box of matches. SALAMANDER, said the box. PATENT SAFETY MATCH 40 COUNT, and a picture of a lizard. The box itself was made of very thin wood. The matches were wooden, too—thick and waxed, with a huge black head. I dragged one down the side of the box; it went off like a firecracker.

Don't normally smoke indoors, said the president, pushing the ashtray to where I could reach it. 'Less it's a smoking room. Grace says it's just making a nuisance of myself. But seeing there's just you and me, and I figured you'd be needing to relax, brought 'em along. He tapped the box with a finger.

I lit the cigar, drawing cautiously. I had been a cigarette smoker until I married, though not a heavy one. At this point I had smoked nothing for six years. The first mouthful was hot and acid, and I expelled it rather too quickly, without dignity. But it perked up my taste buds and got the saliva flowing, and the next draw, though still aggressive, began to reveal the richness of the tobacco. I sat back, the cigar between first and second finger, and crossed my legs. The muzziness was gone. Everything seemed sharp and clear, and only a little unreal.

Where . . . the lady who booked the room. Where is she?

Boston. With her husband. Where she belongs. Fine city, Boston. Very fine police force, as I recall. He regarded me steadily. *Distinguishable from the furniture only when he moved,* according to Mr. Creel. Not so, not so at all. This man had *presence.*

But I arranged to meet her here, I persisted.

I know *that.* Know the whole story. Her boy, too. He's from you, all right. I can see that now. Remarkable likeness, very remarkable.

Yes, yes, he's my boy. My son.

No, sir. The president sat forward, making his point with the cigar. He's *from* you, but he ain't *yours*. He belongs to the people that raised him. His *parents*. He don't know you from Isham Bradley's mare.

The biological parent has rights, too.

Horse manure. The president had sat back. He shook his head slowly. I don't know what this Republic's come to. Seems like everybody's got a right to everything but nobody's got any responsibility for anything. Back in Vermont we knew our rights. Life, liberty, and the pursuit of happiness. But nobody thought he had a right to go plaguing another man's family and creating disturbances. And certainly—he fixed me with a granite stare—nobody thought he had the right to blackmail a married lady into adultery.

I felt myself blushing hot. Mr. Coolidge . . . That is, Mr. President. I never really intended that . . . It was a moment of weakness.

The stare was still locked in. Moment of weakness, he mocked. Moment of weakness, was it? What crime couldn't be excused saying that? Is a man responsible for himself, or not?

Not always, necessarily.

Hngh. Then we'd best send down to the front desk for some pencils and a cartload of stationery, so you can start in rewriting the legal code.

Look. I know I did a wrong thing. It was only that I wanted to be with her. And *she* wants to be with *me!* I could see it. She just needed that little push.

The president's face twitched. Just a little push. My, my. You'd make a fine Philadelphia lawyer, young feller. Got an argument for everything. Just a little push—over the cliff, so to speak.

She wants to be with me. I know she does.

Well, I know she doesn't. She told me plain. And as for your blackmail, she says you may do as you please, she'll square it with her husband somehow. You want to hear it from her, she's home. He indicated the bedside telephone. Call her if you like. He drew two or three times on the cigar, rather fast, and disappeared once again behind the veil.

I did not move. There was no point. This was a man you could not doubt. When he said something was so, it was so. His authority was almost a solid thing, like the table at our side. I burst into tears.

Oh, hey. Hey now. Hey.

The cigar was gently removed from between my fingers, which were covering my face.

Hey. Hey.

I'm sorry. I know . . . you're right, of course. *She . . . she's* right. But it's only . . . I wanted to . . . I don't know. I don't know.

I took out a handkerchief and dabbed at my eyes. Mr. Coolidge had set his own cigar in the ashtray next to mine. He leaned over to the other side and opened a door of the cabinet set against the wall.

Here now. No call to get upset. You did something you hadn't ought to. But there's no great harm done.

From the cabinet he had pulled a very fine looking cut-glass decanter and a small matching tumbler. He set the tumbler on the table by the ashtray and poured a shot.

Glass of Irish'll set you right.

His steady green eyes watched as I downed the whiskey. It did not taste pleasant at all—metallic, somehow—my taste sense possibly distorted by the cigar.

All right?

Yes. Thank you . . . Mr. President.

He nodded, and handed back my cigar. They never brought Prohibition back, I hope.

No, sir.

Good thing too. Damn fool idea, passing a law to make people behave. Never agreed with it myself. I toed the line, mind, when it was policy. Had to. Running in Massachusetts—the damn state half dry, half wet. Heck of a thing to get right. West of the state, they're all Congregationalist, dry as a bone. East side—Irish Catholics, no need to say more. I swung it, though. Went to vote in Northampton with the president of Springfield Brewery on one side of me, our local pastor on the other. They never caught *me* out on issues.

But Prohibition was repealed after you, after your . . .

A wave of the cigar. Oh, I watched it all from the other place. Course, I saw ol' Bert Hoover run his buggy into the ditch before . . . Hngh, before. No surprise there, I always said he was too clever by half. Why, that man gave me unsolicited advice for six years, all of it bad. He was a trier, though, you couldn't fault him on that. But no luck, no luck at all. Grace says I pulled in all the luck of the party to myself, left none for ol' Bert. May be something in that.

Yes. Mr. Mencken called you the Darling of the Gods. Said when you were made Mr. Harding's vice-president people who knew you were openly laying bets Mr. Harding wouldn't survive his term.

A frown. That Mencken—yes, I knew him. That journal with the green cover. Good writer, skillful writer—but you couldn't believe a thing he told you. The man was wild at heart. No bottom, no principles. I was lucky, all right, but you don't get to be president of the United States just on luck. Still, Bert Hoover was *unlucky*, no doubt about it. That damn fool MacArthur! Now how many presidents d'you think *he* was a nuisance to? Did a couple of rounds with him myself, over the Billy Mitchell business. Military men, they're all full of themselves. Then there was that young pup Roosevelt—I remember him when he was secretary of the navy. Come up to Boston to greet Pres'dent Wilson with us when he came back from Paris. Made one of my best speeches there, don't know why they never published it. He was a smart one, young Roosevelt. Sly smart, we say in Vermont. Smart like a fox. Don't agree with the way he tried to stack the Court, mind. If Bill Taft'd been around, he would've nipped that in the bud. Nobody could get anything past ol' Bill. Nobody but his wife, anyways. No, young Roosevelt was wrong on that one. But he used the executive power as he found it, you can't blame him for that. If the people don't want it used that way, the remedy's in the ballot box.

The remedy's in the ballot box. You said that in your speech at the Springfield Chamber of Commerce. Mr. White called the speech a concatenation of clichés.

The president's features softened to something near approval. Well, young feller, you've been keeping track of *me*, all right. As for clee-chays, that's what they always said about my speeches. Clee-chays and platitudes. They weren't wrong either. If you stick real close to the truth, there ain't much you can say that's not been said a hundred times before. Still worth saying it, though. Thing about clee-chays and platitudes is, they're true. Men more often need to be reminded than instructed—who said that?

Dr. Johnson, of course.

Course. See, I've been keeping track of you, too. The president's nose twitched suddenly, like a rabbit's. This Mr. White you mention, I don't know him. Know his type, though. Theorists an' idealists, never satisfied with simple truth. That type's always with us. You can generally take it they're wrong about everything. Important to keep 'em out of government, very important. In my time they were talking up the Bolsheviks in Russia. Mr. Dreiser, Mr. Steffens, Mr. Anderson, Mr. H. G. Wells—how they loved them Bolsheviks! A new civilization! they said. Hope of the future! they said. Hngh! And I said—what? Leaning forward, he pointed his cigar at me to command the answer.

You said Bolshevism would never take root because it was against human nature.

'Sright. And course, they had plenty of sport with that. Small-town lawyer, carried into office in the pockets of business interests—what should he know about the higher strivings of suffering humanity? Hngh! And now, let's see, after all these years, who was right an' who was wrong? *Hngh!* Satisfied, he sat back and veiled himself in smoke again.

253

That's all very well, Mr. President. But if you'd had a more striking way of expressing yourself you might perhaps have left a more lasting impression.

He considered this for a moment, the smoke dissipating. Then: Did y'ever read Mr. Kipling's poem "The Gods of the Copybook Headings"?

I confessed that I had not.

Could be they don't read Kipling now, in this age. Pity if so. Fine poet. Vermont man, too, y'know. By residence, anyway. Had a little house down Brattleboro side, till he brushed his neighbors up the wrong way. My father saw him in the street once, in Rutland. Didn't impose himself, of course. Wouldn't ever have done that. Well, Mr. Kipling wrote this poem, "The Gods of the Copybook Headings." When me and Mr. Kipling were young, you see, we had to do a lot of copying. To develop a good hand. Most everything was written out longhand in those days, so it was important to have a good hand. And to practice your penmanship, you were given copy books. At the head of each page was a motto or a proverb—something improving, as a general rule. Virtue is its own reward. Procrastination is the thief of time. All that glisters is not gold. That sort of thing. Those were the copybook headings. Rest of the page was blank, just ruled off so you could copy the heading, over and over. Boy—he shook his head—you could get weary of some of those headings, copying them over twenty, thirty times. You never wanted to hear the darn things again. But you know—this is what Mr. Kipling says—they were true, all the same. Nobody'll pay you to hear them, but they're true and fundamental. Virtue *is* its own reward. The wages of sin *is* death. You can't argue with 'em. The Gods of the Copybook Headings with terror and slaughter return! Means, you can ignore them for a while, but they'll come back an' get you.

The president turned to tap his cigar into the ashtray. My own was not more than half smoked. I had had enough of it, and would have liked to put it out, but I thought this might be ill mannered, and in any case did not actually know how to do it. Things were shifting again, and my stomach felt unsettled.

Used to read a lot of poetry once, the president was saying. That's from Mother. She loved poetry. Tennyson was her great favorite. Tennyson and Longfellow. D'you know, she could recite "Evangeline" right off—the whole thing!

I wanted to tell him I had memorized *David Copperfield*. Whatever "Evangeline" was, I felt sure it was a less substantial work than *David Copperfield*. But the president now seemed sunk in a brown study, his chin dropping on his chest, and such was his presence that far from being willing to speak, it seemed to me I ought to be holding my breath.

Still stands the forest primeval, muttered the president, barely audible.

I'm sorry?

He raised his head. 'Scuse me. Come close to slopping over, there. The Coolidges never slop over.

In New England, a crime worse than manslaughter.

What? What's that?

Mr. William Allen White. He said that in New England, slopping over was a crime worse than manslaughter.

The president nodded, a faint flicker around the eyes. Well, we do like to keep ourselves buttoned up. What's the use of slopping over? It's a distress to yourself and an embarrassment to others. Best keep things to yourself.

Nowadays people believe that a lot of mental illness comes from holding things in. They think it's good to just vent your feelings.

Oh, that damn feller Freud. I know about him. Blasted crackpot. He thought the human being was a kind of steam engine. Don't let out the pressure, it'll explode. Professor Morse used to say people's imagination is always dominated by the great scientific changes of their time. Freud had to make everything like the steam engine. Or like geology, fossils buried down deep in layers. Some feller nowadays is probably cooking up a theory that the mind is a sort of electrical apparatus. Course, when I say nowadays, I mean the twenties. In your time, I don't know.

Computers, I said. They think it's like a computer.

He squinted. What, like a bookkeeper?

There had been some change in the meaning of words here, I realized.

An electrical calculating machine.

He nodded, clearly not quite sure what I was talking about. Electrical calculating machine. Hngh, well, it's a theory, I suppose. Professor Garman used to say the mind was a mystery that couldn't penetrate itself. Always stuck with that, myself. Not much taste for mental philosophy. Being raised in the country gives you a practical turn of character. That way, I took after Father. He was a practical man. Never saw him with a book, though he liked his newspaper. But for practical skills, country skills, no one could touch him. Carpentering, plumbing, mechanical, toolmaking, horse doctoring, trading, surveying. He could do it all. The things he built endured—why, you've seen for yourself. The lines he laid out were true and straight, the curves regular.

To illustrate *regular* the president traced the perfect arc of a circle, slowly, with his open hand.

Course, I wasn't as practical as Father. Never would have survived as a farmer. Not strong enough. Storekeeper, I would've liked that. You could rest up some. Not like farming, not like being president. Being president, that's an unnatural line of work. No job for a normal feller.

Oh, come on. You liked it. Being in the White House, I mean. You let them play "Hail to the Chief." Mr. Cleveland and Mr. Taft both banned it.

Grover Cleveland banned it? I never knew that. Surprised. Strong sense of style, ol' Grover. Worked too hard, though. Never really got a handle on the job, if you want my opinion. A man shouldn't work so hard. Now Ben Harrison, he never worked after lunch. And didn't do all that much before lunch, from what I heard. Well, yes, I always liked "Hail to the Chief."

Yet you said, "I do not choose to run for president in nineteen twenty-eight." The famous twelve words.

For the first time, he cracked a smile—a full smile, actually showing his teeth. It was a very odd thing, to see this man smile. All traces of clerkishness vanished—he was an imp, a gargoyle.

Yep, had a little fun with that. Nobody knew *what* to make of that.

Because you didn't help out with any explanations.

Why, it warn't their business! If I choose to run, I choose to run, and that's my business. If the American people want to vote for me, they'll vote for me, and that's their business.

But were you sincere? Wasn't that just a tease? You only said you didn't choose to *run*. If they'd drafted you in 1928, wouldn't you have accepted? With another term, you would have been the longest-serving president ever.

With another term, I'd've been dead in six months. Heart trouble, you know. He patted his chest. A small square cylinder of cigar ash fell on the leg of his pants. He brushed at it thoughtfully. I'd had a heart attack—just a small one, mind—that spring. Scared me. Would've scared Grace a lot more, 'cept I never told her.

You never told her about I do not choose to run, either. She heard it from the papers.

No, she heard it from Arthur Capper. Well, if I'd told her beforehand, I'd've had to tell her about the heart attack. Or she'd have sniffed it out. But once I'd made the announcement, she wouldn't bother. She'd just accept it. That's her way.

Still, it's a pity. You'd have got in with no problem. Another landslide, probably.

Oh, I don't know. The warning flags were up, y'know. A lot of us knew what was coming. The whole economic system was unstable. And look: of the five men who came before me, three were killed by the job. And another one hated every minute of it.

You mean Mr. Taft?

Bill Taft, yep. Hated it. His wife pushed him into it. Her and
Teddy. Ol' Bill wanted nothing but lawyering. He loved it.
Never knew a feller loved lawyering like ol' Bill. Happy as a pig
in manure when Warren put him on the Court. Forgot I was
ever president, he said to me. He swore me in, you know.
Nineteen twenty-five, my own term. First time a president got
sworn in by a previous president.

I know. And you were also the first president to be sworn in by
his father.

Oh, but that was illegal, you know. Ol' Harry Daugherty
insisted on that. But he was a publicity feller, ol' Harry. He
thought it would look sort of cute in the newspapers, having
Father swear me in. But the president's supposed to be sworn
in by a *federal* official, d'you see. Father only held notary from
the state of Vermont. So it was illegal. We had to do it over
when we got to Washington.

Did you tell your father you'd done it over?

No, no. But the old feller knew, you may be sure. He knew
enough about the law to figure it out, given time for reflection.
But he wouldn't never have said anything. That wouldn't be
his way.

So you knew there was a depression coming?

Why, I knew the market would break sooner or later. I knew
there was a business cycle. I knew what goes up must come
down. Never thought it would last as long as it did. Thought it
would be 1920 over again. And so it would've been, if they'd
let it rip. Let the economy purge itself. The president shook his

head. But that fool Hoover wanted to hold up wages, and then young Roosevelt wanted to go around socializing everything, and if it hadn't been for the Imperial Japanese Navy you'd still be in depression now.

We're not, though, are we? I mean, the country never went back to your policies, but it achieved great prosperity nonetheless.

He nodded. That's true. But there's been a price. We went off the rails in some important ways. Lost touch with ourselves. See—the president leaned forward again, making his point with what was left of his cigar—the fundamental American principle was self-government. When something needs doing, the people do it. Don't wait for the government, or the nobility, to do it. Do it *themselves*. That's fundamental. He sat back. But that's kind of a chore, you know, and people are lazy. Once they got the idea Uncle Sam could take care of them, they forgot how to take care of themselves. So Uncle Sam gets stuck with everything, and you know it's asking too much to expect folk'll use that much power wisely. You can hire a man to fix your barn, you can hire a man to weed your vegetables; but when you hire a man to run public affairs you can kiss your liberty good-bye. That's when people lose their grip on life. Like you said, a man's not responsible for his actions. Course he's not—he's paid someone else to take responsibility.

I felt this was directed against me, and hastened to defend myself. Mr. President, with respect sir, I did not pay anybody.

You might as well have done. Who's goin' to look after your wife, and that dear little baby, if you abandon them?

I never had the intention to abandon them, Mr. President.

You had the intention to betray them, which is next to the same thing. You know your wife's character. If you cheated her, she'd never live under the same roof with you again. Abandonment, de facto.

But really . . . oh! Can't you understand, Mr. President? Didn't you ever want to kick over the traces? Didn't you ever find the bourgeois life oppressive? Didn't you ever want to break loose? Act on some romantic impulse?

The president stared at me, narrowing his eyes somewhat. He took a long pull at his cigar, which was now burned down low. I had long since had enough of mine, and had been just holding it, letting it burn; but now I drew on it once more. However, I expelled the smoke wrong somehow and made my eyes water.

Well, a man can go to the devil if he wants. It's a free country, and there's a wild style of life for such as are suited to it. Though not half as many are suited to it, if you want my opinion, as *think* they are. What you call the *booj-wa* life— well, Mr. Mencken an' Mr. Lewis an' the others like to sniff at it, and scoff at it, and sneer at it; but it's the most satisfactory way for human beings in general, and your best hope for fulfillment.

Fulfillment, yes. By dint of some vigorous blinking I got to a point where I could see again, more or less. But what *is* fulfillment, Mr. President?

Why, makin' yourself useful. The law of service. Living to some serious purpose. "Whether I shall turn out to be the hero of my own life, or whether . . . whether . . ." Whether what?

"Or whether that station will be held by anybody else," I finished for him. *David Copperfield.* He knew me so well!

261

Yep. That's what your life turns on. Yours, mine, everybody's. Was I the hero of my own life? I believe so. I hope so.

But can you really be a hero if you just stick to the beaten track? If you don't *explore* life? After all—if you will excuse me saying so, sir—you're a long time dead.

His mouth twitched, and he made a little nod in acknowledgment of my impertinence. Oh, next thing you'll be telling me most men lead lives of quiet desperation. That's horse manure. I know those lines, all those lines the young fellers use to excuse their rascality. The road of excess leads to the palace of wisdom. *Dum vivimus, vivamus.* Know 'em all. I was a college man, y'know.

Yes. You gave the Grove Oration your senior year.

'Sright. Very well received it was, too. Though they never printed it up. But horsin' around at college is nothing to do with the main business of life. Explore, you say? Well, certainly. Explore adultery. Explore crime and drunkenness. Explore drug addiction. Explore 'em, and see where it gets you. Skid Row, ninety-nine percent of the time. Or worse yet, Congress. His face crinkled momentarily. But right is right, wrong is wrong, and if you fall off the path you're lost. The Fuller Life is an illusion, just like ol' Kipling said.

> It started by loving our neighbor and ended by loving his wife
> Till our women had no more children and the men lost reason and faith
> And the Gods of the Copybook Headings said: The Wages of Sin is Death.

Reciting these lines, he marked the accented syllables with his cigar hand: tap, tap, tap in the air.

No it isn't.

Hmm? The president had turned to dispose of his cigar, discarding the stub and the cardboard holder, extracting the quill stem, crushing the stub into the ashtray.

I mean, people have affairs with other people's spouses, but they don't *die.*

It's a metaphor, son. *Part* of them dies. We're put in this world for a purpose: to be upright, and give some service to our fellow men. If we don't live the right way, we're as good as dead.

I don't think people believe that now, Mr. President. Most people think our being here is just a matter of chance.

Chance, is it? The president seemed more grave without his cigar. He was sitting back now, straightening his shirt cuffs. The monkey on the typewriter.

I'm sorry?

One of Professor Morse's little tales. Let a monkey dance on a typewriter for long enough and he'll eventually produce the works of Shakespeare.

Well, I think that's true. Following his example, I was crushing out my cigar in the ashtray. Even this seemed to require some art, fragments of burning tobacco breaking off and rolling around in an untidy way, advertising themselves with braided columns of smoke.

All right, let's see.

The president leaned forward again to mark off the stages of the computation on his fingers.

Now, let's see. Shakespeare wrote thirty-seven plays. You can figure, ah, average twenty thousand words a play. Four and a half letters per word average, that's ninety thousand letters times thirty-seven. Hmm, nine sevens is sixty-three . . . three hundred . . . Throw in all the spaces and punctuation, say four million. All right. Now, your typewriter machine's got eighty keys, allowing for capitals and punctuation. So each key, your monkey's got one chance in eighty to hit the right key. One chance in eighty-four million times, that'd be a pretty big number. Fact, you gotta use logarithms. Logarithm eighty is logarithm eight add logarithm ten, that's three times logarithm two add one. Logarithm two is thirty ten so logarithm eighty is one point nine, close enough for government work. One point nine times four million makes seven point six million. That's only the logarithm of your answer mind. So the chance of getting your Shakespeare is one chance in one and seven point six million zeros. Now, that's no chance at all. So you tell me how to get not just the works of Shakespeare, but Shakespeare himself, and the monkeys, and the typewriter and all.

He sat back looking pleased with this somewhat bizarre feat of arithmemania. There, now! And George Olds said I'd never cut it as a mathematician!

So Mr. Gamaliel Bradford was right about you.

Hmm? Why, what'd he say?

He said that with you, the matter of religion was vital.

The president sidestepped. Who was this feller Bradford?

One of your biographers. He practiced a psychological style of biography.

Did he indeed? The president seemed amused. I suppose you've read all my biographers?

Yes, sir. Including your own book.

Hngh. So what's the consensus? About my presidency.

They say it was an honest administration, but short on achievements. (I had not the nerve to bring up the poll of Eminent Historians.)

Achievements? Achievements, phooey. What do you think, the president is some kind of magician-king out of Tennyson? He's an elected official, that's all. If events press on him, he's got to do his best for the country, according to his lights. But if the world leaves him alone, he'd be wise to return the favor. Not go looking for *achievements*. The greatest achievement of my administration was minding our own business.

The door opened, without any knock. It was a woman, slender and pretty, in a calf-length shift, raven black hair cut short in a simple, old-fashioned style. At a glance the woman looked no more than twenty-five; then she smiled, and the lines showed, adding twenty years. Yet they were all laughter lines, and there was laughter in her smile, and in her voice when she spoke, which was strong and melodious.

Isn't it past your bedtime, Poppa?

Then came real laughter—high, merry, and musical, till the door closed, cutting it off. The president stood.

Better hop home.

He walked to the door without another word.

Oh, wait a minute, Mr. President!

He turned, his hand on the doorknob.

Mr. President?

He stood silent, dour—the Coolidge of the photographs, exactly, clearly put out of humor by my calling him back.

Mr. President. I just wanted to ask . . . can you whistle?

He relaxed his expression and let go the doorknob. Without saying a word he brought his top lip down over the lower, pulled his cheeks back, and let fly with such a sound as I hope never to hear again at close range. Done, he took the doorknob again and turned away, unsmiling.

Show me a farm-bred boy that *caa-aa-an't* whistle!

As soon as the president had gone I fell asleep. After a night of confused and meaningless dreams—at one point the bartender floated across the room, then back and out—I woke next morning still dressed, on the bed, the bedspread over me. I felt cold. Also sick—my mouth was furred and my head throbbing. I supposed I must have been drinking, though it was some time before I could assemble clear memories of the night before.

The cold was real. Either from some stumbling act of my own, or because of a mechanical fault, the artificial ventilation system in my room was on full blast. It seemed to operate independently of the heating system, which could not keep up with it. After some fiddling I managed to switch it off. By this time, though I was still in considerable discomfort, the fog was beginning to clear.

President Coolidge! He had been here! I had spoken with him! But that was absurd, of course—the man was sixty years dead. Then what? Reason demanded that it was either a ghost, or a dream.

If a ghost, there would certainly be some traces. A ghost will always leave some reminder of his presence, precisely to show the living he was not a figment of the imagination. Yet there was nothing to be seen. The box of cigars was gone from the side table. The ashtray was clean—in fact (I inspected it closely), it looked brand new.

I stood there in confusion, my head pounding. Cigar smoke? The room must have been thick with it. Yet there was nothing to see or smell. Possibly if I had not slept all night in the room, if I came to it new from outside, I might be able to catch traces of the smoke. Well, I could test this when I got home to Ding. If she remarked on the smell of tobacco in my clothes, then I would know I had entertained a ghost.

I examined the bedside table: no decanter, no shot glass. I scrutinized the carpet for cigar ash: no. A dream then. This was a relief. The less I have to do with ghosts, the happier I shall be.

I left the hotel and walked to Penn Station. It was a bright cold day, and I thought the walk might clear my head, but in this I found only limited success. I did not have to wait long for a train. All the way out, through Queens and Nassau County, I sat looking through the window at the calm suburban streets, the trees all bare now, the neat gardens all bare, waiting for snow.

19.   New Found Land

Lunar New Year fell on a Wednesday this year. I took both Tuesday and Wednesday off—a personal weekend, with none of the drills and responsibilities of the public variety.

It is indeed a very agreeable thing to step out of the common routine like this. On Tuesday afternoon I walked Jip. There was snow everywhere—it had been a beastly winter—but the sky was bright and clear. Some of the retirees were out, shoveling snow or stacking wood. I stopped to greet them, these Americans, stolid old parties in checked shirts and hunting jackets—Wilsonians, Hardingians, Coolidgeans. Down at the further end of the street a younger American (Johnsonian, I would guess) was constructing a snowman for his infant, Bushian, son. Here the houses stop, giving way to loose woodland and little-used lanes. I let Jip off the leash. He ran off ahead at first in pursuit of some scent, but soon came back and trotted along contentedly at my side, leashed by love, trust, and duty.

For dinner Ding made a banquet just for the three of us. There was fish, of course—you must have fish at New Year, because the Chinese word for fish also sounds like *surplus*, so the fish means you won't be hungry in the coming year. There were year cakes made from sticky rice, whose name is another pun, sounding like *top of the year*. There was duck meat neatly chopped, spicy bean curd, lotus in a rich savory sauce. In the Szechuan tradition, Ding had made some *tangyuan*—little flour balls around sweet sesame paste. To flatter my northern palate she had added a plate of *jiaozi*—savory meat dumplings cooked in steamer boxes. One of the *jiaozi* had a red date hidden in it for good luck. Another contained a candy, for happiness. By chance both of them came to me. Or not entirely by chance, perhaps: I have a weakness for *jiaozi*, and ate far more than my share. Hetty took little portions of our food, mediated sometimes by the blender.

When we had eaten all we could we toasted each other in fruit juice. Ding was abstaining from alcohol because of her condition, and I had forsworn it too, from respect for her. Ding's toast was to harmony; mine, to swift success in our applications for citizenship, now in progress.

After this we made calls: to Ding's parents in Chongqing, to my sister, to Mr. Chan. Ding's parents most wanted to hear Hetty, so I held her to the phone and squeezed her chubby little thighs to make her chortle.

I had located my sister the previous month, after some enquiries among more distant relatives. Her husband died of cancer in 1992 and she has not remarried. However, she had already mastered the computer business and so is well provided for. She is in fact stinking rich, at any rate by the standards of provincial China. Between us we are planning to establish a memorial to our parents: a decent tomb, in one of the new cemeteries now permitted on the Mainland, with their names, dates, deeds, places of origin, and some suitable verses cut by a good calligraphist. I shall rest there myself at last: *luo ye gui gen*, as we say—The falling leaf returns to the roots.

Younger Sister has also hired a private detective on my behalf—apparently they have even such things in China now—to trace the daughter of the professor in Shacheng, so that I can make amends to her, if possible. This idea came to me when I was reading the Bible, an exercise I embarked upon in early December with the aid of a study guide. The author of the Psalms asks God to forgive us for the follies of our youth. When I read that of course I thought of my days as a Red Guard. With all proper respect to the Psalmist, it seemed to me that rape stands somewhat outside the scope of normal youthful misbehavior, and that I should attempt some recompense in this life rather than waiting for heaven to take the matter in hand. I spoke of this to Ding, who was wonderfully understanding, and agreed with my resolution—indeed, she insisted on it.

Mr. Chan was sober—it was only midmorning in Hong Kong—and it brought tears to my eyes to hear his dear old voice, his quaint turns of phrase.

Have you cleared your debts? he wanted to know. In our tradition all debts should be cleared before Lunar New Year.

Not quite, I had to confess.

Didn't tell her yet?

Not yet.

Don't procrastinate. It was all a long time ago. She'll be understanding, I know.

I'll tell her. Before Lantern Festival, I'll tell her.

Somewhat to my surprise he asked to speak to Ding when we were through. I handed over the mouthpiece and watched while Ding, blushing slightly, absorbed a long monologue from the other end, herself saying little more than Yes, No, and I understand.

What was all that about? I asked when she had hung up.

He told me to look after you, and cherish our family.

That's all? He took a long time to say that.

He stuck a lot of feathers on it, replied Ding in Chinese, using a Szechuan idiom. Also, he hopes to come and visit us.

Well, I should like that very much, I said cautiously.

I should like it very much too.

After the phone calls we put Hetty to bed and sat by the fire in the living room. In the fury of this winter we had come into the habit of keeping a fire going all weekend, putting one of the largest logs on before we went to bed to keep the fire going overnight.

There was an hour to the TV news, so I put a disk in the CD, some Chopin piano pieces. We sat holding hands, watching the fire, listening to Chopin. I had a book on the table in the study, which I thought I would fetch in a little while. Right now the best thing in the world was to sit here with my wife, watching the flames strip bark from our logs. The book was *Robert's Rules of Order,* which I wanted to master before standing for election to our school board in the spring.

If it's a boy, I said after a while, we shall call him Calvin. And Abigail if a girl. They are good American names.

Calvin, said Ding thoughtfully. *Kaiwen* (pronouncing the common Chinese transcription). Yes, it sounds good. Very auspicious. And Abigail will please Abby. But I thought you'd lost interest in that guy.

Not really. Sort of . . . exhausted him. I got to the point where there was really nothing more to know. But I still believe he was a great man. And a good, and a wise man.

I have felt so much better about myself since seeing President Coolidge in a dream. Life has seemed much clearer and simpler. I shall tell Ding everything when I am sure I have found the words. Before Lantern Festival, at any rate.

The thing I regret, I added, is not seeing that actor.

Actor?

Mr. Ruggles. The one who played President Coolidge. The lady in Plymouth said he was so good. Like Mr. Coolidge reborn, she said.

Oh, you know. The people there would of course advertise the guy. Not advertise, I mean . . . She struggled for the English idiom. . . . Talk up. They would talk up the guy. She seemed to be blushing again—from the warmth of the fire, no doubt. And something else. That flicker of mischief around the lips, which I glimpsed sometimes when playing Scrabble with her. Planning some New Year surprise for me, perhaps.

I suppose so.

Perhaps you should find another old dead philosopher to study.

Mmm. No. I shall concentrate on my election campaign.

This sounded very grand: my election campaign! It was only a school board position, unpaid and with no very great powers of decision. But it attracted me for a number of reasons. Mr. Coolidge was right, of course: we must do these things

```
                    Borders
              Books-Music-Cafe
       5 World Trade Center 212-839-8049
4951    142/0004/04  000267            SALE
ITEM        TX RETAIL DISC  SPEC  EXTND
     SEEING CALVIN COOLIDGE IN DREA
1 CL 1477824 1  22.95 10%  20.65  20.65
                    SUBTOTAL         20.65
     8.250%      TAX1              1.70
1 Item          AMOUNT DUE        22.35
                AMEX              22.35
     373995094991007 0999 647903 16245
                CHANGE DUE           .00
        01/28/97       08:28 PM
     Thank You For Shopping at Borders!
     We will gladly exchange or issue
     store credit for your Bargain 5
                purchase!
     All Computer Software Sales Are Final
```

ourselves, or give them up to despots and bureaucrats to do for us. I had been shocked to discover that school board elections in my town brought out only 7 percent of the voters, though school expenses made up the larger part of property tax—which of course people complained about continuously. And then there was Hetty, of course, and little Calvin-or-Abigail.

There was also the consideration—somewhat arch, perhaps—that Mr. Coolidge himself had once run for a school board position and lost—the only time he was ever defeated in any election. By winning my vote I should not only be doing useful service to my neighbors, I should also be offering satisfaction to Mr. Coolidge in some way. Paying my debt to him.

So, here I am: T. C. Chai, financial analyst for a New York investment bank. Son of Shijie Zhai, engineer, soldier, and martyr, of the town called Willow Palisade in the province called Lucky Forest in northeast China. Forty-eight years old, with a checkered past: revolutionary, murderer, rapist, wife betrayer . . . but incompletely so in every case, and probably not indictable on any count, except perhaps conspiracy to rape. Now living in great contentment with dear wife, beautiful child, and the hope of a second, in America—my new found land. Truly it is a strange road we travel, and what lies at the end of it only God knows.